HEALING LOVE

SAINTS PROTECTION & INVESTIGATIONS

MARYANN JORDAN

Healing Love (Saints Protection & Investigation Series)

Copyright 2016 Maryann Jordan

Cover design: Cosmic Letterz

ISBN ebook: 978-0-9968010-3-4

ISBN print: 978-0-9968010-4-1

For each book, I think long and hard about the dedication. This one is simple and based on what is going on in my life right now as I type. It is to my husband, Michael. He has not only supported me when writing was just a pipe dream, but throughout the process. He never acted like this was a ridiculous hobby, waste of time, or financial loss. He has worked tirelessly beside me to make sure that I am enjoying what I am doing. So for the past thirty-four years of our marriage...thank you.

PROLOGUE

Hiding behind the dumpster in the back alley, the dark night shrouding him in shadows, Cam Perez could feel his heart pound. A slow smile crossed his youthful face as he watched his friends slither out of the back of the small neighborhood store, a bag in their hands. Knowing the sack was filled with cash, he remembered his job and glanced up and down the alleyway to see that no one was around.

At thirteen, he was bigger than most of the guys he hung with...and knew that was probably why they wanted him. Watching carefully, he saw activity at the end of the street and his eyes stayed on the movement, ready to alert his friends if necessary.

This was not the first night spent hunkered down in an alley. In fact, Cam was becoming known as the gang's best lookout. He was not a full-fledged member, but was on his way. He knew if he kept proving himself he would be taken in within the year. *If I can keep my parents out of my business.*

My parents. Thinking of them caused his mind to wander away from his task. Sighing quietly, he imagined them asleep in their beds. *At least, I hope they're asleep.* Rubbing his hand over his face, he knew that was a false hope. The reality was they knew he was out of the house and were anxiously awaiting his safe arrival home. *Mom's undoubtedly on her knees praying right now.*

The thought of his mother praying for his wayward soul reminded him of the story of his parents' romance. He had heard it so many times, the tale resonated in him as his own. And in some ways, it was his story as well.

Cam, the oldest of four children, had been born in a small row house in El Paso, Texas. His father, Henrico, unusually tall and strong, had grown up crossing the border from Mexico illegally for years in order to work for higher wages. Building houses had given his father the money to send back to Cam's grandparents.

Henrico had the honor of working on a church on the outskirts of El Paso. It was a new, modern building and he took great pride in the part he played in the large construction. A trailer was on the property, serving as the church office and Henrico began to notice a beautiful, young woman each morning delivering coffees and small, white pastry bags to the office. She wore a uniform, but he was never close enough to discern where she came from.

One morning, walking around the corner of the building where the office was, he ran into her, spilling the coffees all down the front of her. She gasped, jumping back to keep from being burned. Her pink dress and its white apron, embroidered with Nellie's Bakery on the front, was now covered in the tan stain of coffee.

Mortified, Henrico immediately jerked the towel from around his neck and began to pat her dry, apologizing, as she batted his hands away.

"Stop!" she cried in mortification.

Not knowing what to do, he watched her hustle away, coffee still dripping down her legs.

Turning back to his job, he endured the jeers of his co-workers for the first impression he must have made on the beautiful woman. Determined to make amends, he spent the rest of the day wondering how to do so.

The next morning, he waited outside the trailer once she had disappeared inside with her delivery. A few minutes later as she made her way down the stairs he approached her, holding out one perfect rose. Her steps faltered as she saw him, her gaze bouncing between the flower and the handsome man holding it.

Offering her his sincerest apology, Henrico held his breath as he awaited her response. She did not make him wait long. Her lips curved into a smile that lit up his world. And from that moment on, he knew he had found the one. Pursuing her became his life's mission, as much as working to send money home. But Henrico was up to the task and six months later, they were married.

Marrying Bonita and then becoming a U.S. citizen was the highlight of his life up to that point. Becoming a father to his son, Cam, a year later surpassed all of his dreams.

. . .

Cam had listened to his father talk of hard work, dedication, and falling for *the one* for the past thirteen years. Shaking his head in disgust, he knew his father had no idea how easy money could be made...if willing to get with one of the many gangs.

Just then a police siren pierced the silent night and he jerked as the flashing lights at the end of the street came into view. Shouting to each other, the three friends rushed to the other end of the alley and split up, according to their plan. Cam was smart, having already located a place to hide. His friends...not so smart. They continued running down the street, still clutching the bag. Within a minute, the cops arrested them, hauling them away in handcuffs. Cam stayed hidden...and silent. As the scene unfolded, he waited patiently, his heart pounding.

Dios! Fuck! As soon as the cops drove the duo away, he slipped from his hiding place and headed home. Hoping to stay hidden once there, he was out of luck. As he crawled through his bedroom window the bright overhead light illuminated the dark room as his parents stood at the door. Holding their gazes, he would have preferred their anger. Instead, his mother's face was ravaged with tears and his father's expression held disappointment.

One week later the family moved to Virginia. His parents hoped and prayed that moving in with some of Bonita's relatives in a county outside of Richmond, would keep their oldest son from making the same mistakes he was making in Texas.

But he quickly shunned working on the weekends with his father as a carpenter. Instead, he found a new set of friends to hang with.

(five years later)

Cam celebrated his eighteenth birthday getting drunk, stoned, and screwing willing girls. By now, he was huge. Tall, broad shouldered, and muscular. He loved working out and seeing the results. A natural handsomeness did not hurt either and becoming a pussy-magnet? Icing on the cake.

He had joined a local gang, not nationally known but then, that had never appealed to him. He preferred hanging with his friends, making money on the side with drugs and had discovered a knack for gambling. He had friends, money, status, time to work out, time to make bets on pool, and more than enough time and opportunity to bang whatever pussy hung around their clubhouse.

Kissing his mother goodbye one day, he found her clinging to him a little longer than normal.

"Gotta go, ma," he said, trying to pull away. He loved and respected his parents and watched out for his younger siblings, but he was determined to go his own way.

"Christmas is coming," his mother said, softly.

Smiling, he knew with his money from drugs and

gambling he could afford many presents for the family. "I know. I got you covered," he said boastfully.

Hurt passed through her eyes, but she stood firm. "I only want one thing for Christmas, son. I want you to go see Father Martinez today."

"Ma," Cam started, but halted at the tortured look on his mother's face. Sighing deeply, he nodded. "Okay, ma. I'll go. But," he leaned way back to peer into her eyes, "it's not gonna keep me from my friends."

"Friends? Bah!" his mother spit out. She was silent for a moment, then her chin quivered as her gaze sought his once more. "You think my heart breaks now for you and these so-called friends? You go to jail, it'll kill your father...and me as well."

That afternoon, Cam walked into the neighborhood church, the cool dim interior a welcome respite from the muggy Virginia summer. As his eyes adjusted, he saw the elderly priest coming from one of the side doors.

"Camillo!" Father Martinez called out. "Your mother said she hoped you would come."

Cam walked toward the priest, noticing how much older and smaller the man appeared than the last time he saw him. Cam towered over him and while many people were fearful of the large, rough-looking young man, the priest just smiled up at him.

"Come, sit. You've grown so tall, my neck will hurt looking so far up."

Cam sat, impatiently waiting for the older man to join him. *The sooner we get started, the sooner I can get outta here.*

The priest sat, his gaze on his hands folded in his lap. The quiet of the chapel felt eerie to Cam. Months had passed since he had come to Mass with his parents. The silence was deafening. Unable to stand the quiet any longer, Cam blurted out, "You wanted to see me, Father?"

The priest lifted his head and pierced Cam with his gaze. With a small smile, he shook his head, saying, "No, son. But I think you have need of me."

A frown crossed Cam's face as he cocked his head to the side. "I don't understand—"

"Do you know who you were named for?" Father Martinez interrupted.

"Me?" Cam asked incredulously. He searched his mind quickly, trying to remember the Saints he learned about as a child. He had always hated his name. Camillo. *Jesus, they had to name me after some dumb-ass Saint's name.*

"Camillo," he stated. "A great name for a great man."

Cam shifted in his seat. Listening to a long-winded priest was the last thing he wanted to be doing. He fought the desire to jump up and run out of the church, but his upbringing would not allow him to be rude to Father Martinez. So he made himself a little more comfortable on the hard, wooden pew, and turned to face the older man.

"Saint Camillus," Father Martinez. "He lived in the 1500's. His father was a soldier and he inherited his father's temper. His mother was older and unable to control her son."

At this, Cam's eyebrows raised. He was sure that he

had never heard this story of his namesake. *Ma left this part out. So I was named after a hellraiser!*

"He was exceptionally tall for his age," Father Martinez chuckled as he gazed at Cam. "He actually became a soldier with his father when he was only sixteen years old."

"Sixteen?" Cam asked. "That's two years younger than me right now."

"Oh, yes. Back then, a man was considered a man by thirteen. None of this spending years wondering who we are and what we're going to do. He was a man and was expected to do a man's job."

Once again, Cam squirmed under the scrutiny of Father Martinez, wondering how much he knew about Cam's nefarious activities.

"He ended up as a laborer at a friary with a leg injury, and in spite of his aggressiveness and excessive gambling, the friar continually worked to bring out Camillus' better nature."

Cam's attention was now fully on Father Martinez as he continued the story.

"Camillus eventually had a change of heart and wanted to join the monastery but was unable to. So he traveled to Rome where he entered the Hospital of St. James and began working to assist the ill and injured. Eventually, he founded an Order of health care workers who would assist soldiers on the battlefield. In fact, they wore a large red cross on their cassocks which today is recognized as the symbol of the Red Cross. His works with the ill and his Order spread throughout what is now known as Europe."

Cam sat quietly, not knowing what to say, not moving as Father Martinez continued to tell more stories of St. Camillus. His heart pounded, feeling so heavy that he lifted his hand to rub his chest.

As Father Martinez fell silent once more the two sat facing each other, peace settling over the pair.

Finally Cam found his voice. "Why? Why did you tell me all of this today?"

The smile from Father Martinez exemplified his wrinkled face. "My son, I don't know. Sometimes God lays things on my heart to say. This seemed necessary today. I felt that you needed to hear all about your namesake and the lessons that can be learned. That a man can turn from a wild life to a life of service. A man can change his destiny."

The old Father began to rise and Cam jumped up to assist him. Holding on to him until he was steady on his feet, Cam noted that his own hands were firmly clasped in the gnarled hands of the priest.

"My son?"

"Yes, Father."

"Today, go home. Not to wherever you were going to go. But to home. Sit with your family, if only for this one night."

No knowing why he agreed, Cam nodded. Glancing at his watch, he saw that he had missed the rendezvous with his friends anyway. They were going to hit another store. *They'll just have to hit this one themselves.*

Cam did what was asked, going home and spending the evening with his family. Later that night, news traveled through the neighborhood. His two friends had become embroiled in a shootout with the police as they tried to escape the robbery. One was killed and one was arrested after shooting a police officer.

For weeks Cam could not sleep, his mind continually playing over the *what-ifs*. He had attended the burial of the friend, Jose, seeing the ravaged expressions of the parents' faces. He knew Carlos' fate in prison would be little better than being in the casket.

He did not go out. He did not go see other friends. His parents were worried, but he would not confide his thoughts to them. Finally, he went back to see Father Martinez.

"How did you know?" he yelled, his face torn with anguish.

Father Martinez did not have to ask what he was referring to. Motioning to a pew, the two sat down, very similar to their last meeting. The older, wiser man leaned over, taking Cam's hand into his own. "I can't give you a definite reason, my son. Your mother came to see me and I told her to send you in some time. I had been thinking about you and then about your namesake, seeing such similarities. It just seemed to be the right time to let you know that it is never too late to make a change in your life."

Cam hung his head, unfamiliar tears stinging his eyes. "You heard? About my friends? One dead and the other going to prison on a lot of charges, including shooting a cop?"

Father Martinez nodded his head sadly.

"That coulda been me," Cam bit out. "That shoulda been me."

"No. That was on them. Their choices. God gives us the ability to make what we choose out of our lives. You may have been on that path with them, but you made a choice to come here instead, even if the decision was just to placate your mother."

He held the younger man's gaze steadily while repeating, "It was your choice. You made the decision and it was the right one to make. Now, only you can decide what you will do with your life. Your choice."

Reaching into his pocket, Father Martinez pulled out a silver pendant on a chain. "St. Camillus," he stated, holding the medallion out for Cam.

Cam reached for it, rubbing his fingers over the emblem before slipping it over his neck.

The silence that followed no longer seemed heavy. In fact, for the first time in many years, Cam breathed easier. Sucking in a huge gulp of air, he let it out slowly. Nodding to Father Martinez, he stood and slowly walked out of the chapel. Out into the summer Virginia sunshine, feeling the warmth down deep.

2

10 YEARS LATER

The clink of the metal bar hitting the supports echoed in the early morning gym. Cam was in an old facility mostly used by local boxers and, at this hour, he had the place to himself. He had given up on the other, more populated sports gyms, hating the crowds and the looks that came his way from a few of the women running in designer gym wear on the treadmills. He was not interested; he barely had time for himself and a high-maintenance woman would not fit into his lifestyle. Not that he was against having a relationship—he just had not found the right woman yet. So for now, the occasional fuck-buddy would work just fine.

Cam worked the free weights, pressing as much as he did years earlier. He loved the burn, the time to focus on muscle groups, and the results. A large man, he worked his body like a machine. One that would perform whatever task he called it to.

Swiping a towel from the bench, he wiped his face

before slinging the material over his neck. Glancing at the clock on the wall, he headed home, needing a shower and wanting to have time to grab a bite of breakfast before going to work.

Just the thought of work brought a smile to his face. He knew he was a lucky fuck. *Or maybe luck had nothing to do with it*, he thought for the millionth time, seeing the Saint medallion around his neck. His grades in high school had sucked but he attended Richmond Community College and earned an Associate's degree. He started out as a business major, only because he could not think of anything else that interested him, until he met another man at the gym one morning who was in police science. *Police Science—who would have ever thought that would have interested me?*

Changing majors, he graduated with honors, was accepted into the police academy and worked his way up the police force, finally taking on an undercover operation bringing down a local gang that was making inroads with a national gang.

Last year, his cover had been blown after two years, but the operation was successful. Working undercover had been rewarding, but difficult. And a man his size was too easily recognizable. *I needed a change.* Through his contacts, he met his new boss. Jack Bryant.

Jack's business, Saints Protection & Investigations, was just what Cam had been looking for. A former Special Forces soldier, Jack had brought together a team of men from various backgrounds, including DEA, SEAL, CIA, FBI, weapons and explosive experts, using their combined specialties for a security business that flew under the radar. Private and government contracts provided lucrative enticements but every one of the seven men who were Jack's elite would have done their jobs for a lot less money. The chance to investigate crimes and protect, without the bureaucratic bullshit that hampered each of them in the past? Pure gold.

Opening the door, he stepped into his house, tossed his gym bag onto the floor, and immediately walked toward the bedroom, heading to the shower.

"Oh, so you're here now?" Lisa's sarcastic voice called out.

"What?" he asked, passing by her as he pulled off his sweaty t-shirt, tossing it into the laundry basket.

"*What*? All you can say is *what*?" She stood, her hands on her hips, foot tapping and a glare on her face.

He looked at her stance. Long hair pulled severely into a neat twist at the back of her neck. Designer clothes from blouse to heels. Perfectly applied makeup. There was a time when he would have tried to placate her, but this was not the time. The Saints had been working around the clock on their latest mission and Lisa's hissy-fit no longer mattered. Heaving a huge sigh, he should have known their fuck-buddy relationship was not going to last much longer. A beautiful woman with a business in D.C., Lisa would see him every time she was in town and recently that had been more often.

"Cam, seriously? I got in late last night and I only have a few hours. You're gone when I wake up and," she hesitated as her nose wrinkled up, "you're all sweaty."

Cocking her hip out further, she demanded, "I want to know when you're going to focus on me."

He hung his head for a moment, counting to ten as Father Martinez had taught him to quiet his temper. Sucking in a huge breath, he let it out slowly before lifting his head and staring directly at her.

"Lisa, I go to the gym almost every morning. I'm working on a case and need that time to get my head in the game. I've got just enough time to shower, grab a bite and pick up a co-worker on the way to work. What I don't have time for is this shit. What about that do you not understand?"

She reared back as though slapped. "Shit? That's what we are?"

"You know exactly what we are, Lisa. We're convenient. You come into town and if our schedules allow, we have a few laughs, fuck, and then you head back out again. Since that's all we've ever been, why are you surprised?"

"I changed my hours because of you!" she yelled. "I thought we were going somewhere. I was even thinking of moving my office here, but you're never here either. I want a man that'll be here for me."

"You know my job, Lisa. I'm not a nine-to-five kind of man. And even if I was, we were never going to be more than what we are now."

"You could change jobs. You could even work security for my company," she said, desperation creeping into her voice.

Sighing deeply again, he walked over and placed his hands on her shoulders. Shaking his head, he reiterated,

"That's not me and I'm not giving up me to fit into your world. I liked what we had but that's all of me you will get."

Jerking out of his hands, she stepped back, anger twisting her expression. "Fine. Then I'll say goodbye, Cam. And when I say goodbye, I mean goodbye. You're losing the best thing that could ever happen to you."

It was on the tip of his tongue to refute her claim, but he kept quiet. As the front door slammed, he headed into the shower, his only regret—he was going to miss breakfast.

Fifteen minutes later, swinging into his SUV, he headed toward the Blue Ridge Mountains. Jack's business, Saints Protection & Investigations, was just what Cam had been looking for. He felt as though his whole life up to now had been preparing him for the work he did for Jack. And if he occasionally needed to use his former breaking and entering skills...so much the better.

Picking up Bart, one of the other Saints, he continued toward the compound. A former SEAL, Bart was as tall as Cam, just as muscular, but had sandy hair paired with Hollywood looks that got him noticed by women wherever they went. Bart leaned back in the seat, exhaustion replacing his usual grin.

Looking over at his passenger, Cam remarked, "You look like hell."

Shaking his head, Bart replied, "This case is getting to me. I was out the last three days and just when I think we're getting closer, my leads are goin' nowhere."

The two men fell silent, their thoughts on the

ongoing case that they had been working—a serial killer known as the Campus Killer. Pulling into the driveway after entering through the security gate, they watched the fall leaves on the trees glide by as they made their way down the long path toward Jack's house.

Jack built a huge home on his twenty-six acres that backed to the Blue Ridge Mountains. From the outside, the structure appeared to be a luxury cabin. But underneath the house and four-car garage was the command center of the Saints.

As they parked in front, they saw the other trucks and SUVs of their co-workers and in-between was a small, old sedan.

"She's here," Bart said, his mouth already watering. "I wonder what she's brought?"

Cam laughed but knew his reaction was the same. Bethany Bridwell, the beautiful owner of the rental cabin property next door had caught the eye of Jack and started coming over occasionally. And when she did, she brought something she had baked and always brought enough to feed all eight men.

The two men hustled in, finding the others in the kitchen, all with plates in front of them and the scent of apples and cinnamon wafting through the air.

"You'd better have left some for me," Bart warned as he pushed his way toward the counter with Cam on his heels.

Bethany laughed as she dished out more of the homemade apple cobbler onto two more plates. "Of course I have some left," she replied. Her thick, blonde hair was pulled into a simple ponytail. Makeup-free face, faded jeans and tank-top completed her ensemble.

After his morning with Lisa, Cam appreciated Bethany's fresh appearance...and her cobbler. The group of men, all over six feet tall, dwarfed her on all sides. Her eyes found Jack's and a smile filled her expression.

Cam noticed she smiled most of the time, but when she gazed at Jack she actually beamed. And he had to admit, so did his boss. *Nice. They deserve that.* He knew that Jack had been battling his feelings for the beautiful Ms. Bridwell, saying that his lifestyle and business just would not be conducive to a relationship. But it was obvious—these two belonged together.

The last man to arrive was Marc, a former CIA operative and the group's pilot. Tall, lean with a powerful body, he came in from his morning run, pulling a shirt on as he entered the room. His dark hair still wet only exemplified his piercing blue eyes. Apologizing to Bethany for his appearance, he grabbed the last piece of cobbler before nodding to Jack. The Saints began moving out of the room while Jack walked Bethany to her car.

"You think Jack's really going to go for it?" Chad asked, hope in his eyes that their boss would give the relationship a chance. The former ATF explosions expert was a romantic at heart.

"Hell, if he doesn't, we're all doomed," Blaise joked, halfheartedly. "It's not like any of us are in careers that very many women can deal with."

Bart piped up and added, "Good thing I plan on staying single."

"As many women as you take home from bars, it's no wonder you're single," Luke retorted, balancing his cup of strong coffee with his cobbler plate.

Blaise, a veterinarian specializing in bio-terrorism with Homeland Security, shot Luke a disparaging glance. "I gotta confess, when Jack was talking about how this life doesn't fit any woman needing a white-picket-fence life, it made me wonder if he was just talking about himself...or all of us." Blaise had Nordic looks with his blond hair and, like Bart, easily attracted women when they went out. Blaise's last girlfriend had left him quickly when she saw how many hours he worked and traveled.

Cam knew that besides Jack, the other six men did not have relationships either. A few, like him, had fuck-buddies that they could keep at arm's length or they would hit the bars and enjoy nights of mindless fucking. In this business, whatever they needed to do to keep focused on the job was most important. *But if Jack can combine his business and his heart, there may be hope for the rest of us too.*

Cam's thoughts returned to the morning's scene with Lisa. Not that she was ever a contender for his heart; he knew that most women would react as she did —anger and disgust when he was gone so often. *I'd like to have what ma and pop have,* he realized, his thoughts now turning to his parents. *But this life? Maybe I'll never have that happy ever after.*

Just then Jack walked down into the command

center and they all sat at the main conference room table.

"Boss? You're kinda scaring us," Cam commented. Seeing Jack's raised eyebrow, he continued, "You seem sort of happy."

Jack caught the smirks of the others around the table and hung his head chuckling. "Okay, okay, have your fun." He looked back at Cam and said, "If you bunch of women want your gossip then here it is. I have approached Ms. Bridwell about renewing our relationship and she agreed. There. Now are you happy?"

The men offered heartfelt congratulations accompanied with head jerks in approval before they got down to business.

The Saints began earnestly analyzing the compiled data on the serial killer and reporting on their aspect of the investigation. The meeting lasted for several hours, but Cam did not mind. The chance to get to the killer before he struck again was paramount.

Their data-mining genius, Luke, had left his job with the CIA as a software engineer and now spent much of his time in the command center coordinating their investigations. He was typing furiously, only stopping to slurp more of his potent coffee, trying to enter all of the information from Monty, who was still in contact with his former FBI agents.

The killer was only striking women at colleges. In a lull in the discussion, Marc said, "Spent the weekend at home with my family." His face mirrored the frustration the group felt. "Gotta sister at Dominion College. Sophomore. Pretty. Nice. Decent student."

"Fuck man," Luke bit out.

"Spent the weekend with her and my parents and even though she's home for the summer, we talked about her not going back until this is over with."

"Some serial killers are not caught for years, Marc," Jack said.

Nodding, Marc agreed. "Yep, but I'd rather her not be at risk than to take that chance."

"This is exactly why the governor gave us this task. We've got to find this fucker and shut him down."

Cam's mind wandered back to his family, whom he had not visited for the past month because he had been so busy with the case. *Gotta get back and see the family this weekend.*

Walking out of the hospital after a graveyard shift into the warm, early fall sun, Miriam Delaro's body had to adjust to the temperature change. She tilted her face to the sky, her long, dark ponytail falling down her back. Her blue nursing scrubs provided little warmth. *The hospital is so friggin' cold*, she thought as she climbed into her old car. As she glanced at the mirror, her tired eyes stared back. Driving to the apartment that she shared with her sister, Rebecca, her mind was on overload. *The busy night in the emergency room, the upcoming wedding, needing to find a new roommate, the irritating Dr. Sose...augh!*

Driving on autopilot, she pulled into her apartment's parking lot seeing her sister's fiance's car there.

She liked Thomas—he had a decent job, got along with their parents, and he adored her sister. The two of them were in the process of moving in together, much to the ire of their parents who wanted a wedding before they lived together. *He's just so boring. At least Rebecca has boring—I've got no prospects right now!*

Walking into the apartment, she met him as he was coming out, carrying another box of Rebecca's clothes. Bending down to kiss her cheek, he smiled as he greeted her.

"Hey, Thomas," she called. Looking past him into the kitchen where her sister was already holding out a plate for her, she grinned. "Oh, girl, you're a lifesaver. I didn't get to eat on last night's shift."

Her sister blew Thomas a kiss as he left and then turned to Miriam. "Well, eat up, sis. I need to make sure you don't lose weight or we'll have to have the maid-of-honor dress taken in."

"Don't worry about that," Miriam said, while digging into the scrambled eggs topped with cheese. "I've been eating like crazy lately, so I'll be lucky if the dress doesn't have to be let out!" Her sister handed her a diet soda with a wedge of lemon squeezed into the glass and floating on top.

"How you drink that with breakfast food, I'll never know," laughed Rebecca.

As Miriam ate, she watched Rebecca staring at her. Her sister's dark hair was cut to swing above her shoulders, but her face was so similar to her own that they were often mistaken for twins. Looks were not the only way the two girls were alike—it was as though they could read each other's minds.

"You know," Rebecca began. "Thomas has some nice, single friends—"

"Stop right there," Miriam shouted over her mouthful of toast. "I love Thomas for you, but his friends are just not my type."

"And what type would that be? Tall, dark, mysterious, gorgeous, standing on the bow of a pirate ship or riding over their plantation?"

Miriam blushed, her sister knowing her penchant for reading romance novels long into the night. They used to hide them from their mother and then Rebecca stopped being her reading buddy. Now, she just read them and dreamed alone.

"There's nothing wrong with wishing for the handsome prince," Miriam said, her sharp expression belying the wistfulness in her voice.

Walking over, Rebecca hugged her before taking the plate from her hands. "You can always dream, but just don't forget to be practical."

Looking around, Miriam said, "It's going to be weird not sharing a place with you."

"I know." Rebecca's voice was laced with a mixture of eager anticipation and nostalgia. "You gonna be okay living by yourself?"

Laughing, Miriam responded, "Of course. And it's not like you're terribly far away. Hmmm, let's see? About ten minutes?"

"Okay, smartass," Rebecca grinned.

"Seriously though, I will miss having you around all

the time. But you and Thomas need to build your own life and I've got…well, I'll be fine."

The sisters hugged before Rebecca left the apartment heading to her job as a kindergarten teacher and Miriam walked to her bedroom. After a quick shower, she fell onto her bed with barely the energy to pull the covers up over her. As she drifted off to sleep, she heard the faint sounds of the TV in the living room that Rebecca had left on. Her dreams of a handsome prince became tangled with a newscast about an earthquake in Mexico.

3

TWO WEEKS LATER

Cam poured his coffee into a large Superman mug his nephews gave him last Christmas. His brother-in-law was a great guy but not very large so they considered their Uncle Cam to be as strong as Superman. Chuckling at the thought, he sat down at his table to go through his emails. They had been accumulating since he had been away for the past several days, still working on the serial killer case for Jack. That Saturday dawned beautiful and sunny and he eagerly anticipated a run later followed by a pick-up basketball game with some of the other Saints.

A knock on the door caused him to glance at the clock. Seven a.m. *Who the hell comes that early on a Saturday morning?* Throwing open the door, he was surprised to see Jack standing on the stoop. And behind him were two people he had not seen in over a year. Jobe Delaro and his wife, Mackenna.

He first met them when he was still undercover and assisted in rescuing Mackenna when she was being chased by the gang he was with. Jobe had initially not been happy that Cam had given her a gun to use, but they had a mutual respect for their work. Jobe was with Alvarez Security and a former squad member with Jack when they had served in the Special Forces.

"Cam," Jack greeted. "We gotta talk."

Stepping back, he motioned for them to enter. Receiving a chin lift from Jobe, he noticed that his expression was one of stress...anxiety...*fear?* Once settled in his living room, he looked sharply first at Jack and then at the others, knowing that for them to show up so early on a Saturday morning it was not a time for pleasantries.

"Cam, Jobe's got an issue and I've talked to Tony about the situation. Want to get you in on it and find out your take."

Cam nodded, focusing first on Jack and then settling his gaze on Jobe, noticing Mackenna quietly placing her hand on Jobe's, giving it a little squeeze. The movement was not lost on Cam, nor its significance. Whatever was happening was making Jobe fight to control himself, but he had the love and support of an amazing woman.

"I've got a sister who's a nurse," Jobe began. "Her name's Miriam." He sucked in a ragged breath before continuing. "She usually works in the ER at Richmond General Hospital, but she's also qualified as a Red Cross volunteer nurse. Other than being called for a few local needs, she's never done too much with the Red Cross. Until now."

Jobe's voice faltered and Mackenna spoke quickly, giving her husband a chance to recover. "She's very special. She helped my mother when she had a stroke and lately she's been wanting to do more with her life. More volunteering. So—"

"So two weeks ago, she got a call from the Red Cross looking for nurses to travel to Mexico to aid in recovery when they had that earthquake," Jobe continued. "We, the family...tried to talk her out of taking the assignment. The job just seemed so dangerous but she was determined." He rubbed his hand over his face, pulling his thoughts together. "She had about two days of briefings here in the states with the Red Cross and then she flew to Mexico. She called every day for the first ten days..." his voice broke again.

Cam felt his heart pounding in his chest, fearful anticipation crawling up his throat, threatening to choke him. Knowing where the story was heading, his mind quickly jumped to his own younger sisters. *Fuck, oh fuck.* Steeling his expression, he knew that Jobe needed all the strength he could draw upon. Giving a nod, he turned his gaze to Jack.

Taking over, Jack said, "She's been out of contact for the past four days. The family held out hope for the first day, knowing that Miriam had told them of the horrible conditions, the poor cell reception, and with everything she was doing, calling might be impossible. But two days ago, they got a call from the Red Cross and then the American embassy. She and a few other nurses were abducted."

Cam's gaze shot over to Mackenna as a sob broke through. She was pressing her fingers to her mouth, trying hard not to cry but was unable to hold back. Her eyes were on Jobe, his face becoming more ravaged with each minute.

"What can I do?" Cam asked Jack, giving him the signal that he was ready and willing to do whatever was needed.

"The latest intel is that they were taken by a drug cartel. One of the larger ones, who might normally have their own infrastructure for medical emergencies, but were wiped out with the earthquake. I got Marc on it last night. He used his CIA contacts and found out who has her and where they're located. It appears that several medical personal were kidnapped so that they could provide services for the cartel's workers who were injured."

Jobe rubbed his hand over his face once more as his gaze lifted back to Cam's. "Tony's men are on this, but we've got no one who speaks Spanish. Tony went to Jack and he immediately thought of—"

"I'm on it," Cam said, interrupting Jobe. "Got no reason to ask. You need me, you got me."

Mackenna leaned forward grabbing his hands as more tears slid from her face. "Oh, Cam, thank you."

Jack turned to Jobe, saying, "We got this. I told Tony we would, but I wanted Cam to have that choice. He's got undercover experience, knows the language and we can use Marc as our pilot and CIA contact." His normally gruff voice softened as he continued, "Jobe, man. We've been through a lot together with our squad in Afghanistan. We're brothers till we die. That includes family." He looked back over at Cam and then said, "And Jobe, that includes my Saints. We're brothers as well.

You take Mackenna home, take care of your mom and dad and let us take care of this."

Not used to giving control to someone else, Jobe nodded, drawing in another ragged breath. They all stood and Mackenna moved in, hugging Cam tightly. As she stepped away, Jobe grabbed his hand and then pulled him in for a hug as well. "Find her, please. Take care of her and bring her home," Jobe choked. As Jobe pulled back, he reached his hand into his pocket and pulled out a photograph. Handing the picture to Cam, he grabbed MacKenna's hand and hurried out.

After the two of them left, Jack turned to Cam saying, "You're the best man for the job, Cam. Not just because you're Hispanic—but you have the knowledge and the experience to get down there and blend. But I want you to go voluntarily."

Cam shook his head at his boss. "No worries, Jack. I got this."

Nodding, Jack glanced at his watch. "We rendezvous at the compound in about two hours to plan. Go ahead and pack. Get your gear. And…you'd better let your parents know you're out of contact for a bit."

Cam watched Jack leave his house as well before looking down at the photograph. He sucked in his breath. Not knowing what he expected, he was unprepared for the dark haired, dark eyed beauty that had been smiling at the camera. The photographer had captured her just at the moment when she was about to throw her head back and laugh but was still smiling widely instead. Her eyes were lit with mirth and he found himself moving his finger over her image.

She was perfection and his finger landed on her turned up lips. *Miriam.* A beautiful name for a beautiful woman. Giving himself a mental shake, he slid the photograph into his pocket and picked up his now-cold coffee, dumping it into the sink. Then he did exactly what Jack had directed him to do.

By the time Cam made it to the compound the other Saints were present. Bart clapped his hand on Cam's shoulder and said, "Did missions like this when I was a SEAL, bro. This one'll be tough. Swear to God, if I could go and blend in, I'd do it."

Cam chuckled as he gazed at Bart's surfer looks and Blaise's Nordic appearance and replied, "Sorry, guys. Can't see you being able to blend in."

The men settled around the conference table, having already begun preliminary planning. Luke set up the secure video conference with Marc's CIA contact.

"Todd? Good to see you," Marc greeted the screen. "We're all here and just need to get the latest you've got for us."

The contact nodded and immediately asked, "Hear you've got a man that can get on the inside? Full blooded Hispanic?"

The camera switched onto Cam and he saw Todd's gaze scrutinizing him. After a moment, he nodded and continued with his intel. "Good. The earthquake hit in the mid to southern part of the Gulf of California. Los Mochis, in northern Sinaloa has a huge agriculture economy. Sugarcane, cotton, rice, and the largest exporters of mangoes." He paused and looked directly into the camera before continuing, "And marijuana as well as poppy.

"The Red Cross sent their contingencies through the airport at Los Mochis and then transported them by land to the various farms, villages, anywhere they could set up makeshift hospitals. Our intelligence indicates that several nurses were initially taken, but we've only had visuals of three. One was identified as Sister Genovia, an older Catholic nurse, Sharon Torson, a nurse from California, and Miriam Delaro."

"What can you tell us about the cartel?"

"The goddamn cartels change with every death or capture. They are constantly at war with themselves and I sometimes wish we'd let them just kill each other off if there weren't so many innocent casualties. The largest and one of the most powerful cartels, the Beltran-Leyva Cartel, splintered when a few of the Beltran-Leyva brothers were captured. Right now the area is run by the Sinaloa Cartel, often referred to as The Federation."

Cam and the others were quickly taking notes on their tablets when Todd stopped them. "Gentlemen, let me just tell you that those of us who have been fighting the drug wars have studied this type of information for years. There's no way I can give you everything you need. So let's concentrate on what you're facing."

Jack gave a curt nod and Todd began again. "Their way of life—and it's been this way since they were born, so it's all they know—is blood, violence, killing, viciousness, and getting rid of anything or anyone that even remotely might stand in your way. Women are not valued. They are used for sex, drug carrying, and then killed horrifically."

Cam rubbed his hand over his face, his stomach beginning to churn at what he might find. Looking around the table, he saw similar expressions on the rest of the men.

"But the good news is these nurses were taken because they possess skills and are valued. Chances are they're being housed separately from the masses and well taken care of. The difficulty will be getting to them…and then getting them out.

"Cam? We've got some inside people in place right now. If Marc will fly you down, we can get you to the people who can get you in. You'll be a laborer in the fields, but with so many injuries from the earthquake, they're taking anyone. If you're willing, we'll get the coordinates and send the rest of our report to you right now."

Cam nodded and the video conference ended. Silence reigned around the table. "I gotta get close enough to that hospital," he said. "Whatever we plan, that's got to be my initial goal."

"This isn't going to happen in just a couple of days, Cam," Jack said. "But then, you spent almost two years undercover in a gang, so I reckon you know how to take things slow."

"I got this," he said. *But what shape will she be in when I get to her?* He reached up, fingering the St. Camillus medallion hanging at his chest. *The Patron*

Saint of the Red Cross. Keep her safe until I can take over the job.

In her apartment in Richmond, Miriam was used to the peaceful nights where her sleep was only occasionally disturbed by the neighbors below. But here, in Mexico, the noises of the night kept her awake in spite of her exhaustion.

A fan rotated from the ceiling, moving the mosquito netting around. Shadows danced in the room from the moonlight peeking in through the wooden shutters. The air was hot—stifling. She could hear the gentle snores from Sister Genovia and the tossing of Sharon.

But more than the exhaustion, backbreaking work, lack of sleep, and mediocre food was the constant fear coursing through her blood, entering every breath, and filling her nightmares.

What day is it? Counting backward, she realized that she had been in Mexico for fifteen days. Ten, with the Red Cross in a farming hospital outside Los Mochis and the past five days with a drug cartel. The memory of her first day seemed so long ago.

I arrived at the airport, was transported through streets still strewn with rubble from the earthquake and made my way to the main hospital in Los Mochis. I worked there for three days, in triage and emergency, paired with someone who spoke Spanish.

The Spanish that I studied in high school was too far in the past to assist me now, but I quickly picked up enough words to check on the patients' basic needs. A nearby hotel that suffered few casualties to the structure housed most of the Red Cross personnel. I called my parents every day, filling them in with stories of what I was doing, what I saw of the area and how nice my accommodations were, compared to what they had feared.

On the fourth day, a number of medical personal were bused to a farming community on the north side of Los Mochis. The land outside of the city was beautiful and the effects of the destruction was minimal to the eye. Sister Genovia was among the nurses and I marveled at her stamina for a woman in her sixties. A few of the nurses were unhappy about leaving the city but most were excited to be seeing a different area of the country.

Passing by several villages, I saw crumbled brick buildings, leaving the villagers without any housing at all. Finally, we arrived at the makeshift hospital that was serving a large agricultural area. The line of potential patients was long as they waited to be seen.

Disembarking, we were hustled inside and quickly put to work. The makeshift hospital designated areas for triage, emergencies, non-emergencies and surgery. After a long day, we were shown to our tents. I was assigned to a tent holding ten women in five bunk beds. Sharon proclaimed a bottom bunk quickly and Sister Genovia was given the only other bottom bunk available. I threw my things onto the top bunk before we headed off to the chow hall.

For the next week, I rose early, worked all day and then enjoyed the company of the other Red Cross volunteers in the evenings. They came from all over and the opportunity to serve with them gave me a sense of pride. Making sure to call my parents every evening, I assured them I was fine.

The eleventh day in Mexico would be a day that would live in my mind...and fears...forever. Rising early, we made our way to the chow hall before reporting for our shift. As we walked over to the medical tent, three SUVs careened around the corner. I thought at first that they were bringing in more medical emergencies, but before I could blink, four armed men wearing fatigues jumped from the vehicles. Bandanas covered the bottom of their faces making their eyes seem blacker. But I barely noticed their faces when my focus was on the weapons pointed directly at us.

Ordered into the vehicles, we stood numb until one of the nurses turned and ran screaming back toward the chow hall. Three shots rang out in the morning and to my disbelieving eyes, the nurse pitched forward, falling flat onto the ground, her back riddled with bullets. Another nurse bent over and immediately retched as Sister Genovia grabbed her, holding the heaving woman up.

The shots reverberating through an otherwise calm morning caused other Red Cross volunteers and security to run out of their buildings. Everyone halted when faced with the firepower of the bandits.

What do they want? Drugs? Before I could react to the events taking place all around, four of the armed men ran over grabbing me, Sharon, Sister Genovia, and another woman I had not met yet. The man who had ahold of my arm was surprisingly gentle, but firm. Pushed and shoved over to the vehicle we were forced to stand facing away from the crowed. Oh my God, we're going to die! Someone behind me threw a bandana over my eyes and tied it at the back of my head. Then my hands were tied behind my back and I could hear doors being opened. I was lifted and placed into the seat, feeling someone placed next to me. The door slammed shut and with the wails and screams from the witnesses fading into the distance, the vehicle rumbled forward.

Fifteen days had passed since she had said goodbye to her family in Richmond. Lying in bed, the threat of tears pricked her eyes, but she battled them back, determined not to fall apart. She remembered her last days there at home.

The family had gathered for our Sunday mid-day meal, when I delivered the news about going to Mexico with the Red Cross. When the local RC called, I did not hesitate. Finally a chance to do something different. The hospital shifts were not boring, but for so long I had felt stuck in a rut. The idea of traveling to another country with a group of dedicated volunteers sounded like just the ticket. The hospital would keep my job available while I was gone and with some money saved up, I would take this opportunity to test myself.

Of course, the news went over horribly. Mom burst into tears while my brother, Jobe, immediately looked at me and simply declared, "No, you're not going." His wife, Mackenna, attempted to placate him but Jobe was determined that I wasn't going to go. And I was equally determined to do so.

Rebecca, ever the peacemaker in the family, tried to intervene, but to no avail. Dad finally pounded his fist down on the table and startled everyone into silence. "We will not fight at this table," he announced. He shot me a look of disapproval, but everyone remained quiet. Staring at my plate, appetite gone, I fought the urge to jump up and leave.

Several tense minutes later, dad declared the meal over and told everyone to adjourn to the living room. "Leave the plates," he said gently to mom. "We need to take care of family first. Then you and God can wash the dishes." Mom never wanted an automatic dishwasher, saying that for every dish she washed, she would pray for the person who had eaten off of the plate. She gave dad a small smile, knowing he understood her heart.

The family meeting lasted for a few hours, finally settling down when I got on the computer and showed them the Los Mochis area on the internet. "It's got beaches and farmland right outside. There is an airport that we will be flying into and the Red Cross keeps us all together."

Jobe leaned over my shoulder and with a few taps on the keyboard, he pulled up gruesome photographs of drug murders. "Yes, and it also has a high crime rate and drug cartels."

"Jobe, I'm not going for a drug cartel. I won't be out in the jungle of Mexico! I'll be on the outskirts of town, working in a hospital."

Once again, the family all began to shout, each trying to overcome the madness. Finally, dad stood and brought the room to order once again.

Turning to me, his youngest daughter, he said, "Miriam," gaining my attention. "You are twenty-seven years old and no longer a child—"

"She's my child," mom interrupted, receiving a glare from him.

"Be that as it may, you are old enough to make your own decisions. While my heart is heavy that you would go to an area that is dangerous, I cannot forbid you to go."

Standing, I walked over to dad wrapping my arms around his rotund middle, hugging him closely. "Thank you pop, but it would mean so much if I had your blessing."

He returned my hug and said, "You only needs God's blessing, my daughter. From me, you will take my love with you."

At that memory, Miriam was unable to hold back the tears and she pressed her face into the pillow hoping that Sharon and Sister Genovia would not hear her sobs.

4

Marc flew Cam into the Los Mochis airport, but bypassed the customs office. Pulling into a small, private hangar they were met by Alberto Ortega, their DEA contact. Alighting from the small Cessna, Cam carefully eyed the man sent to assist. As much as he had been prepping about the drug cartels, he found himself doubting everyone. The cartels had even managed to infiltrate Interpol, much less the country and local governments.

Alberto was middle-aged and not overly athletic. He was shorter than Cam and Marc by almost six inches and his tan suit jacket was slightly wrinkled as though it was the only one he owned.

"I can see you evaluating me as we meet," Alberto stated.

"Occupational habit," Cam replied as Marc walked up to the pair.

Alberto nodded. "Understood. For me, occupational hazard."

The three men headed into a room inside the hot, metal hangar and sat in rickety wooden chairs at an old, scarred table. Without wasting any time, Alberto pulled out of his pocket a sheaf of papers and handed them to Cam.

"Here's your ID, papers to keep on you, and there's clothes in that bag," he said as he nodded over to a duffel bag in the corner. "Here is also a cell phone for you. Most of the workers have them so there will be no surprise. The phone's been preloaded with some phone calls and texts so that it looks legit to anyone who takes and searches it. What they won't know is that it can be switched to a secure phone that can reach out to me or to your partner here to contact us as to where to pick you up when you are ready to get out."

Cam looked at him, lifting his eyebrow. Alberto had switched to Spanish and watched him closely. Answering him back in the same dialect of Spanish, he noted with pride when Alberto appeared surprised.

"I see you're not only a native speaker, but you pick up dialects easily."

Cam did not reply, but just nodded in response.

"What have you got for him?" Marc asked, cutting to the chase.

"We've got some inside men working with the cartel, mostly in the fields. We're getting you with them. You'll be introduced as a distant cousin and right now our intel is the cartel won't ask too many questions. So many of their workers have been injured or become sick from the polluted water that they are desperate for workers."

Alberto eyed Cam carefully and said, "The work is hard. Farm work. Long days and hot sun. No privacy and even though they're desperate, there'll be armed guards, so don't fuck up. The only good thing is that some of the guards have been injured as well."

"I got this," Cam answered. Growing irritated with Alberto's daunting outlook, he wanted to hurry the process along.

"I understand you've been undercover before. I get that. What I need you to get is that this world—it's a fuck-of-a-lot different than the gangs in the U.S."

"Understood."

Cam held Alberto's stare for a long minute before the older man nodded and said, "Yeah, I figured you did."

"Tell us about the nurses. What do you know?" Marc asked.

"Right now they're kept in a heavily guarded dormitory inside the main compound." Seeing Cam and Marc's surprise, he nodded. "Yeah, it's true. These animals might not value women but they do value nurses. They desperately need the nurses and do not want them mistreated. So they're inside the compound. We still know of the three, but cannot get a good read on how many others there might be. At least our contact did tell us that the older Catholic nun, Miriam, and another nurse named Sharon are there. We don't know exactly where but our latest intel is that they're in a small building that keeps them together and they're well taken care of."

"For how long?" Cam asked.

Shaking his head, Alberto answered, "There's no way to know. Right now, their skills are needed. If they don't cause a problem, do what they're told, and take care of the medical needs of the injured cartel, then they'll stay there. But…you do realize that if they're not rescued, they'll never be allowed to leave?"

The air grew heavy in the room with the weight of what needed to be accomplished. Cam felt the other man's doubt in his success. "So I need to work in the fields, find a way to get to the area where the nurses are and then find a way to escape in the middle of the jungle and fields with armed guards dogging our every step."

Alberto once more stared at the large man sitting in front of him. Nodding slowly, he said, "Exactly. That's exactly what you'll have to do."

At that, Cam and Marc stood and Cam walked to grab the duffel bag. Holding Alberto's gaze, he said, "Then that's what I'll do."

"It's a suicide mission, you know," Alberto said, standing also.

Drawing himself up to his impressive height, Cam replied, "Never had a mission I couldn't complete. Successfully."

For the first time since the men had gathered, Alberto cracked a smile. "Dios mío. I think you just might succeed."

The day started like the past six days had for the nurses. Someone knocked on the door and then entered, their eyes quickly doing a check to make sure all were present. Another nurse, Lorainne, had been added to the group two days ago and she was not adjusting at all. Crying all of the time, she was pale and Miriam feared that she was making herself sick. Sharon was at the point of wanting to scream every time they were transported from place to place, but so far Sister Genovia had been able to calm her.

After they were awakened, they were allowed time to shower and change clothes. The captors had given them nursing scrubs and they appeared to be clean each day. The four were led by armed guards out to the small courtyard where a table was set up with fresh fruit, muffins, and coffee.

Eating, Miriam was struck once more how surreal the scene was. Closing her eyes she could almost imagine that she was at a resort, eating on the balcony. But then she would open her eyes, see the acute gaze of their armed guards with their guns at the ready and reality slammed back into her.

After eating, the women were led back into the small dorm room where they were allowed to finish getting ready for the day. It was evident that the room had been searched while they ate.

"What the fuck are they looking for?" Sharon growled. "We're stuck in the middle of nowhere and are watched constantly. Where do they think we're going to get the weapons to blast our way out of here?"

"Quiet!" Sister Genovia shushed. "Never let them hear you talk about weapons."

Grimacing, Sharon grew quiet and in a few minutes the guards came back to the door. Escorting the women over to two jeeps, they were taken to the building that had been set up as a makeshift hospital.

Entering the tent, Miriam kept her eyes down as they passed the guards, just as Sister Genovia warned. The words of the nun rang in her head. *Do not underestimate these men. They will respect you for the service you provide, but they demand respect. Keep your eyes down to show them your subservience.* Of course, Sharon had protested loudly when this advice was given, but the gentle nun reminded her of their precarious situation.

Once inside, she glanced around quickly, seeing more people than the day before. The instructions had been to patch the field workers up as quickly as possible so they could get back to work. The initial cases had been similar to what they saw in Los Mochis, but now the families of the workers were starting to come in, having dealt with their injuries for almost two weeks before being allowed to seek treatment.

There were some children, pregnant women, mothers, and elderly. And of course, many suffered from dysentery. The lack of clean water had spread the disease throughout the area.

Sucking in a huge breath, Miriam waded over to the doctor in charge to see what needed to be completed first. Dr. Ernesto Villogas smiled at the pretty nurse that had joined the group. His eyes quickly skimmed the nurse's body, giving her the impression that he was seeing beneath her scrubs. He immediately became professional in his directions, making her feel guilty. *He's just as much a victim as we are,* she surmised. *I wonder if they brought him here at gunpoint also?*

Miriam, determined to be professional in return, smiled back at the doctor. "Where do you need us today?"

He instructed her and the other nurses on their duties. Miriam nodded and headed to the next tent and began working with the children who had been brought in. She could not help but smile at their faces, so innocent of the world around them.

Checking the splints of several with broken bones, removing the crudely sewn stitches in cuts, checking the fevers of others, the morning passed quickly.

Seeing the doctor coming in to check on the patients, she smiled. "Thank you for assigning me to the children today, Dr. Villogas," she said.

"Please call me Ernesto," he replied smoothly.

Nodding slightly, she agreed. At her compliance, he smiled, his white teeth gleaming against his tan skin.

"I noticed that you were tired yesterday, so I thought a day with the children would do you good."

She nodded again before turning back to the next patient. She felt his presence close to her so she glanced over her shoulder, seeing him now standing directly behind her.

"I realize you were brought here against your will, but I can help you, my dear," he whispered. "Perhaps, we can have our lunch together and I will let you know just how much I can be of service. How we can be of service to each other."

He watched her shiver and chuckled. "I see you're interested. We'll talk later."

She heard him walk away as she tried to focus on rolling the bandages on the cart in front of her. *If he had been brought here against his will, he certainly was making himself right at home!* Closing her eyes for a moment, she breathed deeply to still her pounding heart. Thinking of her brother, she pulled his words to her mind. When their sister, Hannah, had been attacked years before and almost raped, Jobe told all of his sisters that they should always use whatever resources they could find to get out of a situation. *Doesn't matter if you lie or scream or fight like hell, just use anything you can. Play it smart and do whatever you need to do to get out.*

Of course, he was referring to being attacked, but Miriam knew this situation was the same. *I've got to keep my head, play their game, and work the system while looking for a way out.* Licking her lips, she knew she was in over her head. Armed guards stood around, although they looked bored. The area was filled with farmland and woods, hardly a place to hide. *Thank God I've got dark hair,* she thought. *I could blend if I needed.* Sighing loudly, she also knew that not being able to speak Spanish would make her stand out. *Jobe, I'm gonna need a miracle to get out of this.*

Just then, she heard Sharon's loud voice berating one of the guards. "I have to get through, you moron."

Miriam glanced into the other room, seeing the guards now alert, watching Sharon with undisguised anger…and lust. Before she could intervene, one of the other nurses hustled over and quieted Sharon, moving her past the guards toward the tent with medical supplies.

Disaster prevented once more, she wondered if talking to Sharon again would make any difference. She had tried to convince her that the way to stay alive was to play it safe, keep their eyes open for possible escape plans, but Sharon had shut her down quickly. "No way am I going to play their game," Sharon had voiced, not seeing the rationale of staying alive until they could be rescued.

Catching the eye of Dr. Villogas once again, she just nodded as she made her way into the medical supply tent behind the others.

Once inside, she saw Sharon being lectured to by the nun. She then looked over to see Lorainne checking the supplies. Walking over, she spoke to the timid woman.

"How're you doing?"

Lorainne nodded in answer, tears threatening to spill once more.

"You've got to hang in there, sweetie," Miriam said, placing her hand on the frail woman's arm. "We have to stay strong so that we can be ready to leave whenever we can."

"They'll never let us go," the other nurse whispered, rubbing her hand over her sweating forehead.

Miriam quickly placed her hand on Lorainne's head and felt the warmth. "I think you have a fever," she said. "Let's check."

Before Lorainne could protest, Miriam whipped out

a thermometer and quickly determined that the woman did indeed have a low-grade fever. "Have you been feeling sick?"

Lorainne nodded and said, "I keep going to the bathroom. I figured it was just the change in water, but…" leaning in to whisper, she confessed, "I'm passing blood."

Miriam turned to look for the doctor, but Lorainne grabbed her arm, hissing, "You can't tell anyone."

Jerking her gaze back to the ill woman, she asked, "Why?"

"Don't you see? They'll kill me. Why would they keep a sick nurse around?"

Miriam wanted to argue, but was afraid that Lorainne might be right. Licking her lips, she looked around quickly, finding the medicine that she needed. "Okay, but let's treat you. Have you taken anything?"

"No, just trying to stay hydrated with bottled water."

Nodding, Miriam walked to the cabinet and scanned the contents. Finding the Paromomycin and an antibiotic, she quickly snatched them. Turning back to Lorainne, she said, "Take these now. I'll take some back to the treatment tent with me. Come find me this afternoon just before we go back to the compound. I'll give you a second dose there and no one will know you're taking them."

Playing her part well, Lorainne took the pills that Miriam rolled into a bandage and, on her way out of the door, grabbed a water bottle provided for the medical staff. Rolling more pills into a bandage, Miriam shoved it into her pocket and then found the drugs she had been originally looking for. Making her way back to the tent, she began her long afternoon.

That night, lying in bed unable to sleep, Miriam tried to figure out a plan for escaping, but it eluded her. *Even if I could manage to escape the compound, how would I ever know where to go to find a way out?* Her mind wandered back to her brother and she sent up a silent prayer once again. *I gotta have help, Jobe. Please.*

5

Cam bent over in the field, sweat pouring down his face as he shoved the dirt to the side. His stained shirt was plastered to his skin and the mud caked on the bottom of his pants made moving difficult. The mountainside was populated with poppy plants hidden with towering pines and fir trees. The creeks nearby, with the pipe irrigation system, normally kept the plants watered. The earthquake had damaged the system and one of Cam's jobs was to dig new holes and re-lay pipes.

Standing, he stretched his broad back and glanced around. The other workers were starting to head back toward the hut for the mid-day break.

He had found the time to send a few cryptic messages through his secure phone but had spent the last three days in hard labor and getting the lay of the land. Most of the workers he was with were healthy, having come from other areas outside the earthquake location and, like his undercover story, were just looking for hourly labor that paid well.

They lived in wooden huts, cooked over a campfire and worked from sunup to sundown. He had started out at a small independent farm, but with his size and ability to work long hours, it was not long before one of the cartel agents sent him to the hillside to work on the irrigation. If the plants were not watered they would die and the cartel was not about to take any more losses than they had to.

"Hey, Big Man," one of the workers called over. "You ready to take a break? You show us up and the bosses will want us to do more."

Cam smiled and lumbered over to the group that was sitting under a tree, water bottles and sandwiches as their lunch. In the couple of days he had been there, he knew that these men were farmers, not cartel members—a great distinction because of Mexico's need for marketable crops. With the legalization of marijuana in many areas, the Mexican farmers could no longer afford to grow it. But with the increase of heroin, growing poppy was profitable. They did not care what they grew or what happened to the crop after they were paid.

But, he also found them to be a source of information about the earthquake and the local hierarchy of the cartel.

"How's your brother?" Cam asked one of the men.

"Haven't heard from him lately but his wife said he was treated at one of the camps. Said they got some doctors and nurses that'll patch 'em up," Andreas answered. "I got me a field that my family works, but came here for the money when they needed some extra hands."

"Who's taking care of your crops?" another asked.

"Got some kids working my small farm. My oldest is ten—he'll work it until I can get back."

Hiding his disgust behind his chewing, Cam thought of the kids working in fields. He watched the men carefully to plan how best to get closer to the central compound where Miriam would be kept. *Slow and steady,* he thought. *Rushing in too soon would do her no good.*

"They got a lot of these camps with doctors and nurses?" Cam asked casually.

"Not many, I don't think. I heard on the radio that Los Mochis had some and I know the workers went to clinics that were closer to the fields. The earthquake hurt mostly where there were buildings." The man looked at the wooden hut behind them and chortled. "As you can see, our dwelling stood tall."

The others laughed and Cam grinned along with them.

"I haven't listened to a radio," he continued. "Was there a lotta' people hurt?"

"Oh, yeah," one of the other men said as the others nodded. "Even the men who own these fields had a lot hurt. Some of their farmworkers or staff were in buildings that would have fallen down."

The men continued to discuss what the earthquake felt like for several minutes. Cam nodded occasionally as though he had been there too, while his mind worked furiously at a plan for getting closer to the compound.

"Anyone ever come up here to check on things?" Cam asked.

"We should be getting a visitor in the next day or so," the old farmer replied. "They come to check on us and see that things are moving forward. In fact, they should come soon to check on the pipes."

"What happens when these pipes are working?" Cam asked. "Don't want to be without work this winter."

Nodding, another man agreed. "Yeah, I ain't got no farm to get back to."

Andreas said, "Don't worry. You'll be taken care of. They always need workers." Glancing around at the sparse living conditions they had, he added, "But some jobs are better than others." He landed his gaze back on Cam and said, "You, Big Man. You could be used for hauling or maybe even get a job driving one of the trucks."

Not going to be around long enough for that, Cam thought, *but I gotta find a way to get closer. Someone coming to check on us will be just the ticket.*

Standing, the men headed back to the fields, the fall sun beating down on their backs once more.

That evening, Miriam and the other nurses were ready for dinner when a guard showed up, ordering them into vehicles once more. *What now,* she thought, fear choking her. With a quick glance, she saw the others had the same look on their faces.

This time they were not blindfolded, but with the dark night closing around her, she had no concept of direction. After about ten minutes, she did notice that the vehicle had left the gravel, bumpy roads and now traveled on pavement. Trying to see through the illumination of the headlights, she finally saw a tall wall up ahead with a heavily guarded, ornate gate. As they stopped at the checkpoint, she blinked away as a strong lamp was shone inside the car before they were waved on through.

Within a few more minutes, they approached a brightly lit, massive home with more guards patrolling the area. The paved driveway circled around a fountain and led toward the front. Once out of the vehicle, Miriam and the others were herded up the front steps of the mansion. As the gold colored doors swung open, the glare of the inside lights blinded her.

As her eyes adjusted, she tried to keep her expression schooled, but found it almost impossible. The inside of the home rivaled the most luxurious mansion seen in any tabloid of the stars' multimillion dollar homes. Floors of marble in the three story entranceway with another fountain in the middle led to dark teak floors extending to the room on the left that appeared to be a library.

To the right was another room, equally ostentatious, and the purpose she could not discern. There appeared to be a great many plants, tall palm trees in ornate pots, and to the side was a large cage. Hearing a growl, she jumped as she realized a black panther wearing a jeweled collar was now pacing in the cage.

"Jesus, how rich are these guys?" Sharon commented, her eyes looking around at the room.

Before she could answer, Miriam turned as a door to the back opened and they were escorted into a dining room with a table laden with food that could easily seat twenty people.

Miriam had to admit that her mouth watered as the smell of the delicacies drifted her way. Angered at how the peasants were given nothing to eat while the cartel leaders lived like kings, she pursed her lips. *Keep a cool head,* she reminded herself. She looked at the others and noticed that Sharon had jumped at the chance to sit as they were instructed. She followed Sister Genovia's lead and sat down as well, near the end, hoping to stay out of the limelight. *It may just be nerves, but I have a bad feeling about this.* Placing her shaking hands in her lap, she continually glanced to the side, keeping an eye on the calm nun.

Other doors opened and a handsome man walked in with Dr. Villogas, two beautiful women behind them and a few others trailing behind. Ernesto's eyes gleamed as they landed on Miriam.

"Juaquim. Let me introduce to you the wonderful nurses that I have been working with," he said smoothly. He called out their names to the other man, who eyed them carefully before breaking into a huge grin.

"Welcome to my humble home, ladies. We are indeed honored that you have come to help our good doctor in this time of need."

Miriam tried to smile but the surreal farce being played out in front of them had her feeling trapped in a tragedy. *I thought Dr. Villogas was a victim also, but he's part of this? He's part of our kidnapping and captivity?*

"You do realize that we were kidn—" Sharon began but was quickly interrupted by Sister Genovia.

"Forgive her, she is unused to our ways," the nun spoke gently. Turning to Sharon, she gave her a pointed look and said, "We should not speak unless spoken to, my dear."

Sharon reddened, but wisely kept her mouth shut.

Miriam watched as she was introduced to the others. Serita, Juaquim's wife, looking bored, gave them a barely-there nod before sitting down at the opposite end from her husband. Her hair was perfectly coiffed, her neck and wrists dripping in jewels, and her clothes were little more than what could be described as slutty couture. It was Ernesto's wife, Consuella's expression that concerned her. She glared at Miriam, unconcealed dislike pouring out toward her as she took a seat next to Serita. While equally drenched in jewelry as her friend, she wore her expensive clothing very well.

As the others settled into their chairs, the waitstaff began serving the multi-course dinner. Miriam kept an eye on Lorainne, knowing she could eat very little of the rich food and not become ill. Sharon dove in to the meal, exclaiming over its deliciousness. Miriam noticed Juaquim's eyes found Sharon's numerous times during the meal and Sharon gave no indication of discouraging it.

Ernesto constantly tried to draw Miriam into a

conversation, seemingly oblivious to his wife's visual daggers thrown her way. Miriam, on the other hand, was very aware. Eating just enough to not seem rude, she tried to keep up with the various players without being obvious. Consuella and Serita chattered amongst themselves, knowing that other than the nun, the nurses did not speak Spanish. Sharon, eyes still wide at the opulence of their surroundings, began talking to the men at the table and for the first time in days was not bemoaning their situation. Poor Lorainne tried not to be sick, and Sister Genovia simply sat as though she did not have a care in the world. *I'm either the only sane person in the room or the only crazy one!*

After the meal, Serita and Consuella excused themselves and left the nurses with the men. Sharon took the opportunity to scoot her chair closer to Ernesto and Lorainne gave a silent plea to Miriam. Standing, Miriam said, "Please excuse me, but Lorainne and I would like to use the ladies' room if possible."

The men immediately jumped to their feet, "Of course, of course," Juaquim said. Snapping his fingers, a petite women rushed in and he gave the order for his honored guests to be shown the bathroom.

Sister Genovia stood and with a nod to their *hosts* she began to follow the other women out of the room. Stopping at Sharon's chair, she said, "Don't you wish to join us?"

Smiling at the men, Sharon shook her head. "No, I'll be just fine here, thank you," she purred.

The other three women followed the servant into a huge marble bathroom appointed with gold colored fixtures. Lorainne immediately turned on the faucet and wet one of the plush towels, using the soft cloth to wipe her face. The servant left them and Miriam turned to the nun and quietly said, "What the hell is—"

"Shhh," Sister Genovia said. Holding on to Lorainne, she said loudly, "Hear, hear now, my dear. You just feel a little over heated and overtired."

Lowering her voice to barely a whisper, she said, "Keep your voice down. This room is probably wired."

Miriam nodded and walked to the sink, beginning to wash her hands as well. Staring into the mirror she also found herself wondering if it was a two-way mirror. Sucking in a shaky breath, she moved to assist with Lorainne. Standing with her back to the mirror, she mouthed to Sister Genovia, *"What is going on?"*

"I don't know," the nun mouthed back. *"For some reason they wanted to prove something to us tonight. Power, money...I don't know, but play their game for now."*

"What about Sharon?" Lorainne mouthed back.

"I'm afraid she now sees this as a way out. What she doesn't understand is that they will use her and then kill her if needed."

Miriam and Lorainne jerked their gazes to the composed Sister, knowing that she seemed to understand the situation better than they did.

"No more talking for now," the nun instructed.

The three women finished using the toilet and then left the room, following the servant who had been waiting outside for them. Taken to the living room, Miriam could not believe the wealth displayed. Her anger at the conditions of the workers compared to the unscrupulous gains of the cartel's leaders had her shaking.

The men, now settled on one of the large sofas in the room, with Sharon close by, stood as the three nurses walked back in. Before they could speak, Sister Genovia walked straight over to Juaquim and, giving him a conciliatory bow, said, "Dear sir, I must request that you allow us to get Lorainne and Miriam back to their room. Both feel overtired and we must take care of the nurses so that they can take care of us. Don't you agree?"

Not willing to argue with a nun, he immediately snapped his fingers once more and said, "Of course, my dear Sister."

Sharon was about to protest, but Sister Genovia answered for her. "Thank you so much and thank your wives for their hospitality."

Miriam spared a glance at Ernesto who was looking less than pleased at the turn of events. She managed a wobbly smile at him, hoping he would be placated enough. Within a few minutes, they four women were loaded into one SUV and taken back through the dark night to their housing near the medical compound. When they were finally back into their rooms and the guards had left them for the last time, they looked at each other.

"You must never forget that you are prisoners here," Sister Genovia whispered, pointedly looking at Sharon.

"I know!" Sharon whispered with emotion. "You think they're ever gonna let us go? I've been looking for a way out since I got here, and this may be my golden ticket."

Lorainne and Miriam looked at each other, neither understanding what Sharon was talking about, but Sister Genovia obviously did.

"You think by getting in bed with someone like those men will get you out of here?" she asked. "My child, don't be a fool."

"I'm not a fool," Sharon answered back. "Getting close to one of those men means better treatment for one thing and then it would be easy to slip out sometime when no one is looking." She smiled as she lay back in her bed. "Did you see the solid gold utensils?"

At that, Miriam startled. *Solid gold? Is that what the bathroom fixtures were also? I thought they were just a gaudy gold color!*

"Do not be blinded by the wealth of their gains," Sister Genovia answered back. "That plan will lead to your destruction as much as theirs."

"Ugh," Sharon bit out, rolling back over to face the others. "I want out of this hell-hole. And if kissing up to one of those men will get me out of here, it's worth it. If I play my cards right, I could easily slip away on some shopping trip. Anything to get out of here!" Her gaze drifted over to Miriam, still sitting on her bed. "You could do the same thing too, Miriam. You're pretty enough."

Miriam, stunned at the entire evening's events, shook her head while her gaze sought out Sister Genovia's.

Before she could answer, the nun ended the conversation. "That's enough, ladies. We're all tired and have another long day ahead." With that, the nun turned out the small flashlight and the room was immediately plunged into darkness.

Miriam lay awake for a long time, the bizarre events of the evening playing through her mind. *What was their game? Why had they been brought to the dinner?* The more she tried to reason it out, the more confused she became. But one thing was sure—Sharon was on a dangerous path, one Miriam felt sure was exactly what the men had wanted them to go on.

Oh, Jobe. Are you close, brother? Have you sent someone for me? I think it needs to be soon...I don't know how much more time I'll have.

6

C am anxiously awaited the cartel's agent that was due to arrive that day. It had only been two days since the men talked about the hospitals, but he knew that time was running out. By now most of the injuries had been addressed from what Marc had told him in their secure texting communications, but dysentery and cholera were the new culprits. While that would possibly keep Miriam safe due to still being needed, she would be more vulnerable to the diseases herself.

Marc supplied him with more intel and Cam was itching to be able to put it to use. Undercover work in the gang back home had fit him—go slow, get the information he needed no matter how long it took and then take action. This was different. This time there was a real person on the other end of the mission. One who had to be scared. Tired. Maybe even sick or injured herself. And if he was honest with himself...one who was beautiful. He had not kept the picture Jobe had given him. It was too risky to have it on him in case he was searched. But he committed her image to memory. Every night when he closed his eyes, he could see her—dark hair...dark, smiling eyes...perfect cupid's bow mouth.

Rubbing his hand over his face, he forced his attention back to the job at hand. The backbreaking digging and laying pipe. Suddenly the rumble of a truck as it was coming up the mountain resounded through the trees. He watched warily as two men alighted from the vehicle and the other workers stopped what they were doing to move toward them. He followed suit, carefully evaluating the newcomers. Medium build, both with weapons slung over their shoulders casually as though they had been born with a gun in their hands. *Probably had.* He noticed their eyes roaming over the group and he was careful to not stare, hiding his antagonizing glare.

The men stopped near the hut and Cam watched as they began talking about the crop and the irrigation system. One of them walked over with the head worker and began inspecting the work. Cam heard his name called and he knew that the worker was praising what he had accomplished. With his size, he had been able to dig and lay quicker than the others. Keeping a neutral expression on his face, he acknowledged the nod he received from the agent.

The men, taking a break, moved toward the hut to offer food and drink to the agents—not that they had any to spare but as a show of respect. *Perfect. Fuckin' perfect.* Cam deftly added the pills he carried in his pocket to two of the crude cups they were using and handed them to the agents, before handing out water to the others. The hot sun beating down through the limbs of the pine trees above made everyone drink thirstily.

Taking a hefty drink himself, he knew the drugs would have a fast reaction. And he was right. Within ten minutes, the driver began heaving, quickly followed by the agent. The workers jumped up, at first concerned and then fearful.

"What is it?" one of them said, trying to assist the first man.

Cam, pretending to be just as confused, said, "Maybe they're not used to our water."

"Will we be blamed?" another frightened worker asked, backing away from the heaving men.

Wanting to place more fear on the situation, Cam adopted a concerned expression as he turned toward the head worker and asked, "Do you think it could be cholera?"

With a gasp, the other workers stepped back. "I got a family," one said. "Not touching 'em."

Cam pretended to work the problem as the workers all backed away, fear in their faces and in their voices. Turning toward them, he said, "We gotta do somethin'. We leave them, someone'll come looking for them and blame us."

"But what? What can we do?" the head worker asked.

"I'll take 'em. In their truck, I'll take 'em to the medical camp."

The others looked dubiously at him and then nervously at each other.

Cam continued, "We leave 'em here and they die,

someone'll come searching and then it'll look like maybe we killed them. Or we get sick too."

The heaving of the two men at his feet punctuated his words.

"Help me load them into the truck, I get them to help and then we're good. No one's pissed at us and then I can get back."

The workers all began to nod. None of them wanted to take the risk, but if the big, newcomer was willing... they were fine with the plan.

Loading the two men into the back of the truck, Cam hopped up into the driver's seat. Looking at the lead worker, he sent him a questioning look.

"Go down the mountain," he was told. "When you get to the fork, go left. If you keep following that and take a left at any fork, then you'll come to the nearest compound I know. It'll be about twenty miles away. I've...I've never been but that's what I've heard. There should be a doctor there."

Nodding, Cam started the engine and headed the truck down the mountain. *Finally I'm making progress!*

With the two men still heaving in the bed of the truck, Cam pulled out his secure cell and placed a call to Marc. Giving him an update, he hung up knowing Marc would call him back as soon as he had more intel from Luke.

With the window down, the breeze blew Cam's hair, now longer and he looked at his filthy hands from having worked in the dirt. *Hell, I'll scare her to death if I find her,* he thought, but realized that his appearance worked perfectly to disguise himself. *Come on Marc. Call back. Time to get the girl!*

Luke, pulling his shift in the Saints main room in the compound, got a call from Marc. *Its about time,* he thought. While patience was definitely a virtue for him, with Cam out in the field alone, the other Saints had been chomping at the bit. Swallowing the last of his now luke-warm coffee he said, "What have you got?" While listening to what Marc was reporting, he quickly alerted Jack. He began working the intel, after fixing another pot of coffee, ignoring the Keurig on the workroom counter. Known for making strong coffee, the others joked that no Keurig was good enough for him. Within ten minutes Jack joined him.

"What've we got?" Jack asked sharply.

"Cam's finally found a way to get closer to Miriam. He used the pills to induce vomiting of two agents and now is on his way with them toward one of the cartel's medical tents. Since we placed him near the last known location of Miriam, that should take him straight to her."

Nodding, Jack ordered, "Get back with Marc and make sure he has Cam's coordinates at all times. Cam'll be planning the mission as he goes and it may be a short notice that Marc will get."

Luke quickly entered the information into his system and called Marc back. Giving him the closest landing field, he had Marc on stand-by. Then he gave him the latest information he could access about the area.

Within minutes, Marc called Cam back. "They still sick?"

"Yeah. Still retching in the back of the truck. They can't hear me."

"Good. Luke says that there's no new info that says that the nurses have been moved. Your coordinates look like you are heading straight for the medical facility that she should be at. Go slow, man. You do not want her to give you away."

Snorting, Cam replied, "Hell, the way I look, the only thing I'm gonna do is scare the shit outta her."

"You may not see her at first. You got a plan for sticking around if necessary?"

"If I gotta, I'll take half of a pill myself, just to become sick enough to get to stay, but I'm hoping it won't come to that. Don't want to be ill if my opportunity comes to get her outta there."

"Right," Marc answered. "Good luck and let me hear as soon as you can."

With that the two men disconnected. Allowing the breeze to continue to blow on his face, cooling the sweat that had been pouring off of him, Cam felt the first sense of freedom in a week. Knowing Miriam had to be feeling the shackles of imprisonment, he wanted that sense of freedom for her too. And wanted to be the one to give it to her.

Miriam started her morning managing to get Sister Genovia alone, wanting to question her further about the events of last night. Finding the older woman in the supply tent counting the stock, she picked up a bag of makeshift bandages and began to sort them.

Whispering, she asked, "What happened last night?"

"It appears the doctor and the...man in charge... were seeking female companionship and hoping to impress us at the same time."

Miriam's eyes grew wide as she stared dumbly at the nun. "Female companionship? Their wives were with them."

"With these men, the bounds of marriage mean little. And their wives are quite content to be taken care of."

"But...but..."

"And the dinner was an exhibition of their wealth. And power."

"But why?" Miriam asked, her confusion even greater than before.

Sister Genovia turned to her, a kind expression on her face. "My dear, I have worked among these men for a while. It was my calling to bring God's grace to whomever I could and if I could save anyone from the clutches of their evil...then that is what I have tried to do."

Miriam looked down at the bandages as a guard walked past the door to the tent. As she heard him move by, she turned her questioning gaze back to the nun.

"I am not a threat, my child. They know that. I am protected by the veil and they know I will not try to escape. Nor am I impressed by their wealth or power.

Those earthly, ill-gotten gains mean nothing to me. But having me along with you last night gave the illusion that it was just a friendly meal."

"But they kidnapped us. They keep us under lock and key!" Miriam whispered harshly. "How can they think we want to be captives?"

"Look around. Are we not kept safe by the men with guns at our door? Are we not fed better than the workers? You see, in their minds, we are being treated well and as a reward for our service here for the cartel, they are willing to bestow upon you some of their wealth. And if you become a mistress to someone higher up at the same time...so much the better for them."

Miriam dropped the bundle, clutching the table in front of her until her knuckles were white. Feeling light-headed, she sucked in a huge breath letting it out slowly. "This is madness," she barely whispered.

She felt Sister Genovia's hand cover hers and squeeze. "Yes, but this is the madness they live in."

Miriam turned her face back to the older woman and said, "What do I do?"

She felt the nun's piercing gaze and held it. Never wavering.

Sister Genovia nodded. "That's good. You're not enticed by the lure of what is here. Sharon is. You cannot persuade her differently and do not try. Leave that to me. They will expect it of me but will look suspiciously at you if you try to talk her out of the path she has decided to go on. But," she squeezed Miriam's hand for emphasis, "do no talk in front of Sharon. She will quickly become an informant if she thinks it will make her road easier. For now, take care of Lorainne. She is ill and becoming weaker. Do what you're told and keep your wits about you."

Lickings her lips nervously, Miriam nodded and then turned her sad gaze back to the nun's. "I'm never leaving, am I? I'll never see my family again, will I?" She battled the tears threatening to fall, blinking furiously.

Another squeeze. "My child, you never know what God has in store for us. But I pray for your deliverance and the deliverance of the others."

"It would take a miracle," Miriam whispered, beginning to feel that there were no miracles in store for her.

Smiling, Sister Genovia replied, "Miracles happen. And I have a feeling that one is just waiting for you."

A guard stuck his head into the tent and the two women quickly began counting the bandage rolls once more. Gathering some in her arms, she walked briskly by the guard and into the infirmary tent, seeing Ernesto and Sharon standing very close together. Sharon was leaning close to the handsome doctor and his eyes were on the woman. Remembering the words of the nun, Miriam gave them a quick smile and continued into the next room.

Please God. I need that miracle. But until it came, she bent over the exam table and began helping the next ill worker.

Miriam heard the noise of a truck pulling up outside and men shouting. Wanting to be as far away from the commotion as possible, she moved toward the back while continuing to check on patients. Pushing her damp hair away from her sweaty face, she bent over the worker who had been retching most of the night. From the looks of him, he might not live through the day.

Dr. Villogas moved beside her and bent over the patient as well, his body too close to hers for comfort.

"I hope you enjoyed the dinner last night," he said, turning his handsome smile toward her. "Mr. Guzman and I were thrilled to have such company."

"It was lovely," she commented. "I hope we did not put your wives out too much."

The only thing that gave away his surprise at her comment was the flash of irritation that moved through his eyes.

"Not at all. Our wives are very...accommodating that way."

Forcing a smile on her face, she just nodded.

"We would love to have you join us again sometime," he said, his voice smooth.

She looked across the room catching Sharon's gaze on her and was trying to think of an answer when she was saved by the yelling from a guard at the door.

Dr. Villagas and she moved to the outside of the tent where a large truck parked, two men in the back being loaded onto stretchers and being brought inside. The doctor immediately moved with the ill and Miriam stayed behind hoping to put some distance between she and him for as long as possible.

Her eyes turned back to the truck, the acrid smell of vomit emanating from the bed of the vehicle. That was when she noticed the driver. How could she not notice him? Compared to most men around, he was huge. Taller than her brother who was six feet, two inches tall, he was built like one of the football players she would see when Jobe dragged her to college games. His black hair curled over his ears and down his neck. His olive skin was covered in the same dust that coated the truck. He had a few days scruff on his face, needing a good shave to go along with a haircut. His cargo pants were muddy at bottom as well as his boots caked in the clay. Other men around seemed to be giving the driver a wide berth, probably wondering if he were going to become sick as well. As her eyes moved back up his enormous frame, she was startled to see that he was staring. At her. Directly at her.

7

Cam could not believe his luck...or fate. *How the hell did I manage to pull up to the exact infirmary tent that she's at?*

He looked away quickly, but not before she had noticed him. Her face, having been committed to memory from the photograph, was now forever burned into his soul from seeing her in person. The family resemblance to Jobe was noticeable, but she was more beautiful in person.

Long, dark hair pulled back into a ponytail. Clean hospital scrubs that did not hide the curves beneath. Her complexion was marred by the dark circles underneath her eyes and he quickly ascertained that she was several pounds thinner than her latest photograph. Her eyes landed on his and before he looked away, he saw the flash of curiosity...as well as fear...in her expression.

Placing his hand over his stomach, he received the desired response of the others moving away. Since no one knew what might be wrong with the agents he brought in, he hoped to keep the others away as well.

Miriam noticed the driver as he swayed slightly and she instinctively moved toward him. Pulling out clean gloves from her pocket, she snapped them on quickly before approaching him. Standing closely, she leaned her head way back to look into his face, noting the grime kept her from telling if he were pale or flushed.

"Are you alright? Do you need to lie down?" Speaking in the broken Spanish that she was picking up.

He grunted his response, "*Sí*."

Nodding, she placed her hand on his arm to lead him inside the tent, immediately noting the muscles bunching underneath her fingertips. Feeling a tingle travel up her arm, she quickly removed her hand. "Come," she said, waving her hand in the universal sign to follow. She moved inside the tent, hearing him directly behind her. Just as she was about to give him one of the free beds, Dr. Villogas approached.

He spoke to Cam in rapid Spanish while Miriam stood by in confusion. She watched as the two men's eyes moved over to the agents and she realized that the driver was being questioned as to what had happened.

She turned her attention to Dr. Villogas as he finished talking to see what his instructions were.

"He says the men came to the camp and became ill, throwing up. I'm putting them in quarantine until we know exactly what's going on."

"What about this man?" she asked, wondering where to put him.

"He'll need quarantining also, but not here. Not with the agents."

She had seen the hierarchy of care given to the ill and injured. The cartel's higher echelon members were given priority and treated at one of the buildings that had been turned over for their medical care. The lower members were treated at the makeshift infirmaries. And the workers from the fields...the lowest of care was given.

Biting her tongue, she said, "But he's been here, so if he's carrying something shouldn't we treat him here? Why send him somewhere else where he could spread an infection?"

She saw the thoughts churning in Dr. Villogas' mind so she pressed her suit further. "He did just possibly save the lives of two agents. I'd hate to see that go unrewarded and have him end up spreading his disease elsewhere."

Finally giving a terse nod, Dr. Villogas agreed. "Put him in the back of the tent. No, there's a spare tent behind this one. Put him in there. If he's well, that'll be good enough. If he becomes sick, he's still away from the rest of us. And if he dies, so be it."

With that, he turned and stalked away and it did not miss Miriam's attention that Sharon was right where the doctor was heading.

She did not realize how long she had been standing, staring at the retreating doctor's back when a voice directly behind her startled her.

"*Señorita?*"

Jumping, she looked back up at Cam and saw him

sway slightly. *"Perdón.* I'm sorry," she mumbled. "Come," she said once more, this time leading him around to the back of the tent.

Cam could not believe his luck. *Jesus, if this will only last,* he thought. For right now, he was going to get a tent to himself and access to this woman. *Gotta make this work. Gotta get this right.*

He followed her to the small tent and passed her as she stood holding the door flap open. He stepped inside before turning to stare at her once more. It appeared that she had gone into nurse-efficiency-zone.

"Clean clothes for you. Put them on," she spoke haltingly, holding up a pair of drawstring pants and t-shirt. *"La ropa,"* she reiterated, as he took the clothes from her hands.

Sliding his fingers along hers, he noticed her jerking her eyes up to his as her brow knit in confusion. *Fuck, she's gonna think I'm a pervert,* he realized as she backed up a step. Keeping his gaze neutral, he watched as she relaxed slightly.

She walked over to a plastic bowl on a small table and picked up a bath cloth, handing it to him as well. *"Lavar,"* she said, motioning to the large water jug next to the bed, indicating for him to wash. She turned and walked to the door flap, before looking over her shoulder again. *"Cinco minutos,"* she said softly, indicating that she would be back in five minutes, before walking out and letting the tent flap wave in her wake.

Cam looked quickly down at his dirty body and knew it would take more than five minutes to get rid of the dirt on him. Jerking his boots and cargo pants off, he pulled on the drawstring cotton pants. Pouring water into the plastic bowl, he pulled off his grimy t-shirt and dipped the cloth into the tepid water. Washing the dust from his arms and face first, he then tried to scrub his hands. Bending over, he dunked his head into the water, soaking his hair to rinse off the dust as well. Standing back up, he gave his head a shake, sending water droplets scattering in every direction. Senses alert, he knew when the whisper-soft sound of the tent flap opened again and heard the sharp intake of breath behind him.

Miriam had stepped inside but halted immediately. She had seen her brother and his friends shirtless many times over the years, but nothing had prepared her for the sight of pure masculinity in its perfection. The driver's dark hair was now wet and tousled. His thick neck was clean and led down to a back that was all defined muscle and sinew. Tapering to a narrow waist, the drawstring pants did nothing to hide the tight ass and the material stretched over his thighs. At the bottom, his lower legs and bare feet peeked out from the too-short material. And his feet were directly in front of hers.

Jumping out of her stupor, she blushed furiously as her gaze lifted and saw he was staring at her, a smile working on his mouth. Caught ogling, she looked away unwilling to allow her eyes to continue to roam over the front of him, which at a glance had appeared to be even more magnificent than the back view.

Cam saw her perusal and while he was accustomed to the provocative glances from women, her blush and

MARYANN JORDAN

gaze aversion was even more interesting. *Got to get her closer.* Pretending to sway slightly, he stumbled toward the bed.

That did the trick, as she rushed to his side and assisted him to sit on the cot. Her assessing gaze noted that his complexion was clear and so were his eyes. Placing her hand on his forehead, she also realized that he was neither clammy nor feverish.

She grabbed the dropped t-shirt and held it up to him. His eyes seemed to be watching carefully. As she started to stand, his hand reached out lightning fast and he clamped down on her wrist. She started to call out to the guards, but his next word had the scream halt in her throat.

"Jobe," he whispered.

Her eyes widened as her knees buckled. Gasping, her mouth formed an "O" but no words came forth.

Cam grabbed her other wrist in a tight, but painless grip. "Keep cool," he whispered. "You gotta be strong."

She continued to stare, her heart pounding in her chest.

"Can you do that for me, Miriam?" he mouthed, not knowing who might be listening outside. Seeing her shock, he gave her wrists a little shake forcing her to blink and focus. He repeated, "Can you do that? Be strong?"

Her head jerked in a nod as her breath was still caught in her chest. She watched as his gaze roamed over her face and then watched as he leaned in.

"Breathe."

Gulping in a gasp, she felt lightheaded and swayed

momentarily.

"Can't take a chance letting you sit down. Someone could come in. You gotta pull it together," he ordered gently. Then as a last ditch effort to get through her daze, he added, "For Jobe."

She blinked and he watched her take another deep breath as her eyes cleared. She said nothing, but he knew she understood that he was sent to help her. Letting go of her wrists, he watched as she stood, solid and back in control.

Her eyes glanced to the door flap but there was no one around. Looking back down at him, her thoughts were a tangled mess. *Jobe sent someone. Someone who looks and sounds as though he belongs here in this hell-hole so he fits in perfectly. What do I need to do? What does he want me to—*

"Stop. Still your mind and let me take it from here. My name is Cam. I'm a friend of your brother."

Sucking in her lips, she gave a slight nod again. "If you're not really ill, you won't be able to stay here."

He answered by reaching down to grab his dirty cargoes off of the floor, digging into one of the pockets and pulling out a small pill. Breaking it in half, he swallowed it quickly before she could stop him.

Her eyes widened again in question, but he said, "It'll just give a man my size some cramps and a little vomiting. Just enough to keep me here till you and I can figure a way out."

Out...he's going to help me get out. Even knowing they had a herculean task in front of them, she gifted him with a blinding smile that had him catching his breath.

Shot straight to the heart, her smile pierced him. *Beautiful. Fuckin' beautiful.* Even in the middle of hell, she was offering him a piece of her—trust. And he vowed to never break that gift.

Within the hour, the nausea had set in and Cam retched into a pan next to the bed. Thankfully, his symptoms were not very strong and he played them up to be worse than they were.

For Miriam, his plan worked to her advantage. With her busy with Cam, Dr. Villogas had not reappeared and the last she saw, he was leaving and Sharon was with him. Sister Genovia came into the tent to check on her and Miriam wanted to confide that the driver was actually someone sent by her brother to rescue them. But Cam had warned her to say nothing and so she kept silent.

"I'll be to dinner soon," she promised the nun.

Nodding, the older woman left the tent and Miriam let out a huge sigh. Turning back to Cam, she wiped his brow, a worried look on her face. "I hate that you had to do this," she whispered.

"I need to stay here long enough to find a way to be assigned to some kind of duty here," he replied. "I need you to tell me everything you can about what you've seen around this place."

While continuing to care for him, she gave him a quick run-down on what she knew. She was able to tell him how often the guards changed, where the nurses stayed, what her schedule was like, who was here with her, and then she told of the events of the previous night when they had been taken to dinner at one of the cartel members' home.

Up until that fact he had been listening, pleased with all of the information she had been able to relate. Hearing that detail and Sister Genovia's opinion of the events, his blood began to boil. *Fuckin' hell. She's now been noticed by someone that can make this even more difficult.*

"Your face scares me," she whispered, seeing his features set in granite.

His eyes sought hers as he replied, "We're not gonna waltz right outta here. I gotta get the lay of the land, then make a plan. My contact's gotta be ready. But what that nun said, you've got the eye of someone who can make this even more difficult."

"What do I need to do?" she asked, her face a mask of fear.

"Play it cool with me. Don't give me any more attention than anyone else. You speak to me in English and I'll act like I don't understand you. I'll try to work a way to be able to stay here and keep an eye on you. For now, sounds like the other nurse is gettin' in bed with the cartel. Miriam, just sayin', I'm not putting you at risk to save her ass if that's how she's playing it."

"I think Sharon's just trying to stay safe the only way she knows."

"Bullshit. From what you said, the dollar signs flashed through her eyes the minute you all showed up at Guzman's mansion."

Sucking her lips in again, her mind in a whirl, she nodded. "We gotta get Sister Genovia and Lorainne out as well. I can't leave them behind."

"Working on a plan, sweetheart."

He peered at her face, seeing the signs of stress and fatigue. In spite of his nausea, he lifted his hand and placed it on her small shoulder. "You need to get outta here. Go eat something and rest. Come check on me in the morning. I'll be safe until then." Seeing doubt in her face, he chuckled, "I'll keep retching enough to keep everyone out."

Answering him with a smile, she followed his instructions. She slept fitfully again that night, but this time her rescuer had a face. One that stayed with her all night.

***

Sharon wondered where Ernesto's wife was, but did not ask. If he did not care what Consuella thought about his activities then she refused to worry about it.

While his foreplay had been caring, once she was naked, he became a very selfish lover. Pounding into her for a few minutes, he pulled out and flipped her over giving her ass a slap. It stung but before she could process this new play, he slapped her hard several more times.

"Ouch, that hurts," she protested, trying to turn around. Used to lovers acquiescing to her every whim, Ernesto's dominance was painful.

"Shut up," he ordered as he continued to thrust into

her. Within a few minutes, he pushed deep one more time as his orgasm overtook him. Rolling to the side, catching his breath, he lay panting.

Sharon, not having reached an orgasm, moved toward him in frustration. "That was our first time, honey, but I've got to tell you that I need a little more to get me going."

The look he gave her would have incinerated other women, but she seemed oblivious. "You seem to misunderstand your position here," he replied. "You come when I call. You service my needs when I say. And if you please me, then and only then will I consider your pleasure."

Those words sunk in and she wisely kept quiet. With a false smile, she just said, "Sure baby."

Thirty minutes later she found herself back in the nurses' dorm, tiptoeing in trying to not wake the others. The evening was not what she had hoped for, but she had every confidence that she could talk him around to whatever she wanted.

Miriam lay quiet in her bunk, hearing Sharon moving around. She had wondered if the other nurse would be gone all night, staying in the luxury of wherever Ernesto took her. Hearing her curse as she stubbed her toe, Miriam guessed that sex with the doctor was not all that Sharon had hoped for.

And even though she was still in the middle of this hell-hole, she could not help but think that sex with Cam would be life changing.

8

The next morning, Miriam wanted to rush in to check on Cam but knew that she needed to see to her other duties first. Once completed she headed to the tent behind the infirmary, her heart pounding in her chest.

Pulling back the tent flap, she saw him sitting on the edge of the cot, his wan expression telling her that he had spent the night continuing to be sick. Quickly moving to him, she reached out to touch his forehead, finding it only slightly clammy.

"How are you? Are you still sick?"

He lifted his hand and gently clasped it around hers. "I'm fine, Miriam. I was careful with what I took. I made sure to retch a little this morning in case someone came in here before you."

He continued to hold her hand as she lowered it from his face. Licking her lips, she glanced nervously toward the tent flap.

"I don't think anyone will come in, since this is quarantined," she said.

Nodding, he asked, "How are you doing today?"

"I'm...I...," she stammered. "I don't really know. I couldn't sleep last night. I'm anxious and scared and excited, all at the same time."

"That's normal," he promised.

"I know they're not going to let you stay much longer in here. They're pretty rough on the workers."

"Yeah, I figured that. I really wanted to make sure I got to see you today, though, so I'm glad you came."

Her eyes darted to his in surprise. "Oh, you couldn't have kept me away," she gushed. "Just the thought that you are here—" Her voice broke as she attempted to regain control over her emotions. She felt his hand rubbing circles on hers as she took a deep breath.

"I'm here for you, Miriam. I told you yesterday that I'm working on a plan. That's true. But I'll need your cooperation as well."

"Anything!" she promised.

"Chances are, when the opportunity presents itself for us to be able to leave, I'll need you to be ready to go at the drop of a hat. Don't know when or how right now, but I'm working on our escape."

"I can do that," she promised again, nodding her head enthusiastically while squeezing his hand.

He glanced down, seeing her small, pale hand still in his larger, tanned one. *So different. So right.*

The next day, Miriam was terrified when she went in the early morning to check on her patients and found Cam's tent empty. Seeing one of the men who assisted with patients nearby, she grabbed his arm. Pointing to the tent, she asked, "Where is the man who was here?"

The older man gave a shrug and said, "He gone."

"I know he's gone," she said, exasperation in her voice, "but where did he go?"

Another shrug was the only answer, so she let go of his arm and allowed him to move on. *Okay, calm. Stay calm. They could have found out he was here to rescue me. Then they would have killed him. But he left. Voluntarily? No, he'd never just leave me. But where could he have—*

"You seem to be in a tizzie," Sister Genovia said, standing nearby.

Startled, Miriam quickly recovered and said, "No, not at all. I just wondered where the patient went who was in here."

The older woman eyed her carefully before saying, "You have a special interest in the man?"

Trying to chuckle but having her mirth come out more as a squawk, Miriam said, "No. It's just that if he's out for a walk to regain his strength, then I don't need to do anything to his room. If he's left for good, then I'll have someone clean the tent thoroughly."

Sister Genovia walked to the open flap of the tent and glanced inside. The interior was spotless, no linens on the bed and fresh water sitting by the bed. Standing and peering back into Miriam's eyes, she said, "Hmm. It appears that he has gone for good. God be praised, he was made whole again." Holding the younger nurse's gaze, she said, "I would think you would be pleased."

"Yes, of course I am. Less work for me, that's for sure," Miriam lied, trying to keep her knocking knees from sounding.

As Sister Genovia passed her by, she whispered, "A big man like that...strong...smart. He'd make a good worker when it comes to re-building some of the damaged buildings."

Miriam's gaze jumped up to the nun's twinking eyes and realized that the older woman knew that she had some interest in the man. Panicked, she asked, "Could anyone else tell?"

Giving a shake of her habit, Sister Genovia said, "Not at all, my dear. I only noticed because I hear your restless dreams at night."

Sucking in a breath, Miriam blushed, but the good nun continued.

"Be safe and be wise. He is close by. You will see him near the loading docks. Whatever you do, plan well. And my prayers will be with you."

Not admitting anything, Miriam simply nodded and moved into the larger tent to begin her day.

Cam had been moving rubble for most of the morning. Declared well enough to work early that day, he had been taken by armed guard to one of the foremen at a building about half a mile from the infirmary. *Goddamn it! I didn't have a chance to touch base with Miriam this morning.* Hoping she would remain calm when she found out he was gone, he made his way down the road.

The foreman looked him up and down, saying, "Agent said you got him and his driver here when they got sick. You got sick too."

Nodding, Cam wondered what they had in store for him. He did not have to wait long. The foreman left and went to talk to another man standing near the trucks. After a few minutes the foreman came back over.

"You're too big to be wasting your time digging irrigation pipelines in the mountains. We need strong backs here working on the buildings. You start here now."

Pretending to be appreciative of the honor bestowed, he nodded and asked who he needed to report to. The foreman introduced him to a few other large men, all hefting the bricks that had crumbled.

As he began working, he noted the trucks hauling away the broken building materials and began plotting what it would take to be able to drive one of them. There was no place to hide the nurses, but that was part of what he spent his day doing besides hauling. He plotted and planned. And thought of her. He tried to remember that she was just a mission. A friend's sister. But the memory of her silky hair as his fingers touched it. Her clean scent when he knew he had smelled of dirt and sweat. Giving himself a mental shake, he once again hoped she would know he was all right. He had seen the older nun watch him as he was taken away and prayed that she would talk to Miriam.

By the end of the day, as the others were finishing

the work, he ambled over to the foreman. Giving him a nod of respect, he asked, "Where do I bunk for the night?"

The foreman turned, yelling behind him. "Joco? Over here."

Another worker came trotting over and was introduced to Cam. "Show the new man here where to bunk. Bring him back here tomorrow." With that, the foreman walked away, leaving Cam to follow Joco.

They made small talk and Cam was pleased to see that as they walked down the road, it was in the direction of the infirmary near the compound.

Before he could get close enough to see if Miriam was around, Joco pulled his attention to the side.

"We bunk in here since the quake. We'll get a meal in a bit and the beds are inside."

Cam nodded and reluctantly followed the man inside. The temporary housing was a tent, similar to what he had been in when ill. The space was large, with cots lining the walls, five to a tent. Nodding to the others, he greeted them and quickly learned their names. He needed to be seen as eager, hardworking, and completely trustworthy.

Stepping outside, he sat at a makeshift picnic table and was given a plate of food by one of the women in the area. From what he could gather, if the men had wives they were kept back home somewhere raising their children. The women around the compounds were mostly the cartel's whores. This became evident when his plate of food was delivered by a young woman with harsh features, who openly propositioned him.

"You want good time? I give you good pussy," she said, her voice almost bored with the conversation.

"No thanks. Not now." Seeing her incredulous look, he mumbled, "Been sick."

She shrugged and was just leaning away from him when he saw a truck drive past, several nurses in the back being taken to their guarded dorm. He caught a glimpse of Miriam's face as she met his gaze. *Fuck*, he thought. *I hope she can see I'm here and close by.*

Eating quickly, he excused himself and headed to the tent taking the cot that had been pointed out to him. Falling down on it, he gave over to the fatigue, his mind on the dark haired beauty that needed rescuing. He had to keep his wits if he hoped to get them out of this hell.

Miriam was stunned to see Cam sitting at an outdoor table with a woman leaning on him. She recognized him immediately—his size made him easy to find. The truck passed so quickly, but not so fast that she did not see the look of recognition on his face as she moved by. His eyes had moved away suddenly and she instinctively knew he had to hide the recognition on his face.

Glancing to the side, Sister Genovia gave her a small smile and then turned back to Lorainne. Miriam looked at the other women in the back of the truck. Sharon had not been summoned away tonight and her mood was foul. Lorainne was not getting better; unable to keep food down, the others were concerned. It was as though Lorainne had given up her will to live.

"We're never getting out of here," Lorainne's weak voice said that evening as they lay in their bunks. "We're going to die here."

"Oh, shut up," Sharon groused. "Maybe you're going to die here, but I plan on finding a way out and I know just how I'm going to make that plan happen."

Sister Genovia turned from wiping Lorainne's fevered brow to the brash young woman. "The wealth you seek, from the men you are after, is not going to be for you. Their wives may be former beauty queen trophy wives, but they are still their wives. You will not have any status, you foolish girl."

"Who needs to be their wife? Certainly not me! But a favored mistress? I could get out of this dump, live somewhere nice, and then get back to California when I wanted."

"A pipedream," Sister Genovia said, shaking her head.

Miriam had been quiet during this exchange, her mind whirling with thoughts. She had now been in Mexico for three weeks, two of those out of contact with her family. *I hope Cam has a way to get ahold of Jobe and let him know I'm still alive.* Hearing Sharon voice her plot to become a mistress of either Ernesto or Juaquim, she frowned. She knew that plan was fraught with disaster but if Sharon would not listen to the wisdom of the nun she certainly would not listen to her.

Moving from her bunk, she padded over to Lorainne. Kneeling down, she took the young woman's hand while Sister Genovia continued to wipe her brow with cool water.

"Please don't give up," she begged Lorainne. "You've got to stay strong so that when we do get out of here, you'll be ready to see your family again."

A tear slid down Lorainne's pale cheek as she offered Miriam a watery smile. "I'll try, she promised. "I'll try."

Later that night, Miriam lay awake after the others had finally drifted off to their own fitful dreams. She tried to see Cam as just her rescuer. Just a friend of Jobe's. Just someone who came to help. But in her dreams he came first as an avenging angel...and then as a lover. Waking the next morning, she was just as exhausted as when she fell asleep, but with one thought on her mind. Rescuer, avenger, or lover...she desperately hoped she could glimpse him once more.

"Got to get the plan moving," Cam whispered into his phone. Managing to find a time to move away from everyone else, he gave Marc his information. "Made contact. Tell Jobe she's alive and well. But don't tell him she's caught the eye of some local cartel leaders, including one of the doctors."

"Fuck," came Marc's response. "How's she dealing?"

"Fine. Strong, smart, fierce."

"She's gonna need to be. Others?"

"One's sick, can't travel with her. The one from California has decided to take up the leaders on their generous offer. The other, an older nun. Can't see her trying to leave."

"That'll make it easier to just get Miriam out."

"Affirmative."

"What do you need?"

"Right now, I'm working about half a mile from her and can see her when she's driven past. Keeping a low profile. Once we get out of the immediate area, I can keep her hidden and we can travel quickly. It's just gonna be getting close to her again. Working on it."

"I'll be in touch. Good luck, man."

Disconnecting, Cam made his way back from his break, no one the wiser.

The opportunity to get closer to the hospital presented itself later that afternoon when part of the building crumbled onto several of the workers. Cam was one of them. Though unharmed, he managed to be taken to the infirmary.

To his good fortune, Miriam came out to greet the truck. Speaking in broken Spanish, she gave orders and he was carried inside. The doctor determined that there were no broken bones, just some cuts and abrasions. Dr. Villogas moved to the other worker, who had suffered a broken leg. Miriam managed to get to Cam, taking over cleaning his cuts and applying bandages.

"Was worried," she whispered.

"Hated leaving without letting you know where I was," he admitted. "You okay?"

She gave a nearly imperceptible nod as she continued to put antiseptic on his abrasions.

His gaze took in the infirmary and then came back to her face. "Don't see the other two nurses."

"Sharon was taken to the main house, supposedly to

take care of one of the leader's children. I…I think she is trying to get out that way."

"She's a fool," he mumbled.

Nodding, she agreed. "Lorainne is very ill. I'm scared for her."

"Just take care of yourself, Miriam. I'm working on a plan, but we gotta move carefully." He watched her as she finished with his leg and arm and then pulled off his t-shirt so that she could bandage his back. Hearing the intake of breath, he glanced over before realizing that she was admiring his physique. He had had a lot of women appreciate his body, but that little gasp from her lips shot straight to his dick. *Down boy. This is not the time or the place…or the girl.* Forcing his thoughts to a halt, he leaned forward so that she could reach the injuries easier.

"Tell me where you sleep," he whispered.

"My room is in the compound and takes about five minutes to drive there," she whispered back. "Down the main road. There is a tall wall around and we go through the gate."

"Gotta have more, sweetheart."

The endearment warmed her insides but shocked her. *Perhaps I've lived in fear so long that any man with a kind word would make me feel this way.* But even as she thought it, she knew her feelings were not stirred by just any man…it was this man.

Licking her lips, she continued, "Once inside the gate, go to the left and we are in the third building, next to the wall. Only has one floor and my room is on the right corner. I share it with Sister Genovia, Sharon, and

Lorainne."

Looking up sharply at him, she asked, "Can you get us all out?"

"No idea, but I'll do my best. Say nothing to anyone."

Nodding her head in agreement, she continued to clean his injuries. As she finished she bent over his body, seemingly to gather the materials from the bed, and whispered, "Thank you for coming. I know you put your life at risk."

He glanced over and saw her battling tears. "Don't cry, baby girl. I'll figure something out." With that, he stood, and with a polite nod, made his way out of the tent and back to his work site.

He had seen the way the doctor stared at Miriam. While it appeared that the man's itch was being scratched by the willing nurse from California, it probably would not be long before he either became bored or realized that she wanted everything she could get... or both. And the beautiful Nurse Miriam would be worth the conquest. Knowing they had a limited amount of time, he worked out an escape route and needed to go over it with Marc the next time they talked.

The following day, with one of the workers out with his injuries, Cam was able to finagle a chance to drive the truck loaded with building rubble and take the vehicle to a dump. He jumped at the opportunity to build upon his escape route.

The trip took him down a dirt road until he was on a paved highway. Several miles away, he turned onto another dirt road and followed it until he came to a river. He could see the pile of rocks and building materials that had been unceremoniously dumped nearby. As he operated the truck bed to unload its contents, his sharp gaze moved quickly in the area. Knowing the river was there, he noted the direction it was flowing. Away from where he had come from and would eventually lead to the ocean.

Calling Marc once more, he said, "Get me the specs on the river that runs nearby. About five miles from the compound. If it works, we can get here and make it down the river toward the ocean."

"Got it. Sending the info to Luke now and will get back as soon as I can."

Disconnecting the phone, he moved the gears so that the truck bed slammed back into place and drove back to his workplace. He noticed the foreman glance at his watch as he backed into the loading space again. *He's watching me,* Cam thought. *Gotta keep giving him reasons to trust me.* For the next two days, Cam helped load the dump truck and then drove numerous trips to the river dumping site.

He made contact with Marc the next day, gaining the intel needed on the river.

"You're talking about the Fuerte River," Marc reported. "You're about twenty-seven miles from Los Mochis. That river'll take you to the Gulf of California. I've got no way of knowing what tributary you're on, but you follow it, it'll get you there."

"Any chance of a pick up before we get to the Gulf?"

"Maybe. It's surrounded by mango plantations and

believe it or not, there are river tour groups, although those ceased after the earthquake."

"Okay. I gotta get her out as soon as I can. I managed to steal a small canoe from a local and stowed it where I go to dump rocks near the river. I'll make contact once we are on our way."

"This may help…or hinder, I don't know. But a large storm is heading your way. Supposed to be about two days of torrential rain. It looks like you don't have a lot of time before bad weather hits."

Cam pondered this new piece of information. "That'll be perfect. Lots of the buildings are weakened from the quake and heavy rain will keep everyone working to shore them up."

"It'll make traveling more difficult," Marc warned. "Especially with someone unused to traveling like that."

"Gotta take that chance," Cam decided. "We're running outta time fast."

Disconnecting, Cam hustled to finish the dump and return to the camp. It appeared that no one was even paying attention to him anymore. *Good. This'll make getting Miriam outta here a helluva lot easier.*

9

That night, Miriam lay on her cot, sleep eluding her as the day's horrors played over and over in her mind.

Dr. Villogas had come to her first thing in the morning, informing her that she needed to accompany him to a nearby village where one of the weakened buildings had collapsed during the night, injuring a number of workers.

Looking around at the infirmary needs, she asked, "Can't Sharon go with you?"

She was surprised at his reaction, noting for the first time the lines of fatigue around his eyes. His face contorted in a grimace and then it was quickly replaced by his typical expression of superiority.

"No," he replied sharply. "I want you with me."

Sighing deeply, she nodded. "Fine. Let me inform

Sister Genovia that she'll be short-handed today," she said testily.

Fifteen minutes later the two were in the back of a jeep bouncing over the rough roads leading toward a village. Neither speaking, Miriam held on to the side of the roll-bar, attempting to keep her teeth from clattering as the bone-jarring pot-holes continued. Tall trees lined the cart path they were on, with nothing but vegetation as far as she could see.

The trees finally fell away and farmland was on either side of the road. A few houses came into sight and, as they rounded another bend, came to the village. She could see the men working to haul off the rubble from the collapsed building. On the ground nearby was a large tarp with several bodies lying on top, the wails of families heard above the workers' equipment.

A man waved the jeep over and they were taken to a makeshift infirmary, similar to what she had seen before. Inside were about seven men with various injuries. She quickly went to work, auto-pilot kicking in. Assess the injuries. Prioritize. Stabilize.

She and Dr. Villogas worked side by side for several hours until the last of the injuries had been seen. Several women from the village came at noon and brought a meal for them. Accepting the food gratefully, Miriam sat in a corner for a few minutes eating the simple fare. One of the women motioned for her to follow and as she did, she was grateful when the woman showed her to a latrine. Smiling her thanks, she was able to quickly take care of her business, glad that the woman anticipated her needs.

A few more hours of work in the early afternoon and then they were back in the jeep, bouncing along. Fatigue was showing and she noticed Dr. Villogas kept glancing her way.

"Are you all right?" he eventually asked.

All right? A rude snort escaped as she turned to look at him. "I don't even know how to answer that."

He had the good grace to look askance before the jeep slowed down to navigate a nasty turn in the rutted road. She noticed that they had taken a different road out of the village than they had going in, but the explanation was only that there may be trouble on the other road. Not understanding the reason, she turned from Ernesto and gazed to her side of the road.

Miriam's eyes latched onto the sight up ahead in the grass. The stench of death rose from the ground... littered with body parts. Hacked off legs, arms, torso... and heads.

A scream erupted from her lips as she clasped a hand over her mouth. Dr. Villogas' eyes darted to see what the cause was when his eyes landed on the carnage.

"Goddamnit," he cursed, then yelled for the driver to get them out of there and then stop. When they had moved away from the site of terror, the jeep came to a jolting halt. Dr. Villogas jumped out and ran to the other side, reaching in and pulling Miriam out of the vehicle.

Dragging her body to the side of the road, he knelt down beside her, holding her head as she retched into the grass. Weakened, she leaned heavily onto him, shaking uncontrollably, unable to sit on her own. After several long minutes, she raised her head looking into his face, which at that moment appeared to be as ravaged as her own.

"Wh...wha..." she stammered, unable to articulate.

Sucking in a ragged breath, he said, "War."

Her brow knitted in confusion at his one word explanation.

"Cartel wars," he added.

The extra word hardly gave her any indication as to what she had witnessed and she continued to stare at him dumbly.

Drawing in another ragged breath, he looked at her face. "Wars are fought all over the world, Miriam. I realize it hasn't touched you, but in many parts of the world wars are a way of life."

She said nothing...just continued to stare.

"I've lived my whole life here in Sinaloa except for attending the University of Guadalajara for college and medical school." He paused before continuing, spearing her with a stare. "My. Whole. Life."

She gave a short nod feeling that some response was expected but still had no idea what he was saying.

"My father was a farmer. Like his father and his father before him. Mangoes until the cartels moved in and marijuana became the crop that was forced on the farmers. My parents tried to resist, but we had to eat. Now that marijuana is legalized, that cash crop has dried up and poppy is now planted on many of the farms that used to supply food to our nation."

"You...you were in college. Why did you come back?" she asked. "You could have gotten out."

"Your white-bread American upbringing," he scoffed. "I was smart. Went to school, got a scholarship, became a doctor. All because that was what the cartel wanted. And the plan was for me to come back and work here."

"But why did you come back when you could have been free?"

"My family was here," he growled. "Here. Under their thumb."

The realization that he had been held hostage at one time, although differently, struck her. "You felt like you couldn't leave."

Shaking his head, he said, "Not as long as my family was here." He saw her expression and bit out, "Don't pity me. I got off the farm. I live in a big house with my trophy wife and sons. I have money, prestige, and don't have to get my hands in the dirt."

Pressing her fingers to her lips once again, she fought back the tears that threatened to come. "Back there?" she asked, nodding toward the road.

"I told you. Cartel wars. The money to be made here is insane. And there's always someone who wants to control the flow of fortune. The...retribution...for that, is what you saw. It serves as not only a way to get rid of insurgents but to publicly display the results as a deterrent."

"You took an oath as a doctor. How can you condone that when you took an oath?" she asked, her voice shaking with fear and anger.

"I don't do that," he growled. "That massacre was not me. You've seen me. I patch them up, not tear them apart." Taking her by the shoulders, he gave her a shake. "Don't you get it? I'm trapped here, just like you are. I work to do what I can to make their lives...the lives of those like my father...better."

"But you take their generosity. You live high, you live well."

The quiet of the moment was broken only by the birds squawking in the tall trees that lined the road. The driver, not understanding English, still sat in the jeep eyeing the two. Letting go of her shoulders, Ernesto leaned back on his heels staring at the beauty in front of him. It had been a long time since he had witnessed that kind of passion. But her naivety could get her killed.

"All it would take is one nod from you, and I can give you that as well. Better food, a better place to lay your head at night. Clothes, jewels. Most importantly...protection."

Her brow once again knitted in question. He watched in fascination as understanding dawned on her. And anger was quick to follow.

"You? You're offering me a chance out of this hell if I become your mistress? What kind of man does that?"

"You think that's a bad thing?" he asked incredulously. Leaning in closely, he said, "You're a good nurse, Miriam, and a good woman. You need to get this though. I am your only way out of here."

Her voice dropped to a whisper as she asked, "You can get me home?"

Guilt flashed across his face before being replaced with irritation. "No. You're never going home again. They can't take that risk. But I can offer you protection and a standard of living that you've never experienced before."

The quiet settled around them once again. Exhaustion was overtaking her as she accused, "That's what you're offering Sharon, isn't it?"

"Yes," he admitted readily. "She's not stupid. She knows what I can offer and is smart enough to take me up on that."

Placing her hand on the ground, she pushed herself up. Standing on shaky legs, she accepted his hand as he stood with her. Looking into his eyes, she pulled her lips in. "You have to know that's not me."

His eyes jerked to the side, his face granite hard. His gaze found hers once more and he said, "I know. That's why I want to help you. Sharon? She's just a fuck. Not really even a mistress that I'll keep but just a fuck I can protect. But you? You're different."

"We need to get back." Turning, she moved toward the jeep and hauled herself into the seat.

Ernesto joined her, shouting to the driver to proceed. She caught him glancing at her during the uneventful rest of the journey. *What does he expect from me? How can he think I would want to stay?* Reaching the compound, she allowed him to assist her from the jeep, not sure if her legs would hold her.

"I can help you," he whispered smoothly. "You're determined to be independent, but this place will eventually break you. And when you crack, I'll be here to pick up the pieces."

She lifted her tired gaze to his, knowing her attempt at a glare was underwhelming. Steeling herself, she pulled her hand from his and walked toward her building. *You're wrong, Dr. Villogas. I won't break.*

Now, it was evening and Miriam lay in her cot listening to the sounds of Lorainne's ragged breathing. Sister Genovia had spent the day working over the injured and ill and the evening hours nursing Lorainne. Sharon was nowhere to be seen after the shift in the infirmary. *In fact, I did not see her after Dr. Villogas left.*

Lorainne was fading quickly, as though once her will to survive disappeared her body was soon following. Miriam tended her for most of the evening and now Sister Genovia was bending over the ill woman, patting her brow with a damp cloth.

The wind outside was beginning to howl and the window shutters clacked against the force.

Miriam's eyes met the nun's as she walked nearby to wet the cloth again. The older woman opened her mouth and closed it quickly several times.

"Are you all right?" Miriam asked.

"I should be asking you that," Sister Genovia said, referring to the tale that Miriam told her when she returned to the infirmary that afternoon.

No words came and the older woman seemed to understand that. Walking over to Miriam, she bent down closely to her face. "I have seen you with the large man."

Miriam gasped, her eyes widened in fright.

"No, no, it is all right. You have been completely

discrete," the nun assured her. "I'm more in tuned to others than most."

Not willing to admit anything, wanting to trust Sister Genovia but the events of the day still too fresh to face betrayal, she just stared into the warm eyes holding her gaze.

"If God gives you an opportunity to leave this place, you must take your chance at freedom."

Miriam's gaze darted over to Lorainne's cot.

"You cannot hold out hope for anyone else, my child. Lorainne will soon be joining God and my duty is to keep her comfortable until that happens. Sharon has made her bed and will lie there until she realizes it is not all that it seems. But you? You must take whatever opportunity you can to find freedom."

Miriam opened her mouth to speak but found no words came, so she sucked her lips inward. A short nod of her head was all that she would give. Sister Genovia patted her arm and then stood, walking back over to Lorainne's cot. Now she knew sleep would not come easily. That was the last thought she had before exhaustion took over and she fell into a fitful slumber.

Marc placed the video conference call to the Saints. Luke immediately patched him through and he could see Jack's face on the monitor.

"What d'you got for us?" Jack asked.

"Cam's going to try to get her out tonight. A huge

storm is coming in and, while the weather will hinder their travel, it will also make tracking them difficult."

"Who's he bringing in?"

"Just Miriam. The others are no longer able to travel," Marc reported. The video camera panned back and he could now see Bart and Blaise at the table as well. "How's your case?" he asked, referring to the serial killer case they had been working on when he and Cam were reassigned.

"Got him. Details will wait until you're home."

Nodding, Marc agreed. "I've got several landing places that I can try to get to once they're out but, until the storm lets up, I'm going to be grounded."

Bart commented, "So the thing that gives Cam a chance to get out will also put you on the ground? Jesus, that's fucked."

"In case my plane can't work, I've got my contact here who says I can have use of a helicopter."

Jack nodded, "Good. Use whatever you can from him. With you and Luke having been in the CIA, he's using contacts to make sure you can get what you need and feeding into your man there."

Finishing their conference call, Marc checked his phone one more time. Nothing from Cam, but maybe that was a good thing—it meant he was on the move.

10

The howling wind began around dinnertime, forcing the men to eat inside of their tent. Cam had just enough of the drug added discretely to the jug of beer sitting on the makeshift table to make the men slightly ill, which would force them constantly outside the tent seeking the latrine.

Within fifteen minutes, one by one of them felt nauseous and rushed outside. By now the pelting rain was coming down, making the paths muddy and forcing all others to seek shelter. *Perfect. This is perfect.*

He slipped out of the back side of the tent, the dark night and pouring rain masking his movements. It took him almost thirty minutes of jogging to approach the compound where Miriam was located. He stayed in the shadows of the trees lining the road, finally seeing the tall wall and gate ahead. The rain pounded his broad shoulders and ran rivulets down his face. Wiping his eyes he could see that the regular guards that stood around the outside of the gate had sought shelter. He scanned the left side, trying to discern the best way to scale the wall. A copse of trees was near the compound on that side, so he headed toward them.

Looking left and right, he was now out of sight of the guard shack but was uncertain if there would be others walking the perimeter. He stayed still for a long time but was finally convinced the perimeter check was not occurring, or it was not going to happen in the dismal weather.

He chose the closest tree and climbed it quickly, maneuvering out to the branch that was nearest to the wall. Tying a thin rope to the limb, he attached the lose end to his belt.

Several attempts later he managed to get his large body swinging so that he was able to propel himself from the limb to the top edge of the wall. He grabbed the concrete with all of his strength, hauling himself up to the top.

Lying flat, he scanned the area once more, blinking the water from his eyes. *Not a soul around.* He leaned over and counted the buildings from the gate. The third one was almost right in front of him. *Right side on the front*, she had said.

Taking the thin rope from his belt he let it drop over the edge of the wall. Not using the rope, he swung his body over and dropped to the ground. Thankfully the small splunking sound his feet made in the mud appeared to go unheard.

The area was cast in shadows, more dark than not, and it was easy to slip between the two buildings. The rain fell in sheets, driving everyone inside. Reaching the front corner, he peered around the corner and saw a small, empty courtyard in front. Unable to believe that there were no guards, he realized that without aid, the nurses would not be able to escape on their own, therefore the security was lax.

He slipped to the window at the right corner room and could see a sliver of light coming from inside. Pulling a knife from his pocket, he wedged it in the slit between the shutters and lifted it slowly. The blade caught on the small shutter latch and as he raised the bar from its catch, he was able to free the shutters. Barely creating an opening just wide enough for him to peek in, he saw the nun kneeling by the bed of the ill woman. Even from a short distance with rain still running into his eyes, he could see the deathly pallor of the nurse.

Moving slightly to the left he was able to see Miriam in a cot, her back to him. Another cot was empty, its blanket undisturbed. Miriam was rolling over, her eyes open and staring at her two roommates. Swinging her legs over the side, she stood and moved toward Sister Genovia.

Knowing time was of the essence, he whispered, "Miriam."

Hearing a noise coming from the window, she looked up at the same time as the nun. They both gasped, grabbing on to each other as he leaned his head in slightly so that the dim light from the candle in the room shone on his face.

"Cam!" Miriam whispered, rushing forward. The

rain was continuing to pelt down on him and she grabbed his arm. "What are you doing?"

Using stealth in spite of his large body, he hauled himself over the window sill and deftly closed the shutters behind him. Turning quickly, drops of water flung off of him and onto the floor.

"It's now. We've got to leave now. The guards are all gone and no one will look for us for a while."

She looked behind her at Lorainne lying at death's door and her gaze flew to Sister Genovia's, who had walked over to the window as well.

"I…can't…I…" she stammered.

"Oh, yes you can," the kindly nun pronounced. "I am old and cannot make the travels, even if I wanted to. My job is to stay and see Lorainne safely to the arms of God."

Miriam's tortured expression tore at Cam as he reached for her. "You cannot help Lorainne by staying here. Sharon has made her choice and," he turned toward Sister Genovia, "I swear I would take you if you were willing."

She smiled and grasped his arm with surprising strength. "No. My place is here. Miriam's place is with you."

He held her gaze for a moment, wondering at the double meaning in her words. Mentally shaking himself, he moved toward Miriam. "Are you ready?"

"I don't know," she whispered honestly. "What do I need?"

He scanned the room quickly. "Do you have some type of bag or sack? I have one that I made but we could use another. One that you can sling over your shoulder or wear as a backpack."

Her eyes immediately widened and she whirled around, rushing to her cot. Reaching underneath, she pulled out the green drawstring sack, emboldened with the Red Cross, she had been given and allowed to keep.

Sister Genovia nodded in approval and moved to Lorainne's cot, pulling hers out from underneath as well. Handing it to Cam, she said, "Lorainne will soon be with God. She will have no use for this now."

Nodding his thanks, he dropped to the floor and placed his items into the sack, thankful that the material was water resistant if not waterproof. Looking up at Miriam, he ordered, "Fill it with any food you have here, your towel, any toiletries you need, and a dry pair of scrubs."

She obeyed without question, her heart pounding in rhythm to the rain on the roof. *We're finally going. I'm finally doing something.* The fear of the scene she had witnessed this morning was fresh on her mind, knowing if they were caught that would be their demise. Still squatting, she jumped as Cam's hand assisted her to stand. Facing him, she forced those thoughts from her mind. *We've got a chance. That's all that matters.*

"Sister?" he said, as the nun turned toward him. "If asked, you fell asleep trying to care for Lorainne and the last you saw was Miriam in bed. She had complained about being sick to her stomach and you knew she had gone to the bathroom several times in the night."

Smiling, she complied. "I can do that easily enough."

"And, I'm not telling you anything about our plans. I can't. You understand?"

"Yes," she agreed. "If I don't know, they can't make me tell them."

"Exactly." Turning to Miriam, he said, "This isn't going to be comfortable, but you gotta know that the worse the weather, the longer we have to stay hidden and get outta here."

"I'm good. I can do this," she promised, gifting him with a small, nervous smile.

He watched as she ran to Sister Genovia, hugging the older woman tightly.

"My children, go with God," the nun said. "I will be in prayer for you. I will know when you are safe."

"How will you know?" Miriam asked, pulling back so that she could look into the Sister's eyes.

Patting her cheek, Sister Genovia said, "God will let me know." Turning to Cam, she implored, "Now hurry and take care of this one. I give her to your trust and protection."

He returned the woman's embrace as well, and whispered, "Always."

And with that, he led Miriam out of the room, down the dark and silent hall to the back door leading to the latrines.

Keeping silent, but wondering why they needed to go this way, she followed him around to the side where the compound wall was. Now that they were out of the overhang, the rain soaked her to the skin almost instantly. Hoisting her sack on her back, she tried to keep up as her feet slipped in the mud. It hurt to look up with the rain pelting on her face, so she kept her eyes down but then slammed into Cam's back as he stopped quickly.

Mumbling, "Sorry," she glanced up to see that there was a slim rope coming down from the wall. *I'll never be able to climb that! Only two minutes into the rescue and I can't get out.*

"I'm climbing up and then you'll tie the rope around your waist and I'll help hoist you up," he said, glad that she seemed relieved for his assistance.

Nodding her agreement, she watched in fascination as he grasped the slick rope in his hands and walk-climbed up the wet wall. Her breath caught in her throat a couple of times when he slipped, but he managed to right himself and continue upwards. She mentally fist pumped when he slung his leg over the wall and balanced on the top, lying flat on his stomach. He gave her a nod and she grabbed the rope, tying it around her waist. Her fingers were so wet that the simple act was taking longer than she wanted. *Please let it hold,* she silently prayed.

Grabbing the rope with her hands, she felt it pull on her waist and she assisted as much as she could by trying to emulate the walk-climb she had seen Cam do. Several times her feet slipped on the wet wall and the rope belt caught her from tumbling to the ground, but it bit into her flesh painfully.

She used to jog for exercise but realized now that she had little upper body strength. *Damn,* she cursed inwardly as her feet slipped once more. The black, star-less night with the pouring rain kept her from being able to see anything other than the wall directly in front of her.

"You're almost there, babe," she heard and spared a glance upward. She could not hold back the smile as she saw his face just a few feet away from her. Two more walk-climbing steps and she felt his hand grasp her arms, pulling her up more.

Finally she was on the top of the wall, lying on her back with his face directly over hers.

"You did it, girl," he enthused, knowing that she had only made it through step one of about a thousand steps that needed to occur, but he was proud of her nonetheless. He quickly leaned over her body further and undid the knotted rope at her waist. Grasping her forearms, he lowered her over the back edge of the wall and when she was as low as he could reach, he dropped her. She only had a few feet to fall and did so deftly.

Snagging the rope, he swung himself into the tree, landing on the branch he had started from. Untying the rope, he quickly coiled it and put in his sack, not wanting to leave any evidence and knowing the odds were that they would need it some other time. Climbing down the tree, he landed at her feet and grabbed her hand.

Checking his solar powered cell phone, he could see the time was only a little before midnight. *Good.* He crept into the copse of trees lining the road again and headed back toward the area where the trucks were parked. The previous trip had taken him almost thirty minutes of jogging in the rain to get to her and he knew they would not be able to go back that fast.

He pulled the baseball cap off his head and tried to put it on hers.

Jerking back, she said, "No. You need it."

He frowned and shook his head. "I'm not wearing it when you've got nothing on your head."

"Cam, you need to be able to see where we're going. I'll just follow you. Please, this makes more sense."

He hated to admit that she was right and it went against his core to keep the hat when a woman he was protecting did not have one, but they could not waste time arguing. Slapping it back on his head, he vowed to find something for her to wear as soon as he could.

Miriam was determined to keep up with him. Once in the trees, he let go of her hand and she followed behind. She found that she could follow the rhythm of his feet and if she concentrated on them and stayed in his path, she did not have too much trouble.

He slowed down after a bit and turned, grabbing her shoulders and pulling her in close. Leaning down to speak directly into her ear, he said, "You're doing great. We're going to go around the infirmary area and over to my workplace. There's a truck that I can hot-wire. We shouldn't be noticed in this storm."

She looked up and nodded, afraid to speak too loudly. Pulling on his arms, she leaned up on her tiptoes and he bent back over. "There's a medical jeep on the far side of the infirmary. It came in today and I think it was still there when I left."

Cam quickly processed this new information. *A jeep parked on the back of the infirmary will be easier to get to and less noticeable than the big dump truck. This just might be a lucky break early in the game.* He felt a tug on his arms again and looked down.

"It's open top though, so I don't know if that will matter to you."

He stifled a grin, then whispered into her ear, "Don't know if you've noticed, sweetheart, but I don't think we can get any wetter."

Just then, in the middle of a torrential storm, in the middle of a drug cartel compound, not close to safety or being rescued, Miriam smiled up at Cam, his words causing her to stifle a giggle. And her smile shot him straight through the heart. They held each other's gazes for just a few seconds and then he nodded.

"Well, let's go hot-wire a convertible." Grabbing her hand, he changed direction and moved toward the dark infirmary tent skirting the outside until they reached the back. And just like she remembered, the jeep was there, with no one in sight.

Cam had Miriam stand back, pushing her under a slight overhang so that she would have a break from the rain hitting her. She wiped her face with her hand, slinging the water from her eyes as she watched him.

Pulling out his knife to use as a screwdriver he bent over the steering column. As he dealt with the wires, Miriam turned her head back and forth terrified that someone would come. Just then, a blinding flash of lightening broke through the sky illuminating the world for a second, followed by the crash of thunder.

Before she knew what was happening, the jeep roared to life and Cam straightened up and gave her a smile. She grabbed his proffered hand and he pulled her over. Lifting her by the waist, he plopped her down in the wet seat and then rounded the front and climbed in himself.

Glancing into the back seat, he pulled out an old hand towel. "Hold this over your head—it'll help to keep the rain out of your eyes."

Nodding she followed his directions as he slowly backed up and then pressed on the accelerator, hurling them down the road. With the towel protecting her eyes she glanced around again, seeing no one. *Oh, my God. I think we did it!*

Cam spared a glance at the woman sitting next to him trying to hold on as the jeep bounced on the slick, muddy road; he could see her slight smile even in the black of the night. They had a long way to go, but if they could get to the river unnoticed, then…just then…they might have a chance.

The jeep traveled quicker than the large dump truck, but with the storm and the dark of night, Cam knew they were not making very good time. *Still... no one's around.* A glance to the right and he saw Miriam holding the towel over her head with one hand and grasping the dashboard to steady herself with the other. While the towel was as soaked as the rest of her, the slight covering deflected the rain from hitting her face. He could tell nothing else about her until a flash of lightening illuminated their surroundings for a second and he saw her grip on the dashboard was tight.

"We've got about five more miles!" he called out, needing to be heard over the storm.

"Where are we going?" she asked, turning toward him for the first time since the jeep had lurched into action.

"I found a place near a river where I would come and dump rubble. I've got a contact that said the name is the Fuerte River. Or at least a tributary of it."

"What'll we do when we get there? Is that where someone will meet us?"

Even over the storm, he heard the hopefulness in her voice. Sucking in a deep sigh, he said, "No. 'Fraid not. We've got to get down the river until we can come to a place where he can land."

"Land what?" she called out.

"He has a plane, but he's got to find a landing strip close enough. He's checking out some of the plantations along the river and as soon as the storm's over, I'll contact him to see where he'll meet us."

"How will you know where we are?"

"Got a chip in me. A tracer. The boys back home will be able to give him my exact location."

At that Miriam became quiet. *A chip? Who has a chip in them?* She wanted to ask more questions but the rain was coming down harder and she did not want to scream over the downpour.

The last mile took forever since Cam had left the main road, following the rutted path toward the river. The lights of the jeep bounced with the ruts in the road but gave off just enough illumination that he saw the rubble he had dumped yesterday. Driving around to the back of the enormous pile, he pulled the jeep into the woods close by.

Miriam watched as he drove straight into the woods, tree branches reaching out to claw at her. Suddenly, his large hand pushed her down in the seat and the limbs moved over her head. Finally he came to a stop and she leaned up cautiously.

"Why are we here?"

He twisted his body toward hers, grinning at the beautiful face peeking up at him from under the sopping towel. "You got a lot of questions," he stated.

Embarassed, she said, "I'm sorry—"

"Hey, don't ever be sorry. Just know I've got a plan even if it doesn't always make sense." Leaning down to catch her eyes, he said, "Here's the deal. I'll always answer your questions if I can, but you gotta do something for me."

"What is it?"

"If I tell you to do something, you gotta do it immediately. No questions. Our lives may depend on you obeying, okay?"

She nodded, completely aware that they were far from out of danger. "I promise."

"That's my girl," he said. "Now, I pulled into the woods to help hide the jeep. It'll be at least a day or so before anyone comes to look for us, depending on how long the storm lasts. They'll know I drove around and will know this area so this junk pile is a place someone will be coming to. By then the tire tracks should be washed away and they'll have to go looking in here to find the jeep. And, hopefully by then...we'll be long gone."

He was turning to get out of his side of the jeep when he felt a soft grasp on his arm. Turning back to look at her, he leaned in to see her face more clearly.

"Thank you," she said, her eyes pleading for him to understand. "I know you didn't have to do this."

He grabbed the back of her head in his large hand

and pulled her toward him, kissing her forehead. "My pleasure, babe. Now let's get a move on."

Literally sliding out of the sopping Jeep seat, Miriam made her way around to the front where she met Cam. Snagging her hand, he led her deeper into the woods, but closer to the river. Her eyes were unable to penetrate the black night, but with the shelter of the trees, the rain was less intense. Keeping her focus on the man in front of her, she tried to keep up without slipping on the forest floor.

He stopped, bent over and she had to halt quickly to keep from running into him. Peeking around to see what he was doing, she could make out a canoe. He grabbed one end and began dragging it toward the sound of the rushing water.

"I nabbed this several days ago from an abandoned shack nearby when I was on one of my solo dump trips. Stored it here, figurin' we'd need it sometime."

The thought of freedom roared in her mind, but soon disappeared as they made the way to the water's edge. The rain-swollen river was rushing and, even though she could only see several feet out, she knew the current had to be dangerous.

"Cam?" she said, looking up at him, her eyes wide.

"Know what you're gonna say and don't worry. I got this. I just need you to get in, sit where I tell you and I'll get us down the river."

"I...I..."

"Sweetheart?" He captured her attention, pulling it away from the river. "What choice do we have?"

He watched in fascination as her lips pursed, she

straightened a little taller and held his gaze before giving him a nod. "I can do this," she pronounced.

Not able to hide his smile, he nodded back. She reminded him of her sister-in-law, Jobe's wife, Mackenna. He met Mackenna when he helped rescue her and thought then how rare it was to find a woman that strong. Now he had once more. *Iron-willed maiden, that's for fuckin' sure.*

Maneuvering the canoe at the edge of the water, he helped her settle. The current was fast, but he knew that could play to their advantage in covering more miles away from the cartel that would be looking for them. The cartel's reach covered the entirety of western Mexico, but with the storm battering the area he was hopeful it would be at least a day, or more, before they were missed.

Pushing off, he quickly sat inside the craft and grabbed one of the paddles. Using it expertly, he kept them near enough to the shore that he could control her safety if they capsized and not so close as to be snagged by the overhanging tree branches.

He knew the dangers of the swift current and canoeing in a storm, but the dangers of being caught by the cartel...he liked his odds on the river a whole helluva lot better. Glancing down, he saw they had taken on about an inch of water.

Miriam noticed it also and wondered if she should try to bend over and splash the water out with her hands, then quickly dismissed the thought. *If he needs to me to do something, he'll tell me.* She also did not fancy her chances of not rocking the canoe if she tried to get the water out.

Losing all sense of time, she had no idea how long they had been going. Not only was the rushing water carrying them along, but when the distant lightening flashed across the sky she saw the trees on the side of the river rush by as well.

Fear threatened to choke her, held back only by the hope that they were getting away. To what and to where, she did not know. *But just away.*

Two hours later, in the wee hours of the morning, Cam steered the canoe closer to the edge where he saw a small opening in the tree line. Jumping out into the waist deep water, he trudged slowly toward the shoreline dragging the canoe behind him. By the time he pulled the front half up on the muddy edge, Miriam was already scrambling forward.

"Hang on, babe," he ordered as he tied off the craft. Then he reached back and plucked her up into his arms and carried her bride-style until they were under the large-leaf trees. The storm was still in effect, but the rain had diminished. Placing her down on a large, flat rock he sat back on his haunches, peering through the darkness at her face.

"How you holdin' up?" he asked gently.

"Good. I'm good," she quickly replied.

Too quickly, he thought. At this close proximity, he could see her hair, naturally thick and wavy, plastered to her head. The navy scrub top she was wearing was soaked and molded to her chest like a second skin. The bottom of her pants were covered in mud and equally as soaked. Droplets of water slid down from her hair onto her cheeks before continuing their path to drip off of her chin.

Instinctively he reached out, cupping her face, using his thumb to wipe the drops. She leaned slightly into his palm and he felt her trust. *Beautiful. So goddamn beautiful.* His mind jumped back to the first time he saw her—or rather, her picture. The vision in the photograph struck him. Now he knew that the camera had been unable to even begin to capture what he saw in front of him. Strength, along with beauty. Character, along with compassion.

Heaving a deep sigh, he felt her eyes on him as she lifted her head away from his hand.

"Are we okay?" she asked, the timidity evident in her words.

"We made it this far, sweetheart," he replied. "Won't lie. We've got a long way to go. I'm gonna try to get hold of my contact and see if we can get picked up somewhere once it's daylight. I'm not keen on trying the river much longer."

"Can't we take it all the way to the coast, if we need to?"

Avoiding her gaze for a moment, he looked back knowing he needed to be straight with her. "Not all the way. There's a significant waterfall and we can't ride that out."

He could see the wheels turning in her mind and

jumped in, wanting to alleviate her worry. "We're gonna rest and have a bite to eat and then get back into the canoe, once I make contact. If I'm figuring right, we should be able to go another hour on the water and then ditch it as soon as he can tell me where there's a farm or field he can land on."

She nodded, then silently turned, grabbing her bag. Reaching in, she pulled out a pack of crackers. "I didn't have much food in the room, but we would take some when we could in case we needed a snack in the infirmary."

Taking the offered crackers, he smiled. "Appreciate it," he said before ripping open the package.

Shoving the crackers into their mouths, while hunkered over to keep them from getting wet, they finished their quick snack. Miriam stepped a little ways into the woods to take care of her business while Cam made the call.

"Marc? Got no fuckin' clue where we are, man. We made it out and into the river. Looks like we were in it about two hours, but with the current faster because of the storm, you're gonna have to get Luke to tell you our location."

"I'm on it already, but gotta let you know that we're gonna have to have a slight change in plans. The storm is larger than anticipated. It's been upgraded to a tropical storm that's hitting the Gulf of California. The good news is that you two can stay hidden for a while 'cause it's taking out a lot of the communication, roads, everything. Western Mexico is almost shut down for the next day. Bad news is that I can't get a plane in and the fields where I could have landed are now mud or washed out."

Cam pondered this news for a moment, deciding to focus on the good. "All right, then here's what we're gonna do. We're getting back into the canoe and continuing on in the river until it gets too hairy. Know there's falls up ahead and I'll get us out before then. I'll call you when we're back on land. We'll get somewhere so that we can hide and rest and then probably travel by land for a bit."

"Don't make too many long range plans yet. I'll get the Saints on the case and get back to you."

There was a momentary pause and then Marc asked, "How's she holding up?"

"Man, you wouldn't believe it. Total trooper. Abso-fuckin'-lutely, total trooper."

"Good to hear. Stay safe and I'll let you know what our new rendezvous will be."

The two disconnected as Miriam was approaching. Her eyes sought his, filled with questions. She appeared lost, the fatigue showing on her face and in the slump of her shoulders.

He stood, reaching out his hand to her. Pulling her in close, he tentatively gave her a hug, having no idea if she was receptive. She melted into him, wrapping her arms around his waist and laying her head on his chest. He figured she was about five feet five or six inches, but that still put her a foot shorter than he was. And with her head nestled against his chest, he rested his head on top of hers. Tightening his arms around her slim body, he rocked her gently.

And in the middle of this fucked up situation, he felt his heart pound. Kissing the top of her head he whispered, "Don't worry, sweetheart. I'll get us out of this."

He felt her head nod against his chest and then heard her whisper, "I know, Cam. I trust you."

For a few minutes they stood, no more words spoken, each drawing strength from the other. Finally pulling back, he said, "We gotta get going again, babe. Can you do that for me?"

Leaning her head way back to make eye contact, she gave him a small smile. "Sure. I can do that. Just lead the way."

They re-entered the water the same way they had earlier. This time Miriam felt more relaxed, having become used to the movement of the canoe. Cam steered it so expertly that even at the pace they were moving, she trusted his control.

Two hours later, the sun was attempting to rise in spite of the clouds and continued rain. The only real difference to Miriam was that now she could see the rain as it pelted down and the trees along the sides of the river. The lightening had stopped and the pain of the rain hitting her arms was not as stinging as it had been. But the long night had taken its toll on her.

Looking over, Cam saw the utter weariness that exuded from her and knew it was time to take another break. Guiding the canoe to the edge again, he jumped into the water, walking it to shore. He repeated his earlier actions, tying it to a tree and then carrying her to a place underneath the leaves of a thick copse of trees to provide as much of an umbrella as he could. He wished it were more, but it was the best he could do.

Walking back, he pulled the canoe completely up on to shore and hid it among the brush as well, just in case anyone else was crazy enough to be out on the water in this weather.

Bone tired himself, he crawled back to where he left Miriam. In the early morning light she resembled a wet kitten. Her tired eyes peered up at his and much to his surprise, she gifted him with a little smile as she lifted her hand to him.

Taking the unspoken invitation, he sat next to her wrapping his huge arms around her, pulling her in close. "Let's get comfortable," he said, sliding down until he was laying on the soft leaves.

She watched him as he got situated and without hesitation she lay down next to him, her head on his chest and her arm resting on his waist. She felt him hug her body tightly and wondered how she would ever be able to sleep…on the ground…in the rain…on a man she barely knew.

Then she fell asleep. And so did he.

12

Cam woke, his mind instantly alert to his surroundings. The rain was increasing in intensity again and he could hear it hitting the leaves overhead. He looked down at the woman he was protectively laying half across, his arms cradling her back and head, one leg pressed between hers, and her face safely tucked against his chest. *Fuck, I must have rolled over her during the night. She must be crushed.*

Then another thought slammed into him. Sleeping with her warm curves beneath him, his morning wood was pressed tightly against her abdomen. He slowly moved his tree-trunk thigh from between her legs, but halted suddenly when her eyes jerked wide open. For the first time he was close enough to notice that her brown eyes were flecked with amber and even a tint of green around the edges. And they were staring straight at him.

Pulling his leg the rest of the way off of her, he rolled to the side, careful to keep his groin from touching her.

Miriam blinked a couple of times, her mind instantly remembering where they were…and who the large man was lying on top of her.

"I'm sorry," he said. "I didn't mean to crush you, but I wanted to try to keep the rain from hitting you directly if possible."

Blushing, she sat up attempting to stretch the cramped muscles screaming at her. "It's okay," she smiled. "I didn't think there would be any way I would have been able to sleep so you must have done something right."

Placing her hand on his arm as he sat up as well, she asked, "Were you able to sleep?"

He looked down at her face, pale skin with dark circles underneath her eyes, and nodded. "Yeah. Looks like we got a few hours of sleep."

He pushed himself off of the ground and stretched his large frame. Her eyes drifted over the muscular body from his handsome face, thick neck, wide chest down to his…*Oh, my God!* The evidence of his erection was pressing against his cargo pants and she immediately jerked her head to the side. *I must be insane. We're far from safe and all I can do is ogle his body!* She dropped her head into her hands and then slicked the wet hair back from her face as she stood up as well. Looking down at herself, she almost giggled.

He turned a questioning gaze to her as a small snort escaped her lips. She peeked up at him, her blush returning and just gave a small shrug.

"You'd think that in our circumstances, how I look would be the last thing on my mind," she explained.

"But I'm standing here soaking wet, covered in mud and leaves, and while we may not be free yet, we're a lot closer to being rescued...and all I can think about is how I'd love a hot bath!" Shaking her head, she muttered, "I know, stupid right?"

He placed his hands on her shoulders, pulling her in gently until her face rested against his chest once more. "Sweetheart, you are one amazing woman and don't you ever doubt that." Pushing her back slightly, holding her gaze, he continued, "You've done everything I've asked and under the worst of circumstances. You've held it together, kept up with me, and not fallen apart one time. Not one fuckin' time."

With the rain starting to fall harder once more, she finally felt her chin quiver as she battled back the tears. "I'm scared," she whispered.

He slammed her back against his chest again, his large hand cradling the back of her head. "I know, baby girl. But swear to God, we're gonna get out of here."

Allowing him to hold her, she let her mind escape for just a minute. *Back at home, him holding me like this as we are dancing. By a warm fireplace. To music that... Stop! He's my rescuer, that's all. A man like him would never be interested in someone like me. He looks like he would go for the tall, big, blonde with lots of attitude kind of woman.*

Sighing, she pushed back from his arms and the moment was gone. Bending down, she snagged her bag, opening it up to grab another pack of crackers. Handing them to him without looking at him, she waited until he took them and then she turned and walked away. "I'll be back," she mumbled as she pushed her way through more underbrush to take care of business.

Cam stood watching her back as she retreated into the woods. Taking his soaking ballcap off of his head, he wiped the water out of his eyes once more. *What the hell just happened? One minute she's all soft and warm in my arms like we are out dancing somewhere and the next she's pushing to get away from me.* Shaking his head as he munched the crackers, he thought, *No way I'm her kind of guy. She's used to the men with business suits or the doctors at the hospital. Not some man built like a tank, that's sweaty, dirty, and has seen the underbelly of the world.*

Hearing her coming back, he quickly headed off to relieve himself. *That's okay. She's my mission. And I never fail.*

Jack and his team of men were conferring with Marc and becoming more frustrated by the moment.

"I gotta give Jobe something more than Cam's got his sister," Jack growled.

"The storm isn't passing over as quickly as was forecast," Marc answered. "That keeps them from being followed, but I can't get a fuckin' plane out to them." His frustration was palpable. *I'm used to being in the thick of things, not sitting on the sidelines waiting for a phone call.* A trained logistician, he used his years as a CIA pilot to make snap decisions, plan missions and above all...be flexible. He loved being active. The sitting and waiting was killing him.

Blaise leaned over Luke's shoulder as the computer guru was trying to locate Cam using the implanted tracker. Looking up, he confirmed, "Looks like he's nearer the falls than we anticipated."

"Is that good?" Monty inquired, pinpointing the area on the map projected to his tablet.

Marc sighed. "The river's current took them much further and faster than we could have predicted. It's away from their captors, but still deep in the Sinaloa Cartel's territory."

"Goddammit!" Jack cursed. The time he spent in the Special Forces taught him to plan and then be ready for contingencies, but this felt different when he was not the one in the field. Having one of his men faced with the ever changing situation—and with a young woman, the sister of a friend no less—made this untenable.

"Marc, what does your contact there say?" Chad asked, interjecting calm into the conversation. He approached everything like dismantling a bomb...slow, methodical, careful.

"Right now, planes are grounded, which normally wouldn't mean shit to me, but the problem is that when Cam was near the plantations that I could have landed in, they were washed out or underwater. The rain has let up some, but now he's further down the river and there's no place to land a plane."

"Helicopter?" Bart asked.

"Working on it. Knowing he's close to the falls means that I probably won't have a landing place even for a chopper."

Jack rubbed his beard thoughtfully, then

commented, "If they can get down the cliff next to the falls, can you pick them up?"

"Not right there," Marc added. "But, if they carry the canoe with them, then they could make it closer to the coast and I can easily pick them up as soon as they're ready."

The silence hung heavy among the six men at the table as they eyed each other all with the same thought. *Two big, strong men carrying a canoe down a steep slope? No problem. One trained man with one petite, untrained woman?*

Looking over the group, Jack growled, "Gotta work the mission, guys."

Luke, jittery from too much caffeine, looked up suddenly from his computer screen and said, "Marc? Can you get your hands on a sea-plane? I can get my contacts at the Agency to help you out if needed."

"The DEA contact here, Alberto, can get that easily for me. What are you thinking? I can't land it on the river the way it's going with the storm."

"No, I was thinking of the ocean. Listen," Luke said, gaining the attention of everyone. "If they can make it to the ocean which, at the rate they're going, should only be another day or two at the most, then we can get a location and Marc can fly in to get them."

Chad added, watching the storm tracking, "The storm will be over by then, at least on the coast."

"What about food, potable water, and any other supplies they may need?" Bart asked, knowing his best friend could handle himself, but worried nonetheless.

Blaise, continuing to check their intel, added, "There

are some villages near the coast. They could get supplies there to last them until Marc can pick them up."

"Still deep in Cartel territory," warned Marc.

Grinning, Bart said, "Not a problem for Cam. He's one of us, but spent time as a kid as a thief. Don't figure he'd have any problem remembering those long-lost skills."

Marc signed off after agreeing to get ahold of Cam immediately with the new plan. Tired of bouncing his leg with nervous energy, he changed clothes hoping a run would help him focus.

The others sat back, satisfied with the mission but not happy at what Cam and Miriam were going to have to go through to get to the coast.

Jack leaned back and speared them with his gaze. "We're still responsible for other cases, but that's one of us out there with one of my best friends' sister. Keep working the problem."

For an hour Miriam had been clinging, white-knuckled, to the sides of the canoe as the water became choppy and rough. The light of day allowed Cam to see where to steer to avoid the rocks, but he knew they had to be near the falls. The rain had intensified once more, but at least that kept prying eyes from seeing them on the river.

As yesterday, he once more jumped into the swirling waters at the edge of the river to pull the canoe to the side. Once he had both the craft and Miriam on land, he flipped over the canoe to let the water drain out and sat heavily on the bottom, patting the seat next to him. She joined him, looking up expectantly, wondering what was next.

"We got a couple of choices and I'm gonna get hold of my contact to see what works best for him."

When he did not say anything else, she just nodded and watched as he stood and made his call. Exhaustion screamed in every fiber of her being. Her skin and hair had been soaked for a full day. While the air was not chilly, the wet penetrated deep inside. She dropped her head to her knees and let the rain continue to pound her back, numb to the core.

Several yards away, Cam listened in frustration as Marc went over the new plan. "Jesus, man. How in the hell am I gonna get our little-ass canoe down a cliff with Miriam? Fuck!"

"Hold it together, Cam. We know and we're trying to make this work. Here's what you need to get—the edge of the river at the falls is rocky, gonna be slippery and impassable for you two. But on the south side, where you are, if you travel inland about a quarter of a mile, you'll have woods to hide in and the terrain is still steep but less so. You should be able to make your way down past the falls."

The idea of making Miriam work harder than ever to get to safety did not sit well with Cam, but without the miracle of a golden rope dropping from the sky and lifting them to Heaven, he saw no other way.

"What else have you got for me?"

At this question, Marc was silent for a second too long.

"Stop stalling just give it to me, man," Cam growled.

"Near the bottom of the falls, there's a village. You're still in Cartel territory, so you've got to figure they aren't friendly. Or at least would turn you in."

Hanging his head, Cam was beginning to doubt the success of the mission for the first time. As he walked back toward Miriam, he saw her sitting on the upturned canoe, leaning over with her head on her knees. As she heard him approach, she sat up, latching her gaze on his.

And then his miracle happened. It was not the golden rope dropping from Heaven. It was much more profound. She smiled. In the middle of a cartel's territory, scared out of her mind, exhausted, soaked to the bone, hungry, and so far from home it was frightening...she smiled. Directly. At. Him. And he knew then, whatever it took, he was getting them out of there.

"I'll be in touch," Cam said into the phone before disconnecting. Walking over he squatted in front of her.

"Babe," he whispered, lifting his hand to cup her face. Once again she leaned into his strength. "We gotta keep going. My contact has nowhere to pick us up here, so we're going to walk in the woods near the cliffs by the falls."

She smiled again, holding his gaze. "We don't have to get back into the canoe?" she said, hope in her voice.

Chuckling, he nodded. "Nope. But here's the thing. We gotta carry it with us so that when we get to the bottom of the falls, we will have it to get closer to the gulf."

The smile slid from her face and shot straight to his heart. "Carry? Carry the canoe?" she asked, new doubt evident in her words.

"*Cariña*," he said. "You are so fuckin' strong. We can do this. And when we get to the bottom, I'm gonna hide you before I sneak into a village and get us some dry clothes and food."

She lifted her eyes, quickly asking, "A village? We can get help?"

"No, babe. I'm 'fraid not. You've got to remember, we're still in Sinaloa." Seeing the confusion, he added, "Still cartel territory."

At that, her breath caught as her eyes widened in fear. "I…I thought we got out miles ago. All this way? We've come all this way and they can still get to us?" Her voice rose with each word.

Sliding the hand that was at her cheek along her neck and into her wet hair, he cupped the back of her head and pulled her forward until her forehead touched his lips. He could feel her body shaking and spoke into her skin.

"*Cariña*, I promise. I fuckin' promise, I'll get you home safe."

Knowing he was calling her sweetheart, she closed her eyes, feeling the vibration of his lips across her forehead right before she felt his lips pressing in. Choking back a sob, she lifted her hands to grasp his t-shirt, fisting it tightly. Her body was jerked up and lifted into his arms as he twisted around and sat on the canoe, settling her in his lap.

Wrapping his arms around her shivering frame, he offered her his warmth, keeping her held tightly, until he could feel her heartbeat next to his. Allowing her a moment to cry, he continued to whisper endearments into her ear. Words his mother had whispered when one of her children was upset. And words he heard his father whisper to his mother when he thought no one else could hear.

After a few minutes, she heaved a huge sigh and lifted her face to his while keeping a tight hold onto his shirt. "I'm sorry, Cam."

"Babe, you've got nothing to be sorry for," he said, pushing the wet strands away from her face as the rain continued to send rivulets of water down her skin. "You're tired and scared but I gotta tell you, you're a fuckin' *mujer de acero*, babe."

Seeing her questioning expression, he chuckled. "Woman of steel. You're strong, Miriam. You can do this. And I'm gonna make sure we make it."

Sucking in a huge breath, she nodded. "Okay, well, I'm down to my last crackers so we'd better fuel up before we start lugging this down the hill."

Chucking her under her chin with his knuckles, he grinned. *Jesus, she's beautiful.* Standing and making sure she was steady on her feet, he moved over to the canoe, grateful that it was not too heavy.

"I'm gonna start by dragging it where we can and will only need you to assist when two people have to get it down a steep slope."

Nodding, she watched as he fashioned a harness from the rope and looped it around his shoulders. Moving forward through the trees near the water's edge he began walking, dragging the canoe behind him. She followed dutifully, keeping an eye on both the canoe... and the man.

13

The first hour was not too difficult but then, as the roar of the falls came nearer, the terrain became more difficult to travel with the canoe dragging behind. Rocks jutted out in the underbrush so Cam moved inland slightly to keep the river within range while being able to continue to head downhill with the woods over their heads.

The ground was soaked and slick but with the cover of the trees, the rain did not reach them as easily at it had when they were exposed in the water.

After another hour, they came to a section where the drops in the path were more significant. He surveyed the land and turned to see Miriam slipping down some rocks to join him.

"How you doin'?" he asked and was rewarded with a smile and a nod. He stood, stretching his aching muscles. "I'd really like to get as far as we can before nightfall. Hopefully the rain is almost at a stop."

"What do you need me to do?" she asked, eying the steep terrain.

"It looks like we can keep moving to the south a little bit, but head inland to skirt these rocks while staying near the treeline."

"If we stay with these rocks can't we just lower the canoe down a bit at a time?" she asked, thinking that would be easier.

"Eventually, we'll have to, but we need to avoid the rocks as much as possible." Seeing her curious expression, he explained, "We'd be more in sight, babe." Keeping his gaze on hers he could tell she did not know what he was implying. "If someone is looking for us and they've got helicopters, they could see us if we stay next to the river on the rocky ledges."

Her jaw dropped open as she realized once the storm passed the possibility existed that someone could come searching for them. "But why? I'm nobody. Just a Red Cross nurse, that's all."

"Babe, you've seen where their main compound is. You've seen one of the local leaders. You've got inside information that they would love to contain."

Miriam turned her eyes to the side, not willing for him to see her fear. Sucking in a deep breath through her nose, she slowly let it out, blinking furiously to keep the tears at bay. Gaining control, she turned back to him. "Okay. Show me what to do."

"*Mujer de acero*," he said, shaking his head. "We keep walking for now."

Several hours later dusk was fast approaching and they ran out of cover. The rain had stopped and they could actually see a sliver of blue sky in the distance.

"Okay, babe, it looks like we can't put it off any longer. Gotta climb down these rocks out in the open. But since we haven't seen sight of anyone looking for us, I'd say we're in good shape."

Walking over to her, he threw his arms around her back, slinging the rope with them, and tied the ends around her waist.

"Gonna lower you down and you walk it just like you did that wall the other night," he instructed.

She looked up in surprise, and with a small giggle said, "Oh, my God. Was that just the other night? It seems like a lifetime ago!"

Chuckling, he agreed. He stood with his hands on her waist for a moment longer than necessary, liking the feel of her in his arms.

"You know, Cam, I don't even know anything about you," she said, her eyes searching his. "You've risked your life for me and I don't even know your last name."

He leaned over and touched his forehead to hers again, whispering, "Perez. Cam Perez. At your service." Then he kissed her forehead once more. "All right, babe, hang on." With that he assisted her out over the edge of the rock cliff and she gave a little scream as her hands and feet scrambled to find their holds. The edges were rough, pointing out in jagged, sharp angles.

She felt as though she did not do much to help since most of her descent was controlled by Cam's muscles. Soon her feet touched the ledge, almost ten feet from where she started, and she called out. Untying the rope about her waist, she let it free so that he could pull it up and then fasten it to the canoe.

Keeping her feet on the four foot ledge, she watched as the canoe was lowered toward her. As soon as she could she grasped the end and guided it to the ledge next to her. Then Cam dropped the rope into her waiting arms.

She watched nervously as he climbed down unassisted over the craggy surface of the slippery rocks. For once she wished his body was small and lean, thinking how much easier it would be for him to maneuver the slippery surface. She could see his back and arm muscles bunch and smooth as he made his way closer.

When his feet touched the ledge, she let out the breath she did not realize she had been holding. He flashed her a grin, chucking her under the chin.

"Worried, *cariña?*"

"Yes," she replied honestly. "Absolutely terrified!"

"Now it's your turn to tell me something," he said. "I told you my last name, now you have to tell me something about yourself."

"What do you want to know?" she asked as he threw the rope around her waist and tied it again.

"Um, how old are you?"

"Twenty-seven," she replied as he tightened the knot. "How old are you?"

Just as he swung her out once more, he called, "Twenty-eight." He kissed her forehead again before she began to crawl down.

Watching her descend, he could tell she was more

comfortable with allowing him to lower her while she guided her body along the wall of rocks. Soon, he was sending the canoe down to her again.

On the next ledge, she chanced a glance down to see that they still had a ways to go and the sun was beginning to set behind them.

"Are we going to be allr—"

"Next question," he interrupted, "And it has to be about me. Not this little vacation we're on."

At that, she snorted, knowing he was trying to take her mind off of their precarious situation. She watched as he lowered the canoe before joining her once more.

"Um...Tell me about your family?" She saw a shadow cross his face and she immediately retracted. "No, you don't have to."

"No, *cariña*, it's fine. I've got a great family. Seems like I'm always causing them worry though." He saw her cock her head to the side while he tied the rope around her.

"Got a great mom and dad. Dad was born in Mexico, near El Paso where he met mom. They had me, two sisters and a younger brother. One of my sisters is married with a couple of boys." Chuckling at the memory, he added, "They call me Superman." After a brief pause, he looked at her. "Your family?"

"My mom and dad are wonderful. I've got an older brother—well, you know Jobe of course. He and Jack were in the Special Forces together. My oldest sister is Hannah. Married, with two kids. Next is Rebecca and she's a teacher." Giving a little shrug, she added, "And then there's just me, the baby."

He halted as he stared at her looking intently at him. The sun had moved down in the sky so that it was illuminating the back of her head, like a halo. *Jesus, she's gorgeous.* He leaned down to kiss her forehead again, but this time her face stayed turned up toward his and before he knew what he was doing, his lips touched hers. A barely there kiss.

Her eyes widened, but before he could get out his apology, she smiled. And he was sucker-punched again.

"So what's your favorite food?" she asked.

"Anything my mama makes," came his quick reply. "But when she makes her Mexican Wedding Cookies at the holidays...I think I've died and gone to heaven!"

Knowing they needed to hurry and get off the side of the cliff, he grinned as he swung her out once more. Going more quickly this time, she descended and then secured the canoe as it came down after her.

"What about you?" he called down. "What's your favorite?"

"Mama makes chicken kabobs that are amazing. I actually just love to eat and will scarf down just about anything."

As he started down, he commented, "You're a tiny thing. You must not eat a lot."

"Oh, I'd surprise you," she replied. "I eat a lot, but drink diet soda. Well, as long as it has lemon in it."

"Lemon?"

"Yeah. I know. My family makes fun of me. But soda is just empty calories so I feel better if I drink diet soda. But the taste is kind of yucky. So if I put lemon in it, then it tastes better."

His feet landed on the ledge and he looked at her, a curious expression on his face. "I gotta confess that I'd like to see you eat as much as you say you do, but the diet soda with lemon? Not too sure about that," he teased.

"Don't knock it until you've tried it, Superman."

Laughing, he looked over the edge. "Looks like we've got about three more of these and then we can start climbing down the rest of the way together where the slope is not as steep. It'll be dark by then but we can find a place to rest for a while.

"So is that three more chances to learn more about you?" she asked shyly.

"You sure you're not talking about three more kisses?"

He watched in amazement as she blushed a deep red from the top of her chest to her hairline, but before he could apologize, she just turned her smile back onto him.

"Well, okay then," he said. For the next hour as the sun slowly set behind them, they continued their patter of descent and learning about each other. She found out that he had been with the Richmond Police Department, had been undercover in a drug gang, and that was where he met Jobe's wife, Mackenna. He played football in high school, but was almost kicked off the team for what he called *nefarious activities*. He admitted that he had been a juvenile delinquent, never caught, and had a change of heart when he turned eighteen.

She confessed that she loved to sing, but only in the shower. Loved to dance, but only in the privacy of her

apartment when vacuuming. He learned that she sometimes hated being the baby in the family, especially
when they got in her business. And she was a great cook
and liked lots of cream and sugar in her coffee.

And each time before he swung her out to climb
down, he kissed her. Light. Soft. A touch of lips that
held no particular meaning…and yet seemed to mean
everything to both of them.

Sitting at the edge of the woods in front of a small fire
that Cam had built, Miriam leaned closer to the flames
as she ran her fingers through her hair. It was finally
dry, but a tangled mess. The extra scrubs she had
packed had been damp, but clean. Laying them on a
branch near the fire was helping them to dry and she
longed to put them on. The fire was welcome and for
the first time since she was rescued, in the middle of the
storm, she was beginning to feel dry. Walking over she
held her fingertips toward the flames, soaking up the
warmth, wondering if they would stay permanently
wrinkled. Sitting down next to the fire, she allowed the
heat to seep into her whole body.

A noise in the distance jerked her from her moment
of respite. She glanced around nervously wishing Cam
would come back. He had left almost thirty minutes
ago, saying he was going to see if he could find something for them to eat. The illumination penetrated the
dark night, but beyond the firelight the night was
frightening. The warmth that gave off comfort,

provided the shadows that danced causing her gaze to jump around, aware that she was completely alone. *What if he doesn't come back? What if he gets captured? Injured? Lost?* Her heart pounded against her ribs as another noise reached her ears. The image of the carnage she had witnessed had her chest heave with fear. Standing quickly as she heard a noise approaching, she grabbed the canoe oar, wielding it in front of her.

Cam came from the underbrush, finding his way back to the campfire. His arms were full of mangoes. Before he could present his bounty to her, she gave a shriek, tossing the oar onto the ground and rushed into his arms, her body bucking with sobs. He barely had time to drop the mangoes in order to catch her.

"Babe, what's wrong?" he asked, wanting to see her face but unable to extract her trembling limbs from his.

Unable to speak, she continued to hold him tightly for several minutes until she was able to catch her breath. "I was scared," she confessed, pressing her face into his neck. "I kept hearing noises and couldn't see anything in the dark. I had no idea if you had been captured, or hurt, or lost, or—"

"Shhhhh," he whispered, as he continued to cradle her body tightly in his embrace. One hand around her middle held her heartbeat next to his. His other hand tucked her head underneath his chin. He held her close until her shivering subsided, then placed her gently back on the ground. "I'm so fuckin' sorry, Miriam, that I had to leave you here alone. I knew I could sneak in and out, getting what we needed and wasn't willing to take a chance that you'd be discovered." He leaned down, holding her face in his hands, "Come on, have a seat and see what I brought."

He maneuvered her closely to the fire again and they sat cross-legged on the ground, next to each other. He noticed she kept her leg touching his as though she were afraid he would disappear again. Reaching behind, he pulled out several mangoes. "I found a grove about a mile from here."

Her eyes jumped to his face, fear still evident in her expression. "Was there anyone around? Did anyone see you?"

"No, no," he assured her. Pulling out his knife, he slit into one handing her half.

Taking a deep breath, she allowed his presence to calm her. Leaning her body slightly onto his, she took another cleansing breath. *He's back and I'm okay.* Taking the offered fruit out of his hands, she bit into the juicy goodness, the taste of the fruit better than anything she could have imagined. He did the same and in a few minutes they had eaten three mangoes, the juice still dripping from their chins.

He had filled his canteen with some water from the river and offered it to her to drink and wash off. She took a drink but hesitated when pouring the liquid over her hands. He looked at her quizzically.

Shaking her head, she giggled. "I know this sounds stupid, but after spending over twenty-four hours being soaked, I almost hate even getting my hands wet again."

He chuckled his agreement, happy to hear her laughing. Standing, he held out his sticky hand to her and she allowed him to pull her up. Walking her to the river's edge, she noticed that he did not let go of her hand the entire way. Squatting at the edge, he tugged her down beside him and they washed the juice from their hands and faces.

Once back by the fire, he used his boot to sweep some debris away and her clean scrubs as a pillow. Patting the ground between his large body and the fire, he said, "Come on, babe. We need to get some sleep and the fire will knock off the chill."

"Won't you be cold on the far side?" she asked, realizing that he was offering her the choice spot between the fire and his warmth.

"Not with you beside me," he tried to joke, but the truth shone out from his expression.

She smiled and nodded, crawling over to lay on the hard ground. He reached over and pulled her body in tightly to his. "Shared body warmth?" she asked, knowing it was a method for staying warm, but felt heat of her blush rise from her chest to her face.

"Absolutely," he agreed.

Once again, neither thought it would happen but, soon they were both sound asleep.

Miriam woke, the pale early morning light surrounding her. As her eyes blinked, she could see that the fire had burned down to embers but warmth still enveloped her body. Cam. He was pressed close to her back, one leg thrown over hers and his arm wrapped around her stomach, tight and protectively. She stretched slightly, wondering what awakened her.

She smiled, feeling something move across her leg thinking that Cam must be awake...or even moving his leg over hers in his sleep. *Sleep. He's still sleeping.* Leaning carefully, she glanced down to see what he was doing, when she saw the red and black stripes of a snake slithering by her leg.

Throwing her body into action while emitting an ear-piercing scream, she rolled over Cam's body. Her elbow jabbed his ribs sharply as she scrambled to her knees on top of him. Grunting, he was immediately alert, trying to move her thrashing body off his.

Unable to reach his knife with her body still mauling his, he grabbed her waist, hoisting her up as he stood. "What?" he growled, before looking down and seeing the snake.

As she turned to grab the oar, he pulled out his knife and flung it expertly toward the snake, spearing it. The snake was dead, his knife plunged behind its head by the time Miriam whirled around, holding the oar over her head to strike.

Staring at her, the bedraggled warrior-woman, Cam smiled. Then chuckled. Then burst out laughing.

Glaring at him, she continued to hold the oar, her eyes darting between his and the ground around.

"I think you can put the weapon down now, *cariña*,"

Huffing, she replied, "Don't think you can *cariña* me. You're laughing. If I hadn't jumped up, that snake could have killed both of us."

Walking over, he pulled the oar out of her hands and

tossed it to the ground. "Babe, you deafened it with your scream...and me as well. Instead of alerting me to trouble and then getting out of the way, you climb all over me, keeping me from doing what I'm supposed to do, which is protect you." Wrapping her in his arms, he pulled her in closely, still able to feel the pounding of her heart. And his.

"Well..." she huffed, unable to think of an appropriate retort, her eyes still riveted onto the dead snake at their feet.

"But," he said turning back toward the fire, "we've now got some meat for breakfast."

"M...meat?"

"This is a Sinaloan milksnake. Not poisonous. Not necessarily all that tasty, but it's meat and we need the protein."

She continued to stay statue-like, watching as he brought the fire back to life from its embers and then turned his attention to the snake. Eyes wide, she saw him pull the knife from the body and make a slit—

Jerking around quickly so that her back was to him, she began to walk a little way into the woods. "I...um... have to...go," she stammered and hurried off to take care of her business hoping that the snake would be gone when she returned.

Several minutes later, she approached cautiously. He looked up, smiling. "The coast is clear, babe."

She could see that he had a slim stick with something sizzling on it, much like the chicken kabobs her mom made. The smell of the meat cooking was enticing, as much as she hated to admit it.

"Have a seat," he ordered gently, nodding toward the upturned canoe. "It'll be ready soon. Why don't you cut up some of the mango left over from last night."

Nodding, she was grateful for the task. While not ashamed that she was scared of the snake, she was embarrassed that she had reacted so outlandishly.

"Cam?"

"Right here, babe."

"Um, I'm sorry," she began.

He stopped what he was doing and glanced over to her. "You've got nothing to be sorry about. You didn't run away, leaving me still sleeping. You reacted immediately and grabbed a weapon. You're a *mujer fuerte* and while we're in a shit situation, I'm fuckin' lucky that I've got you."

Her mind went blank as his last words washed over her. *Lucky to have me?* Before she could react, he handed her a stick with the sizzling meat on the end. She reached out tentatively, her expression unsure.

"Babe? Is a chicken pretty?"

She jerked back in surprise. "What? A chicken pretty? What are you talking about?"

"Just answer the question."

"Um…no. I wouldn't call a chicken pretty."

"But you eat its meat."

Her eyes moved back to the stick he was offering, the smell enticing her senses.

"Just think of it as your mama's kababs," he joked.

Smiling, she nodded in understanding. Taking the skewer, she touched her lips to the meat and pulled it off with her teeth. *I don't care if a chicken isn't pretty, it doesn't slither on the ground.* But after one taste, she devoured the breakfast hungrily, in the face of a grinning Cam.

After they ate, he extinguished the fire while she gathered the rest of the mangoes and put them in her sack.

"I think I'll put on my extra scrubs," she said. "I'm dying to have something clean to wear."

He immediately gave her his back, and while he could not see her body as she changed, he could hear every movement...and imagined every scene. Her top was pulled over her head and landed on the ground. He imagined her standing there with only a bra and, having been around her body for the past couple of days, he had no problem imagining her breasts spilling out of the bra.

He could tell when she slipped the new top on and heard her small moan of delight. His dick jumped and he willed it to behave. Next, he could hear as she pulled her pants down and imagined her kicking them off with her toned legs. As she slid her clean bottoms on, he imagined her gorgeous ass as she bent over. Now his dick was refusing to obey and was painfully pressing against his cargo zipper.

"Oh, my God," she moaned again. "These clothes feel amazing."

Without turning around, he growled, "Gonna go take care of some business. Be right back," and he moved out into the woods.

He returned a few minutes later having willed his

cock back down, but grumpily said, "We need to get going."

She cautiously walked over to him, laying her hand on his arm, asking "Are you all right?" She looked up at him, uncertainty filling her expression.

Jesus, I'm a dick. Smiling back at her, he slid his hand around the back of her neck and pulled her forward. "Yeah, *cariña*. I'm fine." He kissed the top of her head, but before he could let her go she lifted to her toes and raised her lips to his. Her kiss was light but as he moved his arms around her waist, he took the kiss deeper.

His mouth devoured hers and her tongue dueled with his. He lifted her into his arms as she wrapped her legs around his waist. Slanting her head for better access, he delved in as his tongue explored and memorized the taste and feel of her warmth.

Finally coming up for air, he noted her glazed expression, and he wanted nothing more than to see that very expression on her face as he came deep inside of her. Gently forcing her back to the ground, they both stood staring at each other, breath ragged.

This kiss was different. They both felt it. They both knew it. It was not the kiss of two people flirting, or even attempting to forget their desperate situation. This kiss held the promise of a beginning.

An adorable blush began on her chest and crept up her face. "Um, I guess we should be going."

"Yeah," he agreed, slowly moving to the canoe and dragging it behind him. His mind was swirling as much as the water they were approaching. Trying to tell himself that she was still a mission was a lost cause.

She's gonna be mine, he vowed. Glancing behind him, he saw her staring at his back admiringly and then watched as her eyes darted away quickly. *I just hope she feels the same way!*

As they were moving the canoe closer toward the water's edge now that the falls were behind them, she asked, "Cam?"

"Still right here, babe."

"What did you call me earlier? *Mujer fuerte.* Isn't that the name of the river?"

Chuckling, he nodded. "No, I didn't call you a river, babe. It means 'strong'. Yeah, the river is named The Strong River, which we sure as fuck understand. But I called you a strong woman."

Strong woman. Smiling, Miriam did not reply as they placed the end of the canoe into the water and she crawled over into it, taking her seat.

He gave it a push and they paddled their way back into the current. On the water for the first time without the hindrance of pouring rain, she could see the surrounding area. The swirling waters in the daytime did not seem as terrifying as its roar in the dark of the night. She could see the forest along the river's edge with the occasional cleared land where crops were growing.

"Keep your eyes open, *cariña,*" Cam called out. Seeing her gaze land on his, he continued, "Now that we are getting closer to the gulf, there will be more villages around. I talked to my contact this morning to see where we should go and he's getting the intel for me."

"Are we still in danger? Even if we pass a village?"

"Babe, until I get you back home, we're still in danger."

Pulling her lips in, she just nodded, tired of the sick feeling in the pit of her stomach, wishing for this nightmare to be over.

"Don't worry. I'll get you there," came the warm voice from the back of the canoe. Lifting her eyes once more to his, she took in his face that radiated concern... and protectiveness. And for the first time in weeks, began to feel as though she just might see home again.

14

The Saints met in the wee hours of the morning, having given up their night's sleep to help with whatever Cam would need from them.

Luke, talking to Marc, said, "They should hit the beach soon at the rate they're traveling. With the speed of the current after the storm, they will land near the Gulf within the day."

"I can get my hands on a sea-plane—at least that's what my contact says. I have yet to see it, but he swears he can get one by tomorrow."

Chad, following the river's path, added, "They'll beach north of Topolobampo, which is good. Too much drug violence there so we know the cartel could be looking for the two of them."

Bart rubbed his hand over his face, "Jesus, you'd think the cartel would assume they'd be dead somewhere and not traveling down a river in the middle of a storm with a big-ass waterfall to traverse. Hell, after the earthquake and then this huge storm, the cartel should have their fuckin' hands full without trying to chase down these two."

Blaise, former DEA, explained, "Doesn't matter, Bart. Cartel's got money, contacts, and they'll stop at nothing to try to keep Cam and Miriam from escaping with the information they've got."

Monty looked at Jack, knowing how close their boss was to Miriam's brother. "You talk to Jobe recently."

Jack sighed heavily before responding, "Yeah. He's been calling every day and I feel like shit when I can't give him the answers he's looking for. But I told him a few hours ago that they're heading to the coast."

"How's the family?" Monty asked.

"His family's close—taking it hard. I gotta keep him placated so he doesn't go off the charts."

"Shit, boss, we don't need him going rogue."

"I know. I've called his boss, Tony, and made sure his boys are keeping a tight rein on Jobe. They reminded him that he needs to be there for his parents and other sisters and let us and Cam get Miriam out safe."

Luke, still on conference call with Marc, confirmed the sea plane landing area and added, "As soon as we have a lock on their location when they're at the coast, we'll let you know and you can get in and get 'em picked up."

Marc agreed, then asked, "What happens when they get back?"

Jack took on that question. "We'll get them to family and they'll be interviewed by CIA, FBI, and DEA for a while." He added, "I've been in contact with Cam's family also. They don't know where he is but that he's on a mission undercover. I told them that I'll let them know as soon as I hear something."

Bart added, "Jack, I've gotten tight with Cam and his family. If you need me to deal with them while you deal with Miriam's family, just let me know."

Jack nodded, grateful for the offer. Glancing around the table, he discovered that his dream had come true. A group of like-minded individuals, each with their own special skills honed from their various military and agency backgrounds, coming together to take care of what was handed to them.

Sucking in a deep breath, he said, "Okay, Marc. Hang tight and as soon as Cam gets to the Gulf, we'll get you the coordinates."

On track with that mission, they turned their attention back to the rest of their business.

Several times during the day, Cam had Miriam lay flat in the canoe when they were paddling past villages. People were beginning to go about their normal activities and he could see men and women at the edge of the river, getting water, washing clothes, or working in the fields. When the trees lined the river banks, she could be up but as soon as they passed an area that appeared to be populated, he forced her down.

The first time, while immediately obeying, she asked why.

"Cartel probably has put out feelers for anyone seeing a large man and woman traveling together."

"Do you think they put us together? I mean, it's not like we were ever together before," she asked, lying in the bottom of the canoe staring up at him as he paddled.

Glancing down as he paddled, he could not help but notice her stretched out on her back, her head almost at his feet and looking up at him. Her dark brown eyes were moving over his body and he hoped she liked what she saw. He knew he did.

"We were too close together and both new to the area. No way they won't put two and two together and figure that I got to you."

He heard her sigh deeply and wanted to take the worry from her. "Tell me more about yourself," he said.

She giggled and asked, "Why? You buying more kisses?"

"Maybe," he joked. Then added, "But maybe hoping I don't have to buy them anymore."

He held his breath for a second, wondering how she would take that. He did not have to wait long. Her smile lit her face and she said, "You don't have to buy them at all."

He grinned down at her and then said, "Well, all right. So tell me more. Tell me about being a nurse."

"Well, there's really not much to tell. I always liked taking care of people and it's the only profession I wanted to do. I work in a hospital but have to admit that last summer I had the chance to help with Jobe's mother-in-law who had a stroke and really liked that."

"Mackenna's mom?"

"Oh, that's right. I keep forgetting that you met Mackenna. Yeah, her mom had a stroke and by the time

I met her she only needed a little care, but I loved that chance to really connect with a patient. So often at the hospital, even though I treat every patient as important, they're usually in and out so quickly that I have no chance to bond with them."

"So do you think you'll stay at the hospital?"

"I'm sure not going to go overseas with the Red Cross anymore!" she exclaimed. She heard him chuckle and then sobering, she added, "But that kind of sucks also."

"How so, babe?"

Rolling over to her side so that she was still hidden in the bottom of the canoe but could lean her head on her hand while propped up on her elbow, she focused on his face. "I had such high hopes for this trip, Cam. My parents were totally against it and I thought Jobe was going to have a fit. I wanted to do something special. Go somewhere different. Challenge myself." Sighing deeply, she said, "But my plans all went to hell."

Cam glanced around and said, "You can sit back up, *cariña.*"

"My great adventure turned into a great disaster. I could have been killed, or raped, or tortured, or—"

"Stop," he ordered. "Stop right there." He maneuvered the canoe over to the side of the river, where he could pull it in under the low hanging branches of a tree. Tying it off there, he scooted to the center of the craft and sat close to her.

"Don't go there," he warned. "First of all, none of this is your fault. That blame lies squarely on the asshole drug cartel that kidnapped you. You did nothing to bring this on yourself. Second of all, you were a valuable commodity and none of those things were going to happen."

"I saw," she whispered, her eyes large and filling with tears.

His brow wrinkled in question as he took in her ravaged expression. "Saw what, babe? What did you see?"

Licking her lips nervously she looked out over the water, her mouth opening and closing several times without speaking, trying to find the words to describe the horror.

"Dr. Villogas took me to a village to help when a building collapsed. On the way back, there was um…it was…I…" she could not get the words out, but a tear ran down her cheek.

Moving gently so as not to tip the canoe, Cam grabbed her hands and pulled her close, wrapping his arms around hers.

"There were bodies on the side of the road. I'd seen bodies before," she said, looking up at his face. "When we first came to Los Mochis there were bodies piled up from the earthquake. But these were…cut up." Her face grew even paler as her eyes closed as though to force the image from her mind.

He had seen a similar sight and knew what she was trying to tell him. *Fuck! She's seen the cartel's way of dealing with those who break ranks—using hatchets to get their point across.*

"Oh, baby girl. No one should have to see that, especially not you. I'm so fuckin' sorry. If only I'd gotten to you sooner!" he bit out.

"It's not your fault," she exclaimed, cupping his square jaw with her hand, feeling the three day old stubble underneath her fingers. "It's just like you told me. The fault is theirs."

"I'd have given anything to have kept that from you, Miriam," his ragged voice said.

Dragging in a breath, she nodded. Just then, they the heard the sound of a helicopter in the distance. Her eyes brightened as she jerked around, still in his arms.

"Your friend! He must have found a way to get to us," she exclaimed, starting to push back from his embrace.

"No!" he growled. Grabbing the oar, he pushed them back further into the river's embankment, deeper under the overhang of the trees. Seeing her wide eyed expression at his outburst, he explained, "Don't know who it is, but we don't want to be seen by anyone."

"You think they're after us? Just like you were afraid of?"

"It could be a private chopper carrying someone important since roads may be washed out. Could be someone from the government checking out the earthquake and storm damage. Could be any number of people doing any number of things."

She sat quietly as the sound became louder as the helicopter traveled directly over the center of the river and then passed them by. Waiting until it was long out of sight, she looked back up and asked, "But it could have been someone looking for us, couldn't it?"

Cam hesitated, not wanting to cause her any more

stress, but he refused to lie to her. Ever. "Yeah, they could have been looking for us."

He watched the range of emotions play across her face. Sadness. Fear. Anger. *Fuck, she'd better not ever play poker, 'cause her face tells it all.* Then, fascinated, he watched as the final expression settled on her beautiful face. Determination.

Pushing to a seated position once more, she stated, "Well then, we'd better get a move on and get the hell out of here so that your friend can pick us up."

Meeting her gaze, he could not help but smile. "*Mujer de acero, babe.* You got a will of steel."

Finally, by the end of the long day, they could see the shoreline covered with sand instead of mud and the thick trees along the edge thinned out leaving more scrub brush. They had thankfully made it to the inlet near the gulf and had not been bothered by anymore flyovers, nor had they had to pass any more villages. The evening shadows exposed large coral reefs and what appeared to be huge outcroppings of rock formations along the beach front.

"This is perfect for hiding," Cam said, pushing the canoe to the beach. Turning to assist Miriam, he reached out to pluck her from the craft instead of just offering her his hand. Knowing they had been in the canoe for longer hours today, he assumed that she had sea-legs and did not want her to fall. *Hell, who am I kidding? I just want to fuckin' hold her!*

She did not mind and laughed as he twirled her around in the sand. She gazed into his face, his white smile stark against his tan skin, as his dark eyes met hers. Closing her eyes against the intensity of his stare as she grew dizzy from twirling, she could almost imagine being on a beach vacation with Cam. Not in the middle of a drug cartel's zone and running for their lives.

Her eyes popped back open as reality slammed back into her, but all she could see was his face. His dark eyes still staring at hers. His strong arms still holding her tight.

"Where'd you go, baby?" he asked softly. "For a few seconds you were a million miles away."

"I…um…"

Giving her a little squeeze, he gently ordered, "The truth."

"Is this part of the *do what I say when I say it* speech to keep me safe?" she quipped.

Squeezing her again, he smirked replying, "Nope. This is me wanting to make sure you're all right and wanting to know what's going through your mind so that I know what I need to do to take care of you."

Blushing, she admitted, "It was a nice thought, actually." His stare implied that he expected more. Huffing, she said, "Okay, fine. I was thinking that I could almost pretend that this was a gorgeous beach and you and I were on vacation. Not running for our lives."

His smile was her reward and she was blinded with its intensity. Embarrassed, she tucked her face into his neck and felt his chuckle rumble from deep inside of him. He gave her a squeeze again, but did not set her down on the sand. Instead he kept her enveloped in his tight embrace.

"Can't think of anything I'd rather be doing, *cariña*, than be on a vacation with you."

She pulled her head back in surprise and saw nothing but sincerity in his face. She watched as his handsome face came closer just before his lips latched onto hers.

The kiss was deep. Wet. Intense. He slipped his tongue inside her warmth, exploring the recesses of her mouth, tangling with her tongue as well. The world fell away, their cares and worries with it, lost in their connection.

He reluctantly moved his lips away from hers, his cock swelling painfully in his cargoes. Scanning her face, he saw her eyes still hooded with desire, lips swollen with his kiss.

Slowly letting her slide down the length of his body, he steadied her with his large hands on her shoulders before letting them slide down to her waist. Leaning down to kiss her forehead, he said, "Come on babe. Let's get the canoe hidden and find a place where we can be under cover."

After dragging the boat to a small rock outcropping, they explored their private beach. The water was brilliant blue in the inlet and they walked around the beach until they were at the ocean side of the little peninsula. There, the waves were higher but the water was just as clear.

"Cam?"

"Right here," he answered, holding her hand as they walked.

"How will your friend get here?" she asked, looking up into his face, squinting in the bright sun.

Up until now, he kept her informed about what was happening only to the level she needed to know. "You worried?" he asked.

"Yeah. I mean, no. I...oh, I don't know."

"The plan is that tomorrow morning he'll have a sea plane. The group I work for will have the exact location for us through the tracking chip that's embedded in me."

Nodding, she looked around at the beautiful land-scape. "It's gorgeous here, isn't it? This is the Mexico you see in travel brochures."

He twisted his head around also, appreciating the unblemished white sandy beach, blue water, rock formations jutting out around them. Privacy as far as the eye could see. Turning back to her, he said, "You wanna go swimming?"

Joy shone on her face as she exclaimed, "I'd love to!" Then looking down, she moaned, "But our clothes?"

"Your bra and panties probably cover more of you than I would see if you were in a bikini and my boxers will be fine. Afterward, we can go back up the river just a bit to wash the salt off since that's fresh water coming in."

Biting her lip in indecision for only a few seconds, she grinned up at him. "Let's do it!"

They moved back to a small cove with a large overhang, giving them a bit of privacy, and quickly stripped down to their underwear.

Cam's gaze slid head to toe, the view of her body making it hard to be a gentleman. Her eyes darted to the side, the blush starting from the tempting mounds at the top of her bra cups up to the top of her face. Grabbing her hand, he jerked his head toward the bay side. "Come on gorgeous, let's go."

The water was warm but deliciously refreshing. Miriam thought she would never want to be immersed in water again, but this warm swimming pool was not like the cold dunkings of the river.

Walking straight into the clear bay up to their waists, Cam snagged her around the waist and hoisted her out of the water. With a scream coming from her lips, he tossed her into the water. As she rose up, slicing through the surface, she appeared as a water nymph rising from the depths. He watched as her dark hair, smooth and silky, flowed down her back and water droplets fell from her face down toward her breasts. Catching her breath she lunged at him, trying to dunk his head under the water, to no avail.

"That's no fair," she pretend pouted. "You're bigger than me."

"Just noticing that, baby?"

"No. I knew the canoe was tipping up on my side every time you got in!" she laughed.

"You'll pay for that one," he called as he moved quickly through the water as she tried to escape.

Within seconds he caught her around the waist again, but this time instead of tossing her, he turned her until she was facing him and captured her tightly against his chest. The amusement of the moment slowly morphed into something altogether different as her breasts pressed to his chest and his erection was held against her stomach.

She ran her hands through his hair, moving them downward until she grasped his strong jaw. Emotions swirling, she was overcome with the knowledge that he had come for her. And now he held her heart as much as he was holding her body.

Knowing they were not yet safe, the realization of what they had traversed to come this far jolted into their consciousnesses. Neither moved for a moment, each afraid to break the spell. Their eyes locked, hers wide with anticipation and his dropped to her mouth just before taking it.

The kiss was as desperate as the two young people alone in the ocean. One of his hands slid to cup the back of her head, angling her so that he could take the kiss deeper. His tongue easily slipped between her open lips, tasting, tangling...claiming.

She met him thrust for thrust as she wrapped her legs around his waist, still feeling his large erection pressed close to her core. All thought left her except for wanting this man at this moment.

Rubbing herself on him, she knew she could come just by dry-humping...but she much preferred him being inside.

Her arms were wrapped around his neck, allowing him to move his hand to her bra, pulling the cup down. Bending his head slightly, he latched onto her nipple sucking deeply. Hearing her gasp, he continued to suckle before moving to the other side.

Throwing her head back, she jutted her breasts out further toward him making his access easier. The jolt from her nipple electrified straight down to her core. It had been a long time since she had been with a boyfriend and she had never adopted the fuck-buddy attitude. Her long-buried libido roared to life as she continued to press her hips into his erection.

Barely aware of anything other than the call of his dick, Cam walked them out of the water and back to the hidden cove where their clothes had been dropped. Kicking their discarded clothes into a pile, he lay her on her back on top of them hoping they would provide some cushion.

Her eyes, gazing up at him, filled with desire as he leaned over her body, stopping within an inch of her mouth.

"You sure, *cariña*? I want you to be sure," he whispered, holding her gaze. "You gotta understand this is no fuck 'cause there's nothing else to do. This means something. So you gotta be sure."

A slow smile spread across her beautiful face. "Yeah," she breathed. "I'm sure."

15

Cam wasted no time in lowering his mouth the last inch to hers. The sound of the surf provided the backdrop music as he plunged his tongue into Miriam's warmth once again. Not flirting. Not playing. This time...possessive.

Rolling his heavy body to his back with his arms around her, he pulled her on top without losing her mouth. His fingers quickly unsnapped her bra and he moved her just enough to slide the material away, tossing it to the sand. Settling her back on him, he felt her naked breasts pressing tightly to his chest.

Sliding one hand into her panties, he palmed her ass. She was thinner than the picture Jobe had given to him —her time in captivity had taken some precious pounds off of her. He loved the feel of her full breasts and ass but knew that once she was able to gain the weight back...she would feel even more amazing to his roving hands.

Snagging her panties he tugged them as far as they

would go before she moved away from him just long enough to slide them the rest of the way down her legs and kick them to the side. Now completely naked, she lay beside him with her hands on his massive chest. She had never been with a man this large, and her hands continued to glide over the smooth skin covering the ripped muscles of his pecs and abdomen.

"One of us seems overdressed," she giggled, feeling self-conscious.

"Guess I better take care of that," he agreed, sliding his wet boxers down his long legs and tossing them aside. Rolling to his side he pulled her close once more.

"You are fuckin' beautiful, *cariña*," he said, his eyes moving over her body. "Never seen such beauty. Such strength. Such courage."

A smile curved her lips as she watch the handsome man in front of her speak with awe. Moving forward, she kissed him once more as his hands glided from her neck, down over her breasts toward her waist.

She felt him pull her hips in close to his erection and the tingling in her belly zinged straight to her core. All she wanted was this man. *If all I get of this man, is this moment, at this time...I'll take it.* She took over the kiss, leaning her head over his and sucking his tongue into her mouth. She felt him jerk in surprise before he rolled her back and took possession himself.

As his hand slid down over her perfect ass toward the prize, he felt her slick folds right before he moved one finger deep inside. Capturing her moan in his mouth he added another finger, scissoring them until she was quivering beneath him. Within a minute he could feel her inner walls tightening as her body underneath his went taut.

Needing oxygen, she broke the kiss, running headlong into her orgasm as it powered over her. With her head thrown back, as the electricity shot from her core outwards, she gasped for air.

Holding her tight as he watched her, eyes closed and panting, he could not help the feeling of power that washed over him, knowing he brought this amazing woman to her climax. He slowly withdrew his fingers as her eyes opened and watched as they focused on him. A small smile curved the corners of her mouth followed by luscious lips parting in surprise as she watched him slide his fingers into his mouth, sucking off her juices.

His cock was straining toward her as though it had a mind of its own, heading for the place it yearned to be. His restraint was killing him, but without a condom he had no fuckin' clue what she would want. He exhaled a painful breath before rolling onto his back, pulling her along with him so that she was tucked carefully into his side.

Her hand rested on his massive chest as she wondered what happened. One minute she was hurling over the finish line of her first orgasm in a long time that had not been self-induced—and much better than any of those—and now he seemed to have halted. Pulling in her lips, she looked up in surprise.

"Cam?" she whispered. "Did I…um…not do something ri—"

Before she could utter another word, he rolled back over onto his side facing her, his fingers on her lips. She could smell herself on them and closed her eyes for a moment as the beauty of all that was him washed over her.

"It's not you, babe. Fuck me," he groaned. Holding her gaze, he lifted his hand and skimmed her cheek with the back of his knuckles. "You gotta know, it's killin' me. Wanting you so bad."

"I don't understand. What's stopping us?"

"*Cariña*, I got no condom."

Once more, her mouth opened with no sound coming out. The passion rolling off both of them was palatable, and her mind raced to find a solution. "You could…I was on the pill…well, not in the past several weeks, but…"

"Babe, I promise you, I've thought of all of these things," he said, his voice heavy with regret.

"I'm clean," she said, tentatively, not knowing how he felt about that statement.

"I'm clean too," he shared. "We get tested all the time for work, and I gotta tell you that I never go ungloved. Had no one special in years and never trusted a pick-up or, God forbid, anyone when I was undercover for drug task-force."

He saw the hopeful gleam in her eye and hated to crush it once more, but had no choice. Rubbing her face once again, he reminded her, "Right now, the last thing you need is a pregnancy scare."

He watched as her eyes moved back and forth, working the problem. He knew he could pull out…it would kill him to not come inside of her, but he had enough self-discipline to do it. *But this has to be about her. Her choice. What she wants to do.*

"Um…" she began, clearing her throat nervously.

"What, *cariña?*"

"You could…pull out. If you wanted. It would be fine with me. But only if you wanted," she hurried to say, her nervousness showing.

"You sure?" he asked, hope filling his voice.

Smiling, she nodded as he leaned over and kissed her lightly.

"Gotta hear you say it."

"Cam, I've trusted you with my life so far. Why would I not trust you to take care of me now? So yeah, I'm sure." Blushing, she added, "I want you."

Grinning, he moved back over her body, making sure she was lying on the discarded clothes and not directly on the sand. With her head resting on his left arm, he skimmed his right hand along her soft skin, moving from her jaw to her neck, where it paused on her wildly beating pulse. It continued its trail down to her full breasts, nipples hardening as he rubbed his rough thumb over the points.

Bending over to suck one deeply into his mouth, he heard her sigh as her back arched upward toward him. As his mouth worked wonders on her nipples, his hand continued its path until it found her slick folds once more. Still slick. Ready. Waiting.

He shifted his body over hers making sure to keep his weight on his forearms. Watching her face carefully, he moved his swollen cock to her entrance. In answer to his unasked permission, she wrapped her arms around his shoulders and her legs around his waist, lifting her hips toward his.

Plunging inside, he buried himself in her then immediately realized that his girth would stretch her uncomfortably as he heard her gasp. He began to pull out, but was halted by her arms squeezing tightly. She offered him a smile as permission and he let nature take over.

And under a coral formation overhang, on a white sandy beach, finding privacy in the middle of drug cartel country, he made love to Miriam. And prayed to God it would not be the last time.

Moving in and out of her warmth, it was everything he imagined it would be. And more. Forcing himself to not come quickly, he focused on her. Keeping his weight on his forearms, his eyes on hers, he watched the myriad of emotions pass along her face.

She had wanted this from the moment she saw him in the clinic. This gorgeous, mountain of a man, moving over her...in her. The friction increased as did his pace and she felt her slick walls grab onto his cock, eagerly wanting to prolong this feeling.

He bent his head, owning her lips as he was owning the rest of her body. His tongue mimicked the action of his cock, keeping the same rhythm and he loved the feel as her tongue tangled with his.

Letting go of her mouth reluctantly, he moved his lips to her neck, sucking on her pulse before continuing down to her breasts. He felt her ribs and could not wait to get her back home so that she could be safe and healthy once more. But even with the weight loss, her breasts were full and the distended nipples begged for his mouth. The more he suckled, the more she moaned, her hands working his upper arms as she squeezed them tightly.

Miriam felt the pressure building once more, just like with his fingers, only this time it was fuller…more forceful…and then all thought flew out of her mind as he slid one hand down to tweak her clit. Her head fell back to the sand as her orgasm jolted though her, the tingles moving from her pulsating core outward in every direction. Her fingers dug into his back as he continued to power through, no longer pumping slowly, but now pounding in and out of her slick channel.

Within a minute he felt his balls tighten and against his desire to pulsate his seed deep inside of her, owning the last bit of claiming this woman, he forced himself to pull out at the last moment and with his cock pressed against her stomach he roared through his orgasm.

Barely remembering to roll slightly to the side, he dropped onto her after the last of his cum had covered her. Holding her to his massive chest he felt her racing heartbeat, challenging his for beats. Bodies panting, sweating, and sated, they lay in each other's arms for a few minutes until the euphoria was replaced with a calm feeling of content.

Turning his head, he lifted her chin with his fingers wanting to see her eyes. Hoping he would see at least satisfaction and not regret, his heart skipped a beat with the emotion pouring out from her gaze. Like he was a fuckin' hero. *Her hero.*

Smiling widely, he asked, "You okay, *cariña?*"

"I'm perfect."

"Yeah, yeah you are, babe. Absolutely perfect."

Glancing down at the mess on her stomach he stood up, lifting her and their clothes at the same time. Cradling her in his arms, she squealed as she threw her arms around his neck to hang on.

"Where are you going?"

"Wanna take care of you. Get you cleaned up."

"But Cam? We have no clothes on!" she exclaimed.

"We will, but let's get cleaned up first."

Within a few minutes he entered the water coming down from the river that was fresh and cool. Gasping as the water hit their warm bodies, she hung on tightly. He set her feet on the sandy bottom, not letting go, and washed his cum off of her stomach. Moving his large hand between her legs, he gently washed her there as well.

The intimacy of the act was not lost on her as she realized she was not embarrassed. No other lover had taken care of her afterwards. *Not that I've had that many lovers*, she thought.

His words interrupted her wandering thoughts. "Lean back, baby."

Answering her questioning gaze, he added, "Let's wash the sand and salt out of your hair."

Smiling, she allowed him to lean her back over his strong arm, while the other arm ran over the long strands of her hair. As he pulled her forward again, his lips found hers in a soft, gentle kiss. The kind of kiss that speaks volumes. Maybe even more than the wild kisses of passion. This was a kiss that made her think of promises to come.

Once more he carried her out of the water and, taking his t-shirt, dried her body before she slipped her scrubs back on once more. He did the same and then pulled his extra boxers and cargoes on. Walking back to their hideaway, hand in hand, they spoke little. But both knew things had changed.

Lying beside each other, watching the sun disappear into the surf as a brilliant red orb cast colors across the sky, he tucked her closely once more. Having eaten the last of the mangoes and drank more fresh water, they finally settled in for the evening.

Miriam watched as he placed a call to his contact and felt better as she saw that the plans for tomorrow seemed to be on schedule. Cam did not speak much, but as he flipped the phone shut, he turned toward her knowing she wanted to know the details.

"Okay, babe, I can see you're nervous. Right now, we're still on track to leave tomorrow morning, as soon as Marc can get the plane here. He did say that there was a lot of reported activity in the camp where you and I left, and he's had our group back home checking satellite photos. What they can tell is that we're probably missed and they're likely looking for us. They've found the jeep and I'm sure they're combing the river area."

Sucking in a deep breath, she forced her breathing to slow and kept her eyes on his.

He caressed her neck and gently pulled her forward until she planted into his chest. "You're good, babe. I've got you."

He felt, rather than saw, her nod. "Right now, what we've got going for us is that they're still hampered by the earthquake clean-up and the mess from the storm. That's the good news."

She lifted her head and leaned back to look into his face. "And the bad news?" she prompted.

"You've seen one of the major players because he was a dumb-fuck, who thought with his dick, and took you right to his house. He may be buried in this storm, but the cartel's reach is long. And by that, babe, I mean long. So we still gotta get out of here and back home. And then you'll have to meet with the DEA and some others to go over what you know."

"But my family?"

"I'll get you to them, *cariña*. I promise."

"What about when I'm questioned?" she asked, the fear and uncertainty in her voice speaking louder than the words.

"I don't know exactly how that'll play out, but I'll be with you as much of that as I can. They'll be talking to me as well."

She lay quietly for a few moments, her mind racing with all that had happened and her fears of what was to come. *And us? What happens when we go back to our lives?*

"I can see those wheels turning," he accused gently, turning her face toward his with his fingers. "I can keep you safe and I can help you through the shit we gotta deal with when we get back," he promised. "But what else is going through your mind?"

Her eyes skirted to the side, afraid that if she looked at him he would be able to see her questions about *them.*

Before she could deny that there was anything else on her mind, he asked, "You do understand about us, don't you?"

At that, her eyes jumped back to his.

Before he could say anything else, his body tensed and moved quicker than she could have imagined he could move. With a shove, he pushed her further back into the rock formation and rolled so that his body was covering hers, with his front facing outward. Her hand grasped the belt of his cargo pants as she heard the roar of a speed boat engine moving along the coast.

"Who is it?" she whispered, but he did not answer. Afraid to speak again, she just huddled against his broad, muscular back.

Keeping his head lowered, he nonetheless managed to track the boat as it moved along the shoreline, a searchlight dashing around the beach. Several long minutes passed, neither of them moving, before the boat continued out of sight.

Shaking, afraid to speak, she wanted to peek over his shoulder to see if anyone was coming. *I can't go back. I can't do that again.*

Cam finally allowed his breath to slowly let out, feeling the tug on his belt and the quivering body of the woman behind him. Twisting his head to hers, he saw the terror in her eyes.

"It's okay, babe," he whispered, lifting his hand to cup her face.

"I…can't…no…going back," she stammered, eyes wide.

He rolled toward her, wrapping his arms around her still shaking frame. "No one's getting you. They're gone," he promised.

"Were they looking for us?"

Taking a deep breath, he let it out slowly. "Possibly. There's no way to know for sure. But it's dark. They can't see us and Marc'll be here in the morning. I'll contact him to warn him, but he'll get us."

Pulling her face in close to his, he whispered again, "Promise, *cariña*."

Nodding again, she rested her head on his shoulder. "I'm not sure I can go to sleep," she confessed.

"Just close your eyes and listen to the surf. Let it all go, babe. I'm right here."

Breathing deeply, she found that his shoulder was infinitely more comfortable than the thin cot she had been sleeping on. *What would it be like to have this always?* And that was her last thought before she drifted off to sleep.

16

C am slept fitfully, taking short catnaps during the night, staying vigilant, but there was no repeat passing of the boat. *Had it been the cartel looking for them?* He shifted slightly on the bed of sand knowing no comfortable position was possible. But what the hell? In his arms dozed Miriam.

He could barely make out her features in the dark, but knew them by memory. Ebony hair, drying slightly curly, framed her beautiful face. Shadows were under her eyes making her translucent complexion seem pale in comparison. Her cheekbones were more prominent than the photograph he had seen bringing her drastic weight loss of the past month to the forefront of his mind.

The idea of taking her out for a huge, expensive dinner filled his mind as he yearned to take care of her. Smiling, he knew from what he had learned from her, she would rather have a hotdog while watching a college baseball game.

His mind rolled back over the mission, pleased they had made it out, but knowing that without the fortuitous storm it would have been almost impossible. Sighing heavily, his hand moved to his chest where his St. Camillus medallion rested. Patron Saint and founder of the Red Cross. *Jesus,* he smiled, clutching the pendant knowing that they still needed all of the help they could get to make it back home.

Miriam stirred next to him, snuggling her body closer to his in her sleep, tossing one leg over his as one arm landed on his chest, near his hand still holding the medallion.

He reached out gently and held her hand for a moment. *This woman, I could spend the rest of my life with.* He watched her breathe slowly, her face sometimes twitching as she dreamed. *But what of her? Can she love a man with my career? A man who's future is sometimes as uncertain as the missions I take.* Unfamiliar doubt crept in, leaving him with a feeling of uncertainty. *What's better for her...fighting for her or walking away to give her a chance at a normal future?*

He now understood his boss' dilemma over the last year as Jack battled with the knowledge that he had fallen in love with his pretty neighbor, Bethany, and wanting to give her the white picket fence future. What seemed obvious to Cam at the time, was now just as confusing as it must have been to Jack.

As the early morning light began painting the sky with colors, he felt his phone vibrate. He slid quietly away from the sleeping beauty and walked away toward the beach while still staying within the shadows of the rocks.

"Yeah?" he answered, knowing the call was from Marc.

"All's good," came the response.

"Thank fuck."

"Got the plane and got it fueled. Alberto's coming also in case we need some help."

"Why? What's goin' on?" Cam asked suspiciously.

Marc quickly replied. "Intel's that they've been tearing up the compound looking for the missing nurse. They didn't make a connection to you at first until they finally started putting two and two together. With the missing vehicle and knowing you had been to the river, they finally got their search going, and located it. Alberto's been able to find out that they've flown a few passes over the river and even taken a boat out to where the river meets the ocean, right where you are."

Cam sighed, knowing that the news was not unexpected, if unwelcome. "You think you've got trouble with our plans?"

"Don't know. Alberto is coming to provide firepower if needed. From what he can tell, the assumption is that you two are dead, never making it out of the storm, but these fuckers don't want anyone escaping, so they're on the lookout."

"What's your ETA?"

"Give us about two more hours to get everything ready. Got to check in with Jack one more time to make sure our trip home is ready. I've got us cleared with Homeland Security and Blaise has taken care of DEA.

We'll land somewhere unknown and refuel before making it back to Richmond. But warning, bro, it'll be intense once we get back. You may need to prepare her."

"Already on it. She knows there will be intensive debriefing."

"Good." After a pause, Marc asked, "How's she holding up?"

"Like a fuckin' champ," Cam stated, his admiration evident.

The men continued their conversation for a few more minutes, detailing the rescue. As Cam disconnected he remained still, looking out over the surf, his mind focusing on the rescue. Thoughts of her slipped back in, but he pushed them to the side. *Not now. Gotta focus on getting us the fuck outta here.* Sighing once more, he forced his mind to the mission.

Miriam woke, suddenly chilly after having been so warm. She realized that Cam had slipped away and her body missed him snuggling close to her. Blinking in the early morning shadows with the sunrise barely painting the sky, she saw him standing nearby talking on the phone.

His back was to her and she watched the muscles in his broad back as he moved around the beach. His waist was trim but, with his size, even that appeared powerful. His smooth shoulders were burned into her memory as she held them when he entered her. Sucking in a deep breath, she remembered every feel of their coupling. The way he took her with such power…and care. Closing her eyes for a second, she forced her mind to abandon those thoughts.

His black hair, lightly curling on the ends, beckoned her fingers. When he turned his head to the side, she could see the dark stubble of beard on his face.

He exuded danger…a man on a mission. *Me. I'm that mission. How could a man like that ever be interested in me?* She knew she had fallen in love with her rescuer and tried to convince herself that the emotions were only due to their extreme circumstances. But when he held her last night, all doubts flew from her mind and she knew her love was real. Based on the man and not the mission. *Is this one-sided?* Doubts filled her, but she pushed them to the back of her mind as she watched him disconnect his call. His face was etched in thought and she instinctively knew his mind was on the day's necessities.

Forcing her mind to the same, she prayed, *Please God, help us get home.*

Cam walked back over to where he had left a sleeping Miriam only to find her awake and staring at him.

"Did I wake you?" he asked, kneeling in front of her, lifting his hand to tuck a wayward strand of hair behind her ear.

Smiling, she shook her head as she stretched her body from its cramped position. Sitting up, she peered into his face searching for his thoughts. His face blank, she asked, "Is everything okay?"

"Yeah," he replied, wondering how much to tell her.

"There's something you're not saying."

Chuckling, he deflected, "You think you can read me that well?"

Lifting an eyebrow, she cocked her head and answered, "Um, yeah. I think, Mr. Perez, that after the time we've spent together, I know you very well."

Throwing his head back in laughter, he agreed. "Okay, Ms. Delaro. I guess you're right." Lowering his head back to hers, he leaned forward placing a kiss on her cheek. "I reckon you do know me, *cariña*."

Her eyes flashed with desire and he wanted nothing more than to take her again, here on the beach, and prove to her the depths of his feelings for her. But regretfully, now was not the time.

She saw his flare of interest and then watched as it died in his eyes. Sighing, she said, "I suppose you're all business this morning?"

Chuckling again, he replied, "Babe, I'd give anything if we were on this beach as a getaway vacation. Swear to God, I'd be doing nothing but worshiping your body right now in a way that would leave no doubt in your mind how I felt." Sighing heavily, he added, "But I need to let you know that according to Marc, the cartel definitely knows you and I left together."

He watched as her expression hardened and he wished to fuck he could make it soft again. Plunging on, he continued. "It was them doing flyovers on the river and checking out the shore last night." Hearing her sharp intake of breath, he plunged on. "Marc's ETA is about two hours so we need to be vigilant, be ready, and stay on target."

She nodded slowly, letting his warnings take root. "Okay," she said softly. Her gaze moved to the blue waters beyond his back and asked, "How does this work?"

Sliding easily into mission planning mode, he answered, "Marc's bringing our DEA contact along with him to provide extra security. He'll fly in and maneuver as close as he can, but he may have to stay back from the shore. We'll need to get to him."

He watched her face carefully, but so far her expression had not shown concern...just concentration. *That's my girl.* His thoughts stumbled as he realized, *My girl. Fuck yeah, she's my girl.*

"Cam?"

"Right here, babe," he responded.

"Um...I'm a decent swimmer, but not great. And I've never swam in the ocean," she confessed.

"Gotcha." He looked thoughtful for a moment and then said, "As soon as we can, we'll get in the water when we know he's close and then you swim as hard and fast as you can. Once beyond the waves, it'll be just like swimming anywhere else. I'll be right with you and if you get tired before we make it to the plane, I'll get you the rest of the way. Okay?"

Sucking in a huge breath, she agreed.

"That's my girl," he stated firmly, touching his lips to her forehead.

She looked up in surprise at his declaration, hoping

it was more than just a phrase. Smiling, she moved forward slightly and kissed his lips. She could tell he was surprised for only a second until he took over the kiss. Long. Hard. Wet. And full of promise.

At the appointed time, the whir of a plane's engine could be heard over the surf and Cam grabbed Miriam's hand, leading her into the water. They watched as the aircraft flew over and then circled around, its nose aiming toward the water. At the last minute, the plane leveled and the floats touched the surface.

"Let's go," Cam ordered, tugging her further into the surf.

The waves were difficult to manage, but she dove under a few and swam out trying to keep moving. He did not leave her side even though she knew he could have made the swim much faster. A large wave hit causing her to swallow water. Coughing as she came up, she felt his arms latch around her waist and hold her above the surface until she could catch her breath.

"You good?" he asked, worry lacing his voice.

Nodding her answer, they continued to swim toward the approaching plane. Its engines were propelling it forward slowly. *Almost there*, she thought with excitement.

The side door popped open and a man stepped out onto the pontoon. It was hard to focus on him and try to keep her head above the surface at the same time. A loud bang was heard and she jerked her head up at the same time she felt Cam's body stiffen. The other man was pointing a gun toward the back of the plane and firing.

"Fuck! We've got company," Cam yelled. "Go and keep your head down!"

She pushed off, adrenaline coursing through her system and she forced her arms and legs to swim faster than she ever had. She could not see what was happening but was determined to get to the plane.

Touching the pontoon with her hand, she heard the pilot yell through his open window, "Hold on!"

The water splashed over her as the plane created waves on the surf, but she could still hear the ping of the gun.

"Now!" the pilot yelled and before she knew it, Cam was behind, boosting her up. The man with the gun reached down with one arm and easily hauled her out of the water onto her knees on the slick pontoon.

Cam hoisted himself up beside her and with a quick glance to the right, saw a boat veering to the side. He grabbed her around the waist and shoved her through the open cabin door, realizing he was rougher than he meant to be, but urgency was needed. He followed quickly and Alberto jumped in behind as well, shouting, "Go, go!" as he closed the plane's door.

Before the passengers could be seated, the pilot engaged and the plane lurched forward, tossing Miriam against the floor. Scrambling to pull herself up, Cam grabbed her head and pushed her back.

"Stay down!" he yelled, throwing open the window

and firing out of one side while the other man was doing the same from his side.

Cam focused on the boat that had circled around and was making another pass.

"Marc! They're trying to come around to the front."

"Got 'em," came the response.

Miriam could not see anything from her position on the floor, but knew Cam expected her to stay where she was. The plane rattled as it picked up speed and she wondered if they would be able to get airborne. Heart pounding, she clutched the leg of the seat to keep from rolling back again as the aircraft's nose tipped up.

Lifting off of the water, Marc turned the plane toward land to get away from the men firing at them from the boat. As it banked in the curve, Miriam rolled in the other direction, bumping into Cam's legs.

Seeing they were away from immediate danger, he handed his gun to Alberto and crouched over her. "You okay, baby?" he asked, as he assisted her into a seat and buckled her in tightly, noting her shaking.

He buckled into the seat next to hers and threw his arm around her shoulders, maneuvering her body so that it was pulled in close to his.

"Was that them?" she asked, twisting her head to look up into his face.

He nodded, then before he could answer a towel was thrust toward them from Alberto. Offering him their thanks, he dried her arms and face quickly before using it himself.

"Miriam, let me introduce you to our rescuers.

That's Marc up front piloting and this is Alberto. Gentlemen, this brave lady is Miriam Delaro."

"Pleased to make your acquaintance, Ms. Delaro," Alberto said, offering her a blanket, which she took gratefully. Her scrubs were soaked and plastered to her skin. Wrapping the blanket around her body, she tried to calm the adrenaline shivers.

Her eyes shot toward the pilot, who threw up his hand in salutation before looking back, a broad smile on his face.

"Marc," Cam started, "you're one helluva pilot to get us outta there. And Alberto, thank fuck you came along with some firepower."

"You're the one who made it outta the viper's den," Marc said, with Alberto's nod in agreement. "You and Ms. Delaro."

"Please, call me Miriam," she said softly, her voice raspy from the salt water that she had swallowed.

Alberto moved to a chest next to him, saying, "It's not prime rib, but we know you two haven't eaten much." He pulled out water bottles and protein bars.

Her hands still shaking, Miriam took the bar then struggled to get it unwrapped. Cam's hand came over and pulled it from her.

"Here you go, babe," he said, handing the unwrapped bar to her. "Now, eat and drink slowly." He made sure she was taken care of then gratefully accepted the food himself.

Marc moved the aircraft back over the water now that they were safely airborne and the threat from the boat was over. Twisting around, he caught Cam's actions as he hovered over Miriam. "You good?" he asked.

"We are now," Cam sighed heavily, the adrenaline slowly draining from him.

"I…I want to thank you," Miriam said, looking toward Marc. Then she turned to Alberto, adding, "Both of you."

"From what I hear, Miriam, you should be standing up taking bows for how you handled the past month," Marc said sincerely.

"Agreed," Alberto said.

"Abso-fuckin'-lutely," Cam added, throwing his arm back around her once more, making sure the blanket was tucked around her carefully.

"What now?" she asked, chewing the bar.

"We've got permission to land in Texas at an undisclosed airfield. We'll change planes and be flown to Virginia," Marc commented.

Cam watched as a confused look appeared on her face. She kept her eyes on Marc as she asked, "Is that all?"

Chuckling, Marc said, "No, but I was just trying to give you the easy version."

"I think you'd better sock it to me, Marc."

Cam saw Marc quickly twist around and catch his eyes, a questioning look on Marc's face. "You'll find out," Cam explained, "Miriam's as tough as they come, so yeah, go ahead and let us know what's in store, but uh…maybe the abbreviated version."

"You got it," came the response. "All right, Miriam, here's what's gonna happen. When we get to Texas, we'll be in a hangar and the only people around will be DEA and FBI. They've got a doctor and nurse waiting for us and will check you and Cam out first. That may take a while because they will want to be thorough, and then you'll be fed. After that, DEA and FBI will speak to each of you individually."

Cam heard her sudden intake of breath and tightened his embrace. "It's gonna be fine, babe. They gotta find out whatever you know. So you just answer all of their questions and give them as much information as you can. I'll be doin' the same."

His eyes cut over to Alberto, "You know these guys? Don't want any dirty DEAs talking to Miriam." He knew it was a cut to Alberto, implying that there were DEA personnel on the take with the cartels, but every agency had them.

"I talked to the lead investigator. Know him. Know his family. Known him for years. His name's Manuel Reyes. He's clean and his team's clean."

Cam held his gaze and then nodded. Miriam glanced between the three men, not understanding their conversation but trusting Cam enough to take care of her.

Marc continued, "Once that's done, they'll fly us to Virginia. They'll arrange for your family to meet us, again at an undisclosed location. Cam? You want your family brought in as well?"

He shook his head. "Nah, they know I've been working. I'll call them when we touch down in Texas and let them know."

At the mention of family Miriam jerked up, asking, "My family! Does my family know we're out?"

"Soon as we cross into the United States, I'll give the go ahead to let them know," Marc replied.

Nodding, she settled back into her seat and into Cam's embrace.

"Once back in Virginia, you'll still be questioned… and protected," Alberto added. He did not add more after a pointed glance from Cam. The three men knew that her ordeal was far from over, but were determined to protect her as best they could at the moment.

Miriam rested her head on Cam's shoulder, occasionally looking out of the window at the scenery below. *How different from when I flew into Mexico last month.* What had seemed an adventure had turned into a nightmare. *A nightmare that hopefully is over!*

W hen Marc called out that they had crossed into US airspace, Cam gave Miriam a shoulder squeeze and was rewarded with a huge smile that lit her tired face.

She watched as they landed, an hour later, at an isolated airstrip with several large hangars around. The landing was easy and she appreciated Marc's piloting skills. Once the fear of still being within the cartel's reach had diminished, she allowed her mind to take in the reality of their rescue.

Marc and Alberto have been in Mexico ready to get us out, putting their own lives in danger. And Cam—he endured the ultimate risk without even knowing me. Tears stung the back of her eyes as she pulled in a sharp breath.

Cam looked at her face, realizing tears were soon coming and knew she was overwhelmed. Keeping one arm around her shoulders, he leaned forward and cupped the back of her head with his other hand, pulling her face into his chest. Holding her tightly, he offered her his warmth...comfort.

"Thank you, Superman," she said softly into his shirt.

"I'm no Superman, sweetheart."

She leaned her head back and peered into his eyes. "You're my Superman," she said simply.

His heart skipped a beat as he continued to hold her tightly.

She stayed there for a moment as the plane taxied into one of the large hangars and the heavy doors were closed behind them. Sucking in a deep breath and letting it out slowly, she managed to control her tears. Wiping her face quickly, she offered a weak smile to Cam as he loosened his hold to unbuckle her seatbelt.

The door to the small aircraft was opened and they saw a group of people standing around. Nerves hit her and she stood woodenly instead of exiting the plane.

Cam reached over, linking his fingers with hers, offering his strength. Alberto stepped out first onto the pontoon and then quickly hopped to the concrete floor. Cam followed but, as soon as his feet touched the pontoon, he turned and swept Miriam up into his arms. She clung to his shoulders as he made the jump to the ground and then gently lowered her to a standing position. Marc followed, landing right next to them.

She jumped when the small assembly began clapping and tears sprung to her eyes once more. Overwhelmed, she allowed Cam to turn her into his embrace again. Sucking in a huge breath, she pulled back and then walked over to Marc and Alberto.

"I haven't thanked you enough...for everything," she

said, her voice wobbly. Turning to Alberto, she added, "I have no idea what you do, but just shooting at the men in the boat so that I had time to get to the plane..." her voice hitched, "saved our lives." She rose on her toes and kissed his cheek.

His eyes were warm as he said, "My brave Miriam. You, my dear, have my deepest admiration."

Pulling herself together, she then turned and looked up into Marc's kind face, his green eyes filled with warmth. His dark hair was longer than Cam's and a lock fell over his forehead. No longer in the cockpit, he appeared much larger than she had imagined. "Cam spoke of you, so I know you're friends. I...thank you," she cried, unable to hold back any longer now that her feet were once more on American soil.

Marc took her slight weight, allowing her to cling to him as he folded his huge arms gently around her body. Holding her there for a moment until he could tell her shaking had subsided, he then turned her toward Cam's embrace.

Cam pressed kisses to the top of her head while murmuring assurances against her hair. She finally pulled back, her watery face looking up at his. Offering her a smile, he then looked beyond her at the gathering. "Got some more friends I want you to meet."

She turned in his arms and watched as three handsome men approached, smiles filling their faces as well.

"These are more of my co-workers, Miriam. I'd like you to meet Blaise, Bart, and Monty. They've just finished up another case with Jack and came here to meet us."

The blond Nordic god, Blaise, came forward and shook her hand, smiling a panty-melting smile that Miriam was sure had worked on many women. She caught the twinkle in his blue eyes as they darted between her and Cam, causing an even larger smile to break out on his face. Bart was simply huge, like Cam, only with sandy-blond hair. As he took her hand in a sincere greeting, she continued to get the feeling that he was amused at seeing Cam's arm around her shoulders. Then Monty approached. Tall, dark haired, distinguished. Just as gorgeous, but more suave.

After the three greeted her, they immediately turned their attention to Cam who let go of her only long enough to accept their man-hugs and congratulations on a successful mission.

Another Hispanic man approached Alberto and pulled him into a hug as well. "You kept this one a secret, man. I had no idea what was going on until we got your message that you were in the air."

Alberto smiled, saying, "We had to keep this mission from getting out but, thank God, it was successful."

The two men chatted for a few minutes until Cam walked over and Alberto introduced him to Manuel Reyes.

"Cam, I've known Manuel for a long time. He'll take good care of Miriam."

A voice cleared behind the group and, turning, Cam knew that the welcome was over. Stepping back to Miriam, he placed his hands on her shoulders and peered down into her questioning face. Heaving a sigh, he looked back down, saying, "It's time, *cariña.*"

She understood and wiped her tears with her fingers. Facing the small assembly, she nodded and said, "I'm ready."

Two hours later Cam sat with Bart, Blaise, Monty, Marc and Alberto at a table while they ate, waiting impatiently for Miriam.

"Bro, she'll be out soon. Go ahead and eat before you have to be interviewed," Bart suggested.

"Not eating before she gets out here." He rubbed his hand through his hair. His medical examination had gone quickly—he had lost a couple of pounds and needed fluids, which they said would be taken care of with his meals. His eyes cut to the door leading to the makeshift examination room where they took Miriam. "What the fuck is taking so long?"

Marc and Alberto shared a glance, before Marc softly asked, "Cam? Did she say anything? About being..." His voice trailed off and Cam's gaze jerked over to his.

"Sexually assaulted?" Cam growled. Gaining Marc's nod, he let out a deep sigh. "No. She didn't say anything and her actions never seemed like there was a problem." He looked down at his food and let his mind wander over what she had explained to him. "The offer was there...to become the mistress of whoever the fuck was in charge of that area of the cartel...and the fuckin' doctor also."

"Jesus," Marc bit out, at the same time as the other

men had the same reaction.

"She said that was what one of the other nurses was doing. The one from California. That's why I only got Miriam out. I know that she was the mission, but I would have gotten out anyone I could."

None of the Saints said anything, knowing the man in front of them would have tried to rescue anyone possible.

"When I got there, it was just Miriam, the older nun nurse, and the other one who was literally at death's door. The nun didn't want to go anywhere, knowing the other nurse was dying. She told Miriam to go with me."

He allowed his eyes to travel over his friend's faces, knowing there was something they were not telling him. "You all just show up to give us a warm welcome?"

Blaise spoke first. "Partially...yeah. You've had a time of it and we wanted to make sure you were all right. We finished the last major case and Jack sent us here to keep an eye on you and Miriam."

"Think there's gonna be trouble?"

"Don't know," Bart stated. "Blaise is gonna get a feel from the DEA questioning her as to whether or not she may need protecting."

"Fuck," Cam breathed.

"She might not," Monty added. The former FBI agent was cautious by nature, but did not want to be an alarmist.

Just then, the door opened and Miriam walked out, her long hair hanging damp, wearing clean jeans that were slightly baggy and a t-shirt that was two sizes too large. Her eyes darted nervously around until they landed on Cam and then he was gifted with one of her smiles.

Next to him, he heard his friends murmur under their breaths and in the back of his mind, he knew they were appreciating the view, which shot a bolt of jealously through him. Glancing around, he knew for sure the other men in the assembly had the same appreciation. Taking his gaze back to hers, he saw...she only had eyes for him.

Standing, he moved over, stopping directly in front of her, watching her head lean way back as she held his gaze.

"You okay?" he asked.

She heard the concern in his voice. Nodding, she said, "Yeah." Giving her shoulders a little shrug, she added, "I got the full examination. They're concerned about the weight loss and dehydration, so they gave me some IV fluids for a bit." She looked down at her clothes and giggled. "I'm afraid I will have to buy some clothes in a couple of sizes smaller than when I left."

Tagging her hand, he led her over to the table. "You hungry?"

Looking at the table loaded with deli meat, fresh vegetables and fruit, as well as several types of bread, she nodded enthusiastically. "Oh my God, I could eat everything."

He assisted her into a seat between his and Blaise, and across from the other men, all who greeted her kindly. "Gotta eat a bit at a time and slowly, *cariña*."

"I know," she agreed, but dug in heartily nonetheless. She saw the looks by the DEA agents in the room and she knew they were chomping at the bit to get her to finish so they could begin their questions. Determined to eat her fill, she just smiled at them and dug into the food, ignoring the churning of her stomach.

By that evening, Miriam wished that she had just kept eating and not stopped to deal with the DEA. The questions had continued until she thought she would scream. Separated from Cam, she knew he was also being questioned, but his were more about the operation that he had witnessed. Hers was about the kidnapping, their containment, who she saw, who she interacted with, the doctor, the visit to the leader's house...*on and on!*

She answered every question as thoroughly as she could but exhaustion set in and her head was pounding. The door to the room flew open and before anyone could speak, Cam stalked through.

"She's done," he growled.

"Now hold on," one of the DEA investigators spoke, "We're not—"

"Yeah, you are. She's fuckin' exhausted and has given you everything she's got to give. You need to cut her a fuckin' break."

Not sure what was expected, she glanced back at the three men at the table and then back up to Cam. Before she could speak, he scooted her chair back and leaned down to take her hand. He was moving away, giving her no choice but to follow.

As she allowed him to lead her away, he called over his shoulder, "We're heading to Virginia in an hour. Ya'll are gonna be on the plane with us, so I reckon that gives you another crack at her for about four hours. Then she's gonna have a reunion with her family and you'd better be finished 'cause she's gonna be getting back to her life."

"Does he speak for you, Ms. Delaro?" one of the DEA agents growled.

She turned her head back to stare at the man and then up to Cam. Smiling wide, she nodded. "I can always speak for myself, gentlemen. And have been for a couple of hours. But in this? Yeah, he speaks for me."

With that, she threw her arm around his waist as he tossed his arm over her shoulders and pulled her in tight, grinning down on her.

As the couple walked out into the main room the other Saints watched them, smiles on their faces. Having heard and watched their friend carefully, they nodded approval.

"Looks like another one of us has found something good," Blaise said, as the men moved over to stand with the couple.

***

Cam chuckled as he watched Miriam bouncing in her seat. The DEA plane had just touched down and taxied to another undisclosed hangar.

"Will they be here? I can't see anyone," she said, leaning over Cam's lap to look out of the window.

He smiled, knowing that her family was just inside one of the offices waiting on her. Marc had talked to Jobe and he had gathered her parents and sisters to meet them.

Once again, he held her hand as they alighted from the much larger aircraft, his eyes carefully scanning the area, unable to shake the feeling that she might be in danger. His mind trailed back to the conversation they had before the flight had taken off.

Blaise had spoken to the DEA agents and then talked to Cam afterwards, when Miriam was not with him. "She's given them a lot of information and while most of it they knew, it helped getting both of your descriptions of the compound, location, and inner-sanctum hierarchy. While none of it was really new, you two solidified some of their intel."

"So, what do they think of her safety?" Cam asked, concern in his voice.

Blaise watched his friend struggle, understanding what Cam felt for Miriam went way beyond rescuer. Placing his hand on Cam's shoulder, he answered, "They don't think that she needs protecting. She was never in a position to gather more intel than what they had, she had no dealings with anyone who was here in the US, so they think she's good."

"What about the media?" Monty asked, walking up and catching the end of Blaise's explanation.

"They're keeping her name out of it and advised her to do the same, which as you can imagine, she has no intention of blabbing to anyone about her ordeal," Blaise continued.

Bart looked at his friend and asked, "Cam? What's the deal with her? You involved more than a mission? Were the looks I saw pass between the two of you just looks between a rescuer and victim? Or is there something else brewing?"

Cam looked away, running his hand through his hair, seeing Miriam standing to the side talking to one of the nurses who had examined her. "Fuck if I know," he admitted. "She's amazing, strong, smart, and I'll admit only to you all, I'm falling hard for that girl and think she feels the same. But..."

The silence hung between the Saints for a moment and then Monty prodded, "But what, man?"

Cam turned back and looked at them. "What if that's all this was? She may have just been reacting to an intense situation when you don't know if you're gonna live or die. I want to explore it. See if it's real. Hope like hell she does too, but...now that we're back and she'll have her own life, then I don't know."

Bart clapped him on the shoulder, saying, "Tell you the same thing we told Jack months ago. You find something like that, you just don't let it slip through your fingers. Work at it, man. Work to see if what you discovered back there in the wilds of Mexico is something that you can build on here."

Now they were back in Virginia, off of the plane, and walking toward the office where she would be reunited with her family. He was glad...this was what the mission had been all about. *So why do I feel so fuckin' afraid?*

18

The door from the hangar's office flew open as Jobe threw it against the wall, his eyes on his sister. Miriam jumped at the sound then immediately saw him, followed closely by the rest of her family.

Screaming, she left Cam's side, running to meet Jobe, jumping into his arms at the last minute. She hit him so hard that as large as he was, he had to take a step back when her body crashed into his.

She could barely catch a breath as he twirled her around, before becoming aware of the crying of her mother, Rachel. Jobe set her down only to have her engulfed by her mother and father. Joseph Delaro had thought seeing each of his children as they were born was the most beautiful sight he had ever seen...but nothing matched holding his daughter once more after they had feared the worst. Miriam's sisters, Rebecca and Hannah, crowded in as well, a group hug that made it impossible for the observers to tell whose arms belonged to whom.

Choking back tears, Miriam assured over and over, "I'm fine, I'm fine."

As the family continued its reunion, Cam and the others stood back giving them privacy. He wanted to join…wanted to walk over, interrupt and say something stupid like, *Here's your daughter and by the way I'm in love with her.* Instead, he stood rock steady, the doubt of what they had in the wild and what they could have in the real world creeping in.

Jobe separated from the family and walked over to Cam, his arm stretched out. Cam took his hand, then found himself pulled into a man-hug.

Jobe's voice choked, "Gratitude man, you gotta know it."

Cam wanted to offer comfort but knew that if anyone had taken one of his sisters, he would be beside himself with worry and overjoyed to have her returned.

"The last month's been hell on my family. Never knowing. Jesus," Jobe continued, pulling back to hold Cam's eyes. "Owe you. Whatever, whenever. I owe you."

Shaking his head, he reached around placing his hand on Jobe's shoulder. "Nah, man. I took this as a mission, but I gotta tell you, your sister's fuckin' amazing. She held her shit together, did what she had to do to survive and then, when I got to her and we got out, she was right on point. Never wavered. Never faltered."

Jobe nodded, but added, "I can't begin to imagine what the hell you two went through." He turned to watch Miriam smiling with her parents still hovering. Turning his gaze back to Cam's he asked, "You think she's gonna be okay?"

Nodding, Cam responded, "Yeah. She's gonna be fine." He glanced over at the DEA agents still in the area. "They've questioned her pretty hard and she was checked out by the medical staff when we first landed. She's exhausted but, for the most part, she seems fine." He watched Jobe carefully, knowing Jobe had faced issues with PTSD after his time in Afghanistan. "They mentioned that she should seek a trauma counselor and I don't think that's a bad idea."

Jobe's gaze shot to his immediately, a heavy sigh leaving his body. Rubbing his hand through his hair, he nodded. "They're right. No matter how she's coping now, this is gonna fuck with her head."

Cam wanted to tell Jobe that he would be around. That he would be seeing to Miriam personally. That he would take care of her himself. But the words caught in his throat as he continued to watch her with her family. *She needs time with them. I need to back off...for now.*

Miriam's tears ceased as she convinced her parents she was not going to disappear in a puff of smoke. While talking to them she watched her brother approach Cam and smiled as the two hugged. She wondered when he would reunite with his family. *But he was on a mission, not kidnapped, so his family might not have even known he was out of the country.* Biting her bottom lip, she allowed her mind to wonder if he did this often—go to foreign countries to save maidens in distress. *Maybe so, but I was special...what we shared was special...wasn't it?*

Fatigue and emotional exhaustion crowded into her thoughts, making them a jumbled mess instead of the clear knowledge that the man who had held her through the night was hers. Hers to still lean on, still need, still...*love.*

Her thoughts were interrupted when her father declared, "We need go. We need to get Miriam home. My girl has been through enough."

Jobe walked over, hearing his father's words, and pulled his sister back into another embrace. "We're done here, sis. Let's go."

"I...I have to say goodbye to Cam."

Walking away from her family she approached Cam tentatively, seeing that he was standing with his co-workers. The wall of muscular testosterone in front of her was impressive...and intimidating, but she only had eyes for Cam.

He stepped away from the others and met her in the middle of the hangar, aware he wanted to spirit her away from the curious eyes all around and take her somewhere private. They stopped two feet apart, her head still having to lean back to look into his eyes.

"Hey," she said softly. "I...I guess my family is ready to go."

"Yeah," he answered, suddenly unsure of himself and who they were now that she was safe.

She picked up on his reticence, sucking her lips between her teeth in nervousness. "I want to make sure you know...um...well, how much...well, thank you for everything." Her words sounded lame to her, but with a crowd surrounding them, she did not dare throw herself into his arms and declare her undying love.

Her uncertainty screamed out to Cam and he lifted his hand toward her, saying, "The pleasure was all mine, Miriam. I'm glad you're with your family now and… well…it was very nice to get to know you."

She looked down at his outstretched hand and, not knowing what else to do, placed her much smaller one into his, accepting his shake. *No Cariña. Just Miriam.*

He watched her carefully, looking for a sign that she wanted more, but only saw her looking down at their clasped hands.

She battled back the tears, wishing he would pull her in for a hug…something to indicate that what they shared was special to him as well.

With half-hearted smiles, they dropped their hands, neither saying anything.

"Well, um…goodbye, Cam," she said, trying to make her voice sound stronger than she felt.

Nodding slowly, he added, "Goodbye, Miriam."

With that, she turned and started to walk away, when he called her name again. Smiling she moved back. Looking up expectantly, she watched as he pulled out a pen and piece of paper from his pocket. He scribbled something and then handed it to her.

"It's my phone number, in case…well, if you ever need anything."

She stared at the paper as she had his handshake a moment earlier, before looking up. Steeling her expression to mask her confusion, she nodded her thanks before walking back to her family. Accepting Jobe's arm across her shoulders as they walked to their vehicle. Once inside, she spared a glance at the assembly, but only had eyes for the large man who had rescued her... and stolen her heart. And she watched him until he was out of view and another tear slid down her cheek.

The DEA agents, including Alberto, were packing up as Marc walked over to Cam, clapping him on the shoulder. "You wanna tell me what the hell that was?"

Cam's lips tightened into a thin line as he let out a deep breath through his nose. "Don't go there," he warned.

Bart, Blaise, and Monty joined them, each quietly observing their friend.

Marc ignored the warning and pushed, "You can't tell me that what you feel for that woman is going to be shoved aside 'cause you've got some idea that she's better off without you."

Sending a blazing glare toward Marc, he answered, "You think I'm ever gonna be able to fit into her world? Sweet girl, with a sweet job? Hanging with someone who never knows where the next mission might take him? She's got family that wants to keep shit from happenin' to her. You think Jobe would welcome a rough *hombre* like me into the family?"

"Cam—" Bart began.

"Fuck!" Cam growled. "What the fuck was I thinkin'? I should've kept my mind on just the rescue instead of..." he trailed off.

"Falling in love with a beautiful woman?" Monty finished for him.

Cam's eyes darted over to Monty's as he sucked in a sharp breath, ready to retort. Then stopped and let the breath out slowly. Dropping his chin to this chest, he nodded. "Yeah. I fuckin' fell in love with the mission."

"No," Bart said, watching his best friend closely. "You accomplished the mission. You fell in love with the girl."

The cavernous hangar was silent for a moment as the five men stood in solidarity.

"Jesus," Cam said, his voice laced with frustration. "Now I know exactly how Jack felt when he first met Bethany. Miriam deserves a man who can give her a nine-to-five life and not have to relive her nightmare every time he heads off to work."

"So you're gonna make that decision for her?" Blaise asked. "Cause from what I saw, that woman wanted you. When we were on the plane coming here, there was no doubt she was making the same statement that you were—that you two were together."

"She needs to be with family. They gotta heal as a family. They gotta see to her...for them as much as Miriam. And I gotta step back right now to give them that."

Marc nodded, saying, "Okay, man. I can see that play. You giving her family a time to reconnect. But then what? Are you seriously gonna let her just walk out of your life?"

Before he could answer, Monty added, "Or rather, are you going to walk out of her life?"

Cam's gaze cut back to his, and Monty continued,

"That's what's going through her mind. Not that she walked away, but that you did."

Rubbing his hand over his face, the exhaustion was overwhelming. Cam nodded and said, "I get where you're coming from. Right now, I've gotta walk away to give her what she needs. Down the road? Who knows?"

Recognizing their friend's need to recuperate, they moved toward their vehicle, deciding to drop the conversation.

"Jack wants a debriefing as soon as you're up to it," Blaise said.

Nodding slowly, Cam said, "Tomorrow's good. Just let me sleep tonight and I'll be there."

With that, the five Saints climbed into the SUV and Bart drove them away. Cam leaned his head back, wishing that sleep would overtake him but, instead, visions of a dark haired, dark eyed beauty filled his thoughts.

As the taillights of the SUV left the hangar, hidden eyes followed it as it disappeared from sight before a phone call was placed. Then the mysterious caller slipped unnoticed into the night.

Instead of going to her apartment, Miriam was not surprised to see that her father drove the family straight to her parents' house. The lights were on, both inside and outside, and the minute they entered the driveway the front door opened and Jobe's wife, Mackenna, and Rebecca's fiancé, Thomas, ran out. More greetings and tears followed, before Jobe and Joseph managed to herd the women inside. Rachel wanted to feed her daughter, but Miriam caught her in the kitchen, saying, "Mom, I honestly just need to sleep."

"You should eat. Look how thin you are," Rachel exclaimed, worry etched on her face.

"I know and I promise tomorrow, I'll eat. Right now, I just want a shower and to fall into a soft bed."

Rachel pursed her lips, but relented. Cupping her daughter's cheek, she peered deeply into Miriam's eyes. "I prayed. Every minute of every day since you've been gone." Her voice broke, but she powered through. "I prayed God would send someone to save you. And He did."

"He did, mom. He sent a Saint to watch over me," Miriam whispered, hugging her mother for the hundredth time that night.

An hour later, tucked in the bed she slept in as a child, Miriam's thoughts moved back to Cam as sleep was overtaking her. *Did I read the signals wrong? Was it just me that wanted what we discovered to last longer than the rescue?* The night provided no answers and as exhaustion overtook her, she dreamed of the large, handsome man who had plucked her from danger and stolen her heart.

19

Jack eyed his group carefully as they met the next morning in the main conference room at their compound. He took his responsibilities as their boss seriously, not only wanting to know about the mission, but keeping a pulse on his men as well. Cam, hair and beard trimmed closely again, sat stoically at the table waiting for the meeting to begin.

"Good to have you home, Cam. We've read the reports coming in from Marc, but we'll get to your assessment in a few minutes." Jack reported the ending of the recent serial killer case that they had all been working on, including Cam before he was re-assigned. The case had just been resolved. Much to Cam's surprise, it ended much closer to home than any of them had anticipated.

Jack divvied up the newer security assignments, pleased that none of them required travel at this time except for a few visits to Washington, D.C. for a couple of them. Turning back to Cam, he said, "Okay, let's hear it. I'll still need your written report, but until then, give us your version and where we need to go with this."

Cam recited his observations of the mission, the camp, the compound, and the rescue. His words were precise, clinical. Non emotional. He noticed the glances of the others around the table, but he was not going there. *No fuckin' way are they getting more.*

Jack listened, taking notes as Cam spoke. When the report was given, he turned to Blaise. "What does DEA say? More security needed?"

Blaise answered, "The agents I talked to yesterday seem to think that this is over. Miriam and Cam's interviews didn't provide any new information, just confirmation of what the DEA already knew. Juaquim is the local leader of that area. Made a shit load of money on the backs of the farmers who barely make enough to feed their families. Miriam was able to give them some information on his private compound and the activities of a Dr. Villogas, but, other than that, they felt like she's in no danger. Nothing that would make anyone want to come here to harm her."

The group was silent as their eyes gravitated toward Cam. Jack turned back to Cam and asked, "What's your opinion?"

Sighing heavily, he said, "Got no reason to think that she's in further danger. We've got Alberto and Manuel working on having the DEA keep her out of the media, but that's not to say that it won't be noticed soon. Probably everyone she worked with at the hospital knows she was missing and when she shows back up, they're gonna have questions. How was the local news?"

Bart replied, "News reporters camped outside her parents' home for a while until Jobe and the rest of Tony's men convinced them they needed to move along. When no news was coming, the reporters left looking for bigger stories. Now that she's back? Don't know."

"I'll stay in touch with Jobe to make sure the family is covered with security, although Tony's probably already taking care of his needs. I want us to work with Alvarez Security on that," Jack added. The others nodded and he saw a flash of gratitude in Cam's eyes.

"Then are we all agreed to keep Miriam Delaro on as a security risk for now?"

Absolutelys and fuck yeahs were heard around the table. Eyes twinkling, Luke grinned and said, "Right. Then I'm gonna set up a continuous intel link into Juaquim's setup." He looked over at Blaise and said, "What I find for DEA, it'll be your call to let them know, but I'm only keeping an eye out for anything that pertains to Miriam."

The others chuckled knowing how Luke lived for hacking into the computer systems of those they were investigating.

Blaise nodded in agreement as Jack noted that he would inform Jobe and Tony about their plans.

The meeting adjourned and the eight men headed upstairs to the main level of Jack's house. As soon as they reached the living level the scent of cinnamon filled the air. Bethany, was standing in the kitchen having just pulled out a huge apple cobbler from the oven.

"Jesus, I missed this," Cam exclaimed, rounding the breakfast bar to get a better whiff.

Bethany turned her face toward him and, once she set the hot dish on the cooling rack, she walked over, offering him a hug. "Welcome home, Cam."

He returned the hug, saying, "Hear a lot happened while I was gone."

Letting go of the large man and turning her attention to Jack as he prowled over to her, she smiled. "Yeah, it's been kinda crazy. I guess Jack filled you in?"

Cam nodded and watched his boss kiss the top of Bethany's head. *Jack thought he'd never be able to fit Bethany into his world. Guess he found out that she fits perfectly with him.*

Offering a sincere smile, he said, "Good to see you two together."

Jack accepted his congratulations, before saying, "You'd better serve this up, babe, before the crowd gets restless."

Laughing, Bethany dished out hearty servings of the cobbler to the Saints and they all retired to Jack's large deck overlooking his property with the Blue Ridge Mountains in the background.

The group settled into comfortable conversation, Bethany joining right in, as they devoured the treat. Jack often held post-meeting gatherings here or in his massive den. Having served in the Special Forces, he knew the importance of bonding with the men who needed to have your back and understanding them so that you could have theirs.

The conversation slowly turned toward Cam's latest

mission as Bethany asked, "Tell me about Miriam once you escaped? How did she handle everything?"

"She was great," Cam responded quickly. "Never complained. I told her straight out that she needed to follow my every command, even if she didn't understand it. She had no problem doing it and it probably saved our lives several times. She ate what I had for her, slept when we could. I did the paddling, but she worked to keep the canoe afloat when the rain was pouring down. When we had to climb down a steep mountain side, taking the canoe with us, she did everything just right."

The group fell silent listening to their comrade describe his admiration for Miriam.

"Sounds like an amazing woman," Bethany said softly, seeing the struggle in Cam's expression. "Like someone worth knowing. Maybe even...worth fighting for."

"Babe," Jack warned, giving her a little squeeze.

Cam's eyes jumped quickly to hers, but instead of seeing mirth, he saw understanding. Nodding slowly, he said, "I agree, Bethany. She is someone worth fighting for. But the right person needs to be doing the fighting."

He watched as Bethany cocked her head to the side and knew the other men had stopped eating and were watching him carefully.

Jack spoke first. "Sounds a lot like me a couple of months ago, thinking that my life had nothing to offer a woman like that."

Bethany put her hand on Jack's chest, glancing at

him before turning her gaze back to Cam, who was staring off in the distance.

"We shared something down there," Cam finally admitted. "Something special. Not gonna talk about it, but I will say it gave me hope. Hope that someone like her could be happy with someone like me."

The group said nothing, waiting for the big man to gather his thoughts.

"Watched her last night with her family. They're tight. Tight as my family and I didn't think anyone could be that tight. She's good. They've got her covered. Just not sure I see myself fitting into her world right now."

"But—" Bethany started, but Jack once more gave her a squeeze.

Cam continued, "She saw shit down there. God-awful shit that no one, especially a sweet nurse, should ever have to see. Down there? I was her rescuer. Now that we're back? I might just be a reminder of what all she went through."

Bart, feeling his friend's pain, said, "Man, you're taking that choice away from her just like Jack was with Bethany. You're deciding what she'll feel. What she'll remember. Maybe that's not what she wants at all."

Sucking in a deep breath, Cam looked down at his empty plate. Standing, he looked at Bethany saying, "Appreciate the cobbler. It's just as good as I remember." He walked to the sliding glass door that led inside before turning once more toward his friends. "I get what you're saying. But that's gonna have to come from her. I'm not about to walk her back through those memories unless she wants me to."

With that he left Bethany and the other Saints still on the deck.

A week later, Miriam lay in bed after a shift at the hospital. As tired as she was, she hated closing her eyes. Waking up night after night, fear clutching her heart, she would sit up quickly in bed. Each time the nightmares came, she would get up in the middle of the night and head to the kitchen, getting a glass of cold water to soothe her sweat soaked body.

She talked to the hospital counselor once but decided that she would not return. *I'm a nurse. I know what the hell PTSD is and that I need help.* But the realization that her experiences in Mexico were so far removed from anything the counselor could imagine had her refusing to go again.

Standing at the kitchen sink, she glanced at the clock on the stove. Two a.m. *Damn.* Forcing her mind from the nightmares that awoke her, she turned her thoughts to her day at work. *Like that's any better,* she thought remorsefully.

Remembering the reasons behind her decision to go with the Red Cross to Mexico, she realized they still existed. The fast pace of the ER did not allow her time to bond with any of her patients. On top of that, it appeared that she had received some level of notoriety since she had last been there. The staff was pleased she was back, but full of questions that she had no intentions of discussing with any of them.

Returning to her bedroom, she threw herself across the bed, turning off the lamp on the nightstand, trying to battle the nightmares.

Her mind rolled back to the weeks that she helped take care of Mackenna's mother who had a stroke. She loved that experience—working with a patient she had the opportunity to get to know.

It was not just the hospital that was getting on her nerves. After two nights of sleeping in her old room in her parents' home, she was ready to move back into her apartment. Jobe had his coworkers at Alvarez Security come by to set up security. Rebecca had insisted on spending the night, but Miriam finally convinced her to return to the apartment she now shared with Thomas. Jobe wanted to stay...then her mother.

Earlier in the evening she almost lost her composure but maintained, knowing her family loved her. "Guys, you've got to let me get back to my life. I love you, but the only way I'm going to move on past what happened is if I can get back to what's normal!"

They relented reluctantly and now she found herself lying in bed, the moonlight casting shadows around the room and her heart pounding as she tried to steady her breathing. *I'm in my home. Safe. No one is threatening me here.*

As always when her mind cast back, she thought of her time with Cam and wondered what he was doing. It was hard letting go of him, not understanding why he walked away. Rolling from one side to her back and then over to the other side, she wondered if sleep would come.

She knew her brother saw Cam as nothing more than her rescuer...not a lover. *Oh Jesus, what would he say if he knew?*

Her phone vibrated on the nightstand and she grabbed it, not looking before she answered. Rebecca, Hannah, or Jobe had taken to checking on her at night. As soon as she said, "Hello," and heard silence on the other end, she immediately recognized her stupidity. *With the media still trying to get a story, I should have never answered.* With her finger over the off button, she heard a man's voice, thick with an accent, "You left. That was not very nice of you, was it?"

Bolting upright in bed, she gasped, "Who is this?"

Only a deep chuckle was the answer before the phone call was disconnected.

Heart pounding, she stared at the phone in her shaking hands. Her mind raced trying to make sense of his words and who to call. She had programmed Cam's cell number into her phone, remembering his parting words. *In case you ever need anything.*

Hitting her contacts, she saw Cam's name.

He answered sleepily, "Yeah?"

"Cam?"

"Miriam?" Hearing the fear in her voice, he quickly asked, "What's wrong?"

"I got a call, Cam. I got a call from someone. Someone who knew I left and...and...and they said it wasn't nice of me to leave."

"Fuck!" he growled instantly alert. "Where are you?"

237

"In bed," she replied, eyes darting around as though the shadows in her room would come alive.

"No, no, I mean what house are you in?"

"My apartment."

"You alone?"

"Yes. I told my family that I wanted to get back to my life and not to hover."

"I'm on my way. Stay locked in."

"My address is—"

"I know it, *cariña*. I know where you live."

Disconnecting, she leaned her back against the headboard, drawing her knees up to her chest and resting her chin on them. Her mind was racing. *Who could that be? And why?*

She looked back down at her phone and considered calling Jobe, but with Mackenna pregnant, she did not want to disturb him. *He'll lose his shit when he finds out anyway but, for now, he needs to be with his wife. And Cam? He may not want to be with me, but he can protect me.*

Before she knew it there was a knock on the door. Startled, she ran through the hall to the front door but stood numbly, afraid to answer.

"Babe? It's me," Cam's voice carried through the wood.

Throwing open the door, she grabbed his hand dragging him in quickly before shutting the door and throwing the bolt.

Twirling around to face him, she blurted, "I'm sorry I called. It's just I was scared and didn't want my brother to lose his shit, not when his wife is expecting and I thought of you and knew that no matter how you felt about me, you'd help."

Cam grabbed her shoulders pulling her toward him. Her long, dark hair flowed down her back, framing her pale face. Her eyes, large and unblinking stared up at him. "Babe, slow down. I'm here and fuckin' glad you called. I'll handle Jobe, but right now I need to see your phone."

She handed it to him and watched as his fingers quickly flew over the keys. He then pulled out his phone and placed a call.

"Jack? It's Cam. Sorry to disturb you but I'm at Miriam's. She got a warning phone call on her cell, then she called me. I want to meet tomorrow. Everyone? Yeah. No, I'm taking her with me. Not leaving her here." Signing off, he turned back to her and said gently, "Babe, I need you to get changed and pack some shit. I'm taking you to my place."

She stood and stared, unable to process what he was saying. *Babe? He's taking me with him?*

He stepped closer, lifting her chin with his fingers. "*Cariña*? Breathe," he ordered gently, and she felt the air whoosh out of her.

"I don't understand, Cam. Why are we going?"

"I know Jobe had your apartment wired for security, but I don't want to take any chances. I want you to pack up whatever you need for a couple of days and I'm taking you to my place for the night. Tomorrow morning, we're going to Jack's where all the guys will meet. I want Luke to have a crack at your phone to see what he can tell about the caller."

She licked her lips nervously, glancing around. "I...I should call Jobe."

Cam stepped closer. "You already said you didn't want him upset with Mackenna pregnant right now." He watched as she nodded her head slowly in agreement. "Why'd you call me?" he asked.

Her eyes sought his and she answered honestly. "I...I knew you'd come for me. I knew I could trust you."

He stepped closer so that her front was almost plastered to his. "Why'd you really call, baby?"

Her chest heaved with each breath as she replied, "Because I wanted you. I know you wanted to get away from me once we were back but...I just wanted to feel safe and you're the only one I would really feel safe with."

He cocked his head as he stared at her for a long minute, then quietly said, "Get dressed and get your shit, babe. I'll take care of Jobe...and I'll take care of you."

She nodded and headed toward the bedroom, stopping as he called her name.

"I got stuff I need to handle to make sure you're safe first but then we're talking. We've got things to talk about and I'm not letting you walk away again without taking care of all our business. You with me, *cariña*?"

She sucked her lips in and stared before giving a quick nod and doing what he asked. He watched her, noticing her pink sleep shorts with the matching polka-dotted camisole. Forcing his mind to the problem and not her ass, he moved about her apartment making sure it was secure before they left.

Fifteen minutes later, she handed him her suitcase as she slung her laptop bag and purse over her shoulders, following him out into the night. She had no idea what he wanted to talk about. But as long as she was with him, she knew she'd be safe.

20

Cam woke the next morning, his mind instantly alert and focused on the woman sharing his bed. Her long, dark hair lay across his pillow and her face was relaxed in slumber. His mind wandered over the night's events, resulting in Miriam in his bed...where he wanted her but had been afraid would never happen.

As soon as Cam had her in his SUV, he called Jobe. "Bro, It's Cam. Keep your shit, but I've got Miriam. She got a threatening phone call and called me. I called Tony to keep an eye on your cameras and I was there in fifteen minutes." Cam heard Jobe immediately go into protective brother mode and he interjected, "Nope, not happening. She called me. She's coming to my place, not some lock-down at Alvarez." Pause. "This is a courtesy call, man, 'cause I know you're tight with your sister, but she's already decided she's not bringing this shit to your doorstep with you havin' a pregnant wife."

It took a couple of more minutes to get Jobe under control, but Cam finally convinced him that it was for the best. They agreed to meet at Jack's compound the next morning. Disconnecting, Cam looked over at Miriam, seeing the concern on her face.

"He lost his shit, didn't he?" she asked.

"Yeah," he nodded. "But if it was one of my sisters, I'd be losing my shit too."

They drove in silence for a couple of minutes, Miriam staring out of the window into the darkness. She lived on the western side of Richmond in an apartment complex that was close to the hospital where she worked. They passed several neighborhoods before he turned the SUV onto one of the highways that took them farther west outside of the city. About five minutes later they exited and she saw that they were already in a less populated area. A few more twists and turns took them to a street with few houses on it, each with several acres around.

"You live out here? There's so much land around and you're not that far from the city," she said, surprise in her voice.

"I consider it to be the best kept secret around. The neighborhood is old and small with only about twenty houses, but we all have some land around so there's still a sense of privacy. I'm twenty minutes away from the city and about thirty minutes away on the other side from Jack's place." Chuckling, he added, "And just about ten minutes away from a grocery store."

They pulled into a long driveway lined by trees and

then she got a glimpse of a small, two story house before the garage door opened and they drove inside.

Cam led her into the laundry room from the garage and then into the kitchen. While not large, it was updated with new appliances. An arched doorway led into the combination dining room and living room. Having only seen him in the wilds, she could not help but look around in curiosity at what his home represented.

She saw old, comfortable furniture that appeared to be second hand while clean and neat. The table could seat eight, which seemed strange before she remembered that he also had a large family. The informal living room was filled with an overstuffed sofa and chair angled to face the brick fireplace and large screen TV mounted over the mantle. The space was definitely male—no nicknacks, no frills, but warm and inviting all the same.

Cam placed her suitcase in the hall that led toward the stairs and turned to see her looking around. "It's not much, but it's home…and it's wired for security as well as anything Jobe could offer you."

She offered him a small smile, saying, "I'm sure it is. I feel…completely safe here with you."

As he watched, he saw a shadow pass over her face and he decided that talking was the first thing on his list of what they needed to get out of the way. He walked past her, taking her hand in the process, and led her over to his sofa. Sitting down, he twisted his body so that as he pulled her down next to him, he was facing her.

"You want to talk about the phone call?" she asked.

"Nope," he declared. "I want to talk about us."

Her head cocked to the side as her brow creased in question. "Us? Um...I don't know what you mean," she said nervously.

"Look at me, *cariña*"," he ordered gently and her eyes immediately sought his. "I'm a simple man, Miriam, so I'm gonna lay it out as plain as I know how. I don't see the reason to drag this out or have either of us unsure of what we are and what we have."

He watched carefully, seeing her gaze remaining on his although the questioning expression was still on her face.

"Okay," she said, dragging out the word in hesitation.

"We met under strange, intense circumstances and sometimes people get so caught up in that kind of world that they act in ways that lets them know they're alive and then the emotions get all tangled up in that as well."

She sucked in her lips, listening to him sound so dispassionate about what their relationship had been.

"But that was not us, babe," he declared, seeing the surprise on her face.

"What we had down there was real. What we learned about each other. What we did. And especially when we made love...it was not fucking. It was not just getting off on each other because of an intense situation. I felt it. I knew it. And I fuckin' want to keep exploring where it's gonna go now."

"But...but you seemed so distant when we said goodbye," she said, confusion warring with hurt.

"I screwed up, babe, and I see that now. The last thing I wanted to do was interfere with your family reunion. They needed that and so did you. And I knew you needed time to get back into your life. And I admit that I wondered if there was any place for me in your real world."

"My real world?"

"Yeah, the world where you live, work, meet with friends…you know? This world that doesn't involve running through woods and over cliffs and down rivers."

Silence descended on the room for a moment—not uncomfortable, just each to their own thoughts.

"But I need to know what your thoughts are," he admitted.

"Cam, I assumed that when we returned, we'd see each other. Um…like date…or something." Her voice was a mixture of strength and hesitancy and he realized that he had a shot, but before he could speak, she continued.

"But when we got back, you seemed too distant. I thought maybe you were embarrassed in front of your friends or when my family showed up, that you didn't want to be seen with me."

"Looks like we both made wrong assumptions," he said, with a smile.

"So what exactly does it mean when you say you want to see where we go?"

He shifted her body so that she was straddling his lap, one hand resting on her ass and the other hand drifting under her hair. His thumb rubbed her neck as his hand pulled her forward slightly until their lips were a whisper apart.

"It means that as of right now, no more misunderstandings. No more giving you space. No more stepping back. You want me, you tell me now and then I'm claiming you, *cariña*. Publicly, to our families, to our friends, to the world."

He watched her eyes drop to his lips but he continued to hold them apart until he got the answer he was looking for. "What's it gonna be?" he prodded.

"Yes," she breathed into his mouth. "I want you."

With that he pulled her in, capturing her lips, immediately diving into her warmth. His tongue thrust inside, exploring and claiming. She met him, sucking on his tongue, drowning in the intensity of the feeling.

The hand that held her neck drifted down her back, pulling her body flush against his. Her breasts were pressed into his massive chest and his erection was plainly nudging against her core.

He moved his hand back to her neck and gently pulled her away, something his body did not like and he could tell from her mewl, she did not either. "Hate to do this, but now that we got us squared away and we take this further, which I gotta tell you involves you being naked in my bed, me having a condom so I can come while buried deep inside you, and then you sleeping beside me...we gotta talk about the phone call."

Her face scrunched in displeasure, but he soldiered on. "Tomorrow morning, we go to Jack's place where the others will meet us. We'll get some info from you, but mostly you'll be hanging with Jack's woman,

Bethany. I'll get your phone to Luke, but he's already gonna be working on it, probably before we get there." He watched her eyes carefully, keeping a check on her emotions, but she seemed to be holding it together. *That's my girl. And now, I can fuckin' say My Girl!*

Continuing, he said, "And until we get things figured out, you're staying with me. We'll use the Saints and Alvarez Security to make sure you're good at the hospital."

Miriam nodded slowly and then said, "Um, I guess you should know that I turned in my notice to the hospital."

Eyes wide, he did not even have to ask before she jumped into her explanation. "One of the reasons I took the Red Cross offer was because I was no longer happy at the ER. Too much red-tape, not getting to know my patients, and the crazy hours. I felt so burned out. And now that I'm back? Lots of curiosity seekers on top of the same problems as before. I can't handle the stress," she admitted.

"I think that's a smart move, babe."

"Yes, but now I'm unemployed."

"You take the time to find the job that you really want and in the meantime, you're safer here anyway."

Her teeth worried her bottom lip and he moved his rough thumb pad over the plump redness. "What's got that look on your face now?"

Sucking in a deep breath through her nose before letting it out slowly, she admitted, "My family's going to have a fit if I'm living here. Jobe'll lose his mind again and that doesn't even begin to explain my parents' reaction. They blew a gasket when Jobe and Mackenna moved in together before getting married and again when Rebecca and Thomas did. But at least they were all engaged."

"I told you that I'd take care of it, and I will. The most important thing is your safety and they feel that too. My job will be to explain just how safe you'll be here. And then to keep you that safe." He squeezed her hips slightly, keeping her attention on him and not whoever the fuck was out there scaring her. "You with me, *cariña?*"

Her answer was leaning forward and licking his lips. Surprised, he instantly dove in for another kiss, this one more than claiming. It was complete mastering.

Quickly standing, her in his arms and her legs wrapped around his waist, he walked up the stairs to his bedroom, trying to decide if he wanted her to slide slowly down the front of his body or toss her onto the bed, pouncing after her.

She tightened her grip on his hips with her legs, bringing her core in direct contact with his swollen cock. Making his decision, he tossed her backward onto the bed but, before she could bounce, he was on top of her with his weight held up by his forearms.

Her eyes lit with the promise of what was to come and he battled to take things slow. *First time in my bed... this is all about her.*

He lifted one hand to her breast, kneading the mound and flicking the nipple through the material. Seemingly in a hurry, her hands moved to the blouse, but he pushed hers out of the way. Slowly undoing each button he eyed the prize as it was slowly unveiled. Once he could pull the material away from her breasts, he allowed her to shift forward so that he could strip it off of her body, leaving the light blue, lacy bra all that lay between him and the luscious mounds. He moved her hands above her head and held them there with only one of his while shifting his weight partially to the side. With her arms trapped above her, he slowly licked her breasts, tracing the blue lace.

With a quick tug on the cups he freed her breasts, pulling a rosy nipple into his mouth, sucking deeply, eliciting a moan from deep within her. She began to writhe on the bed as he slid one hand down, unzipping her jeans and slipping his fingers in, finding her folds slick and ready.

Releasing her nipple with a pop, he moved back to her swollen lips, his tongue thrusting in rhythm to his fingers embedded in her sex.

Once he released her hands, she found the bottom of his t-shirt, maneuvering it up toward his head. Desperate to feel his solid chest muscles against her naked breasts, she wrestled with the material.

Chuckling, he broke the kiss, sitting up on his knees as he jerked the shirt over his head. "What's the rush, babe?"

Unsnapping her bra was her only response and as she tossed it to the side, he watched her full breasts bounce as she lay back down.

Her hands moved to the button on his jeans, but getting them unzipped over his impressive cock was proving difficult so he rolled over to quickly divest himself of them as well. Shucking his boxers, his dick was standing at attention as he turned his gaze back to the gorgeous woman lying in his bed. *His bed. Just where he imagined she would be.*

If he were honest, he imagined her there since he first saw her picture. But this was so much more than the lusty thoughts of just any gorgeous woman. Determined to make love to Miriam, he moved slowly, licking and sucking from her lips to her neck to her breasts once again. His fingers found their refuge deep inside as she felt herself climbing higher and higher.

The taste of her was intoxicating as the kiss went deeper. Giving each breast attention, he elicited moans from her as her hips began to press against his body.

"Patience," he chuckled, his mouth moving lower. Leaning up on the bed, he pulled her jeans down, snagging her matching blue panties as he went. Tossing the clothes onto the floor, he spread her legs wide as he completely exposed her pink sex to his eyes. With a growl rumbling deep in his chest, he dove in, licking her wetness before sucking her clit into his mouth.

"Aughh," she moaned again, her hips rising. He moved one of his hands up to her stomach and gently pressed her back down.

Plunging his tongue inside, he continued to lap her juices, loving the taste of her. His hand on her stomach rose higher until it palmed her breast, pinching the nipple lightly.

"I need..." she panted, feeling the coil of tension deep inside her core ready to spring. "I..." was all she managed to say as he gave each nipple a tug as he sucked her clit deeply with his mouth. Her inner walls clenched and her orgasm raced through her, sending all of her nerves tingling outwards. Throwing her head back, she screamed his name once again.

He finished licking her glistening sex before kissing his way back up her boneless body until he plunged his tongue back into her mouth.

"Please...I need you inside of me," she begged, tasting herself.

Growling, he grabbed a condom and rolled on top of her, stilling his cock just at her entrance. Holding her legs apart, he looked down at all her beauty. Pale skin gleaming in the moonlight. Dark eyes looking into his. *Mine. She's truly mine.* A sexy smile lit her face and he swore his heart stopped as her arms rose up to him.

Plunging to the hilt, his dick reveled in the soft warmth of her body, remembering the feel of her on the beach. Leaning over, his hands on either side of her head, he pounded deeply, trying to reach the innermost part of her soul. Hanging on to his self-discipline by a thread, he was determined for her to come again.

"Close, baby?" he panted.

"Yes, yes." She grabbed his shoulders, holding on for all she was worth. The sparks shot from her womb out through her limbs as her orgasm rocketed. Digging her fingers into his arms, she cried out once again.

He followed her, his neck thrown back as the cords of muscles strained. Continuing to thrust until every last drop was drained, he fell to the side taking her with him. Holding her close, he wrapped his arms around her trembling form, pulling her tight into his chest.

Legs tangled. Arms wrapped. Breaths mingled. Heart-beats pounding in unison.

Slowly awareness crept in and he looked back into her face, seeing her smiling at him.

"Are you okay, baby?" he asked.

"Oh yeah. I couldn't be happier," she whispered back.

Pulling her back tightly to him, he threw his leg over hers as his arm wrapped around her waist. Tucking her sated body next to his, he allowed the sound of her deep breathing to lull him to sleep.

Now it was the next morning and Cam watched her slow, even breathing as she slept. He glanced at the clock, noting the time and wondering how long it took her to get ready in the mornings, when his thoughts were interrupted by a loud knocking on the door. *Who the fuck was here that early?*

Sliding from the bed, tucking the covers back around her, he pulled on his jeans and padded out to the front door. Looking through the doorviewer, he saw Jobe standing on his front porch.

21

C am threw open the door and stepped back to let Jobe in.

"I know it's early and I'm sorry, but I need to see my sister. I figured she didn't sleep any last night and I gotta make sure she's alright."

"I told you that I was taking care of her," Cam stated, but before he could say more, he saw Jobe's eyes move down the hall.

"Jobe? What are you doing here so early?"

Jobe's gaze raked his sister up and down, seeing her dressed in nothing but Cam's shirt, and then back to Cam, who was only wearing jeans, the top buttons unbuttoned.

"You fuckin'—"

"No!" Miriam screamed, flying down the hall as Jobe landed a punch to Cam's face.

Cam rocked back, determined to let Jobe have that one punch for his sister's sake knowing he would have the same reaction if he walked in on one of his sisters.

Cam rounded Jobe to keep him from landing another punch when Miriam tried to get behind her brother, taking his cocked elbow right in the forehead.

Dropping to her knees, she cried out in pain as she saw stars.

"Oh, fuck, Miriam!" Jobe exclaimed.

Cam scooped her up in his arms before Jobe could react, and hustled her to the sofa. Setting her down gently, he said, "Baby, let me see. Move your hands so I can see."

As she lifted her head up, he quickly assessed that she was just bruised on her forehead. "Thank God it's not your eye," he said. Yelling over his shoulder for Jobe to get ice, he brushed her hair away from her face. "Babe, never and I mean fuckin' never get between two men who are fighting."

The nausea from the pain was slowly receding and she wanted to glower but it hurt too much. "I couldn't let him hit you."

"I let him get that punch in. I knew if I was the brother, I woulda done it also."

Jobe walked over with ice in a plastic bag with paper towels surrounding it. Handing it to Cam, he sat on the coffee table trying to ascertain her injury. "Sis, swear to God, you know better than that."

This time she managed a glower in spite of the pain and bit out, "How is this my fault? You two should be ashamed of yourselves."

The two men eyed each other warily, both knowing she was wrong when it came to men and both silently agreeing on a truce...for the moment.

"Jobe, I didn't say anything when we got back because I wasn't sure what Cam and my relationship was, but we're together now."

Jobe glared at Cam once more, saying, "You took advantage of my baby sister at a time when she was vulnerable?"

"No!" Miriam exclaimed, not allowing Cam to speak.

He turned and said, "Jobe, you want to step outside with me?"

"Fuck yeah," was the response.

Miriam tried to rise from the sofa, but Cam gently pushed her back replacing the ice pack on her head. "Babe, I once told you to do exactly what I said because it could be life or death. Right now, plant your ass on that sofa, keep the ice on your head, and do not move. Jobe and I are gonna have a chat and when we get back, you'd better not have moved."

"Fine, just go kill each other and see if I care," she groused, angry at both of them.

The two men stepped through the front door onto the porch, Cam closing the door behind them. "Gonna lay it out and then you do what you gotta do. I'm a brother also, so I get where you're coming from but, just letting you know, that was the last punch I'll let you land."

Jobe pursed his lips but, for the man who saved his sister's life, he was willing to hear what Cam had to say.

"The picture you showed me captured me from the moment my eyes landed on it, but I told myself it was just because it made me angry to think of a woman being snatched and scared. Got down there and swear to God, she had a will of steel and she was all I could think about. I kept my mind on the mission and we made it. Along the way, we got to know each other real well. Talked a lot, shared a lot. It started as a way to pass the time and try to keep her mind off of what I figured was following us."

At this, Jobe's eyes gave away the distress he felt at having his sister in such danger.

"But it wasn't until the end that we decided we wanted to see if what we had could go anywhere."

"Did you two—"

"Not goin' there, bro. Whatever happened was consensual and between two adults. If Miriam wants to discuss it with you, that's her choice, but I'm not going to stand out here on my front porch with my woman inside on the couch with a knot on her head and discuss any particulars."

Jobe held his gaze for a moment, his emotions warring inside for the woman he still felt like was his little sister and the realization that she was the same age as his wife. Heaving a sigh, he lifted his hand in conciliation toward Cam, who shook it willingly.

"Now, let's get down to what's happening. In just a bit, I'm taking her to Jack's where we're all meeting. Jack'll keep you and Tony in the loop. We'll get on it with our DEA, CIA, and FBI contacts and see if we can identify who made the call. My place here is wired, watched, and fuckin' impervious. She's quit her job at the hospital—"

"What?" Jobe growled. "Shit, she's not telling the family a goddamn thing!"

"I think it's just happened, but she can talk to you about that. Bottom line, she's escorted at all times and we're keeping you aware of everything."

Jobe nodded as he rubbed the back of his neck with his hand. "I appreciate it, man." Sighing heavily again, he said, "I'd better go in there and make up with my sister, before heading back to my pregnant wife who's gonna flip out when I tell her I clocked Miriam in the head."

Cam chuckled, not envying the man having to deal with two irritated women. "Come on in. I'll get the coffee."

While Cam poured the coffee, Miriam sat with her brother, trying to stay mad but, the truth was, she knew he cared.

"My head is fine," she assured for the third time, taking the ice pack down to show him that she was not sporting a bruise.

"I just want you safe, sis. I'm not having you get rescued only to have you live in fear."

"I'm trying to find a counselor now, but I want one with victim experience. And PTSD experience," she added. "Just because I'm a nurse and understand about PTSD doesn't mean that I'm going to conquer it quickly."

"How bad is it, sis?"

Sighing deeply, she glanced over at Cam, receiving his reassuring gaze. "Some anxiety, a few panic attacks, nightmares. Sometimes just a general irritability with people. That's what I felt all the time at work."

Jobe walked over, enveloping his sister in his arms. Kissing the top of her head, he reiterated, "I want you safe."

"I know, I know," she said, as Cam handed her a cup. She took a sip and immediately smiled at him. "Cream and sugar?" she asked.

"I seem to remember hearing that somewhere," he grinned.

"Okay, I can see you two don't need me, but Cam—"

"I got you covered, Jobe. As soon as we are at Jack's, he's gonna patch into Tony's place."

Jobe nodded his agreement, leaned over and kissed Miriam and then headed out of the house. Her eyes followed his departure before turning back to Cam. "So, are you going to tell me what you two talked about on the porch?"

Cam lifted her up from the sofa, twisted with her in his arms before he sat down and settled her on his lap. His eyes drifted up to her forehead where he was pleased to see only a slight bruise, before coming back to meet her gaze.

"I laid it out for him, how it was for us down there. How we got to know each other, talk, and discover that we wanted to take a chance on building on that."

Sucking her lips in, she asked, "Did you tell him that we—"

"No, *cariña*. That's yours to share if you want to, but for me...that night was just for us."

Smiling, she took a sip of her coffee, fixed just the way she liked it. "Good answer," she mumbled.

Glancing at the clock on the TV, he said, "We've got to get going, babe. You jump into the shower first, don't worry about getting fancy, and I'll be right behind you."

"Fancy? I think after most of your friends saw me looking pretty rough, just having clean clothes and clean hair will be fancy enough."

She stood and walked to the hall entrance before turning to look over her shoulder, her gaze pinning him to the spot. "Cam, thank you...for taking care of me."

He walked over and kissed the top of her head. "I'd take care of you no matter what. But you're mine and I definitely take care of what is mine."

Miriam's eyes were wide as Cam turned off the road, stopping at a security gate to gain entrance before driving down the long driveway toward Jack's house. He had told her about Jack's place but it was different seeing it in person. The cedar, oak, and maple trees were thick on either side of the drive until they came into a clearing and she saw a huge, two-story, log cabin with a wide front porch. Two chimneys, one on each end, stood as sentinels to the imposing structure. Several trucks and SUVs were already lining the circular driveway in front and Cam pulled his right up next to the others.

Licking her lips nervously, she wondered what she

had gotten herself into. Before she had time to blink, Cam was at her door assisting her to the ground.

Throwing his arm around her protectively, he said, "Come on, babe. You'll be fine."

Stepping through the front door, she looked around at the cavernous space. The living room on the left was two-stories with a stone fireplace on the inside wall and large windows on the two walls facing the outside. The panoramic view of the mountains behind Jack's woods was spectacular. The furniture was oversized but, considering the size of men lounging on it, she knew it had been bought with them in mind. Dark, exposed wood was everywhere and the few pieces of artwork on the walls were expensive but not ostentatious.

Mixed in with the very masculine décor were some colorful throw pillows, flowers on the mantle, and a few knick-knacks that she assumed belonged to Bethany.

One of the men—tall, dark, with a thick, neatly trimmed beard—stood and headed directly to her, with his hand out. "Miriam? Jack Bryant. Welcome to my home."

Smiling up at him, she said, "Thank you. It's absolutely breathtaking here."

He smiled back at her before shifting his gaze to Cam. "You got her phone?"

Cam pulled it out as the other men were gathering around. "Luke, see what you can get out of this," he said.

Luke was a handsome, dark-haired man, not nearly the size of Cam, but Miriam easily recognized his strength in his lean, muscular body. He shook her hand as well and then disappeared down the hall.

Bart, Blaise, Monty, and Marc had all met her before, each kissing her cheek in greeting, before they followed Luke.

The last man walked over, a huge smile on his face. "I guess I'm the last one to meet the lovely and, from what I hear, very brave Ms. Delaro. I'm Chad." Of all of the men, he seemed the one that would smile the most, easily cracking a joke or just enjoying himself with friends.

"It's nice to meet you, too," she said sincerely, then watched as he also followed the others. *I wonder what's down that hall?* Before she had time to think too long on it, she heard soft footsteps coming from the right. Turning her head, she saw a long, heavy, wooden table in the dining area and just then a beautiful woman came from the kitchen carrying a tray.

"Here, babe, let me get that," Jack said, walking over to take it from the woman. While he moved to set it on the coffee table near the large sofas, the smiling woman rushed over and engulfed Miriam in a hug.

"I'm so glad to meet you," she exclaimed. "I'm Bethany." By this time Jack had returned and, with his arm around Bethany, pulled her front into his side.

"Hi," she answered, smiling at the warm greeting. Unsure what to do next, Miriam glanced up at Cam who caught her expression of uncertainty.

"Jack and I are going to head down to where we all meet and work on finding out who called and where the threat is coming from. You and Bethany will have a chance to get to know each other and then we'll come back and probably have some questions for you."

263

Nodding, she said, "That's fine. You go do...whatever it is that you do."

Laughing, he leaned over and gave her a quick kiss before following Jack down the same hall.

The two women made themselves comfortable on the sofas, finding that they could easily curl their legs up under them with all the room.

Bethany grinned as she said, "I'm just getting used to living in a house with what I call giant furniture."

Laughing, Miriam nodded as she looked around the beautiful room once more. "I'm glad to hear you say that. Whenever I meet one of Cam's friends, it seems as though they are all as big as him! I feel like a shrimp!"

"I hear you," Bethany smiled. "Me too!"

"Cam told me a little about you, but I didn't know that you two had gotten together."

"That's right. I met Cam when he was working on a case with Jack and then he left to go get you just before the other case was solved."

"Is it weird, having Jack's business right here at his home?"

Laughing, Bethany exclaimed, "Oh, not at all. I own the Mountville Cabin rentals and wedding venue on the property next to Jack's and so I'm used to living where my work is also. And I'm safer when he's traveling."

Seeing Miriam hesitate, Bethany also added, "And let's face it, I've got the best eye-candy to look at when they're here meeting!"

Unable to contain her laugh, Miriam nodded, "Oh, yeah. I noticed that."

After a few more minutes of casual conversation, Bethany asked, "I understand that you're a nurse?"

"Yes. Well, an unemployed nurse at the moment." She watched the other woman cock her head to the side in question, so she continued, "I turned in my notice at the large hospital. I was just burned out and have decided to find a position that seems right for me."

"I think that's wise," Bethany agreed. "Do you have something in mind?"

Taking another sip of coffee, Miriam responded, "My sister-in-law's mother had a stroke and needed some in-home care for a while. I did that in the evenings just to help out and discovered that I really enjoyed it. I actually like working with geriatric patients and so I might see what's available."

"You know, my grandmother is in a memory care nursing home near here. She was just placed there a little while ago and I visit several times a week. She still remembers me most of the time...unless she thinks I'm her sister, Helen. You ought to visit with me sometime. I know they're looking for nurses."

Miriam felt a spark of interest that she had not felt in several weeks. "I'd like that...a lot, actually."

22

Downstairs in the large conference room, the men sat around the table, faces grim at the news from Luke.

"It's definitely from a stateside phone," he said. "Burner. No trace."

"Can you tell from where?" Jack asked.

"Got a read from the towers. Call came from Texas, near the Houston region."

Luke pulled up the intel provided by the DEA on the Sinaloan cartel's reach into the United States and sent it to the tablets each man had in front of them.

"Jesus, they're everywhere," Bart said. "I wasn't going to believe that this was a real threat from close inside, but the cartel has their hand in most of Texas."

"They've got ties into almost every state," Chad stated, carefully checking the information.

"That's not all," Cam growled. "Look in Virginia."

Monty, pulling up intel from the FBI, agreed.

"They've got a far reach, even into rural Virginia counties."

"So, we're not looking at the call necessarily coming directly from Mexico, but could be one of their co-horts here?" Marc asked.

Jack looked around the group before his gaze landed on Cam's hard face. "Right now, with what we've got, looks like she needs more security at this time instead of investigating the call."

The other men nodded, but not happily. Each would rather be actively finding the threat instead of waiting to see when it would rear its head once more.

"She staying with you?" Monty asked, looking at Cam.

He nodded, his jaw still tight with anger. "Yeah, gonna keep her at my place. She's not working right now since she quit the hospital." Seeing the surprised expressions, he explained, "She needs a change of scenery."

Chad stated, "That'll actually be good, man. Easier to keep up with her when she's not in a hospital."

Cam looked down at his hands for a moment, then shook his head. "Jesus, this is fucked. Down there, I was doing something. Active. Working toward getting her the hell outta there. But this? This is like waiting to see what's gonna happen next. We've got no fuckin' thing to work on."

Monty spoke up, "There's been no overt threat yet. The words spoken in the phone call were to unsettle her. Make her nervous. That's where you come in, bro. You take that on."

"He's right. We provide security while working the problem the best we can, but you take her emotions. You give her what she needs to feel safe," Jack agreed.

Cam silently nodded, but wondered if that would be enough.

Bethany and Miriam had just shared cell-phone numbers and arranged a date to visit when the men returned upstairs.

Jack nodded to Bethany before asking Miriam to join them at the large dining room table. Cam sat next to her, pulling her chair close to his. The other men settled around as well.

"Okay, here's what we have and it's not much at this time," Jack started. "We can tell the call did not come from Mexico. In fact, it came from Texas."

"Texas?" Miriam exclaimed. "I don't know anyone from Texas."

Cam squeezed her shoulders and she twisted up to look at his face. "No, *cariña*. It came from somewhere in Texas, but the threat is still from someone in Mexico."

Her forehead crinkled in thought as she slowly shook her head. "I just have no idea what's happening." Looking around the table, she said, "I was just a nurse. No one of importance. I treated whoever came in, but they were mostly workers, farmers, guards, and some others that were dressed nicer, but still...no one."

"Tell us about that night you were taken to dinner at the main compound," Jack prodded. "We know you talked to DEA, but their interest was more cartel related. I'd like to hear your version, focusing on the people there."

"It was...uncomfortable." She lifted her gaze back to the men as she continued. "You know when you're in a social situation but you don't know what role you're supposed to play and you're stomach feels hot inside because you get nervous?" At this point, none of the men appeared to recognize what she was talking about at all.

From behind, Bethany spoke, "Yes, I do." She caught Jack's eyes and moved toward the table. "I don't suppose you men experience it, but sometimes women do. You go to a work party and the boss seems flirtatious. You've got no idea what to do. Is he being polite? Is he coming on to you? Do you flirt back or is that a big no-no? Sure, some women eat that up but, honestly, there are a lot of us that when we're in a situation like that, we just get nervous and don't have a clue how to act."

Miriam was nodding her head emphatically. "Yes, Bethany, that was exactly it!"

"Okay," Jack said slowly, "Why don't you just tell us what happened...and how it made you feel."

"Once we got there, we were all in awe at the place. It was almost palatial and looked completely out of character for its surroundings. When we sat down to dinner it was Dr. Ernesto Villogas and his wife and then he introduced us to Juaquim Guzman, who seemed to be in charge. Also at the dinner table was his wife." At this she wrinkled her nose slightly.

Bart chuckled. "I take it you weren't too impressed?"

Blushing, she admitted, "The women were...um... well kept. They were dressed in what looked to be expensive clothes and there we were, four nurses dressed in drab scrubs. The whole dinner was weird!"

"Describe weird, baby," Cam gently ordered.

"You don't already see the weirdness?" Miriam asked, looking up at him.

"Yeah, I can. But we need to hear exactly from you what your impressions were about the people around that table."

"Oh. Well, Dr. Villogas was always very professional in the infirmary, but kind of flirty, and he continued that at dinner. With his wife sitting there! And Mr. Guzman? He looked like he would like to devour us, and his wife was sitting right there also. The two women talked to each other in Spanish, looked at us like we were bugs to be squashed, and their husbands flirted right in front of them. And even though the women glared at us, they soon left the table and we never saw them again."

"How did the night end?" Blaise asked.

Sighing, she said, "Sharon definitely had dollar signs in her eyes and she began flirting back. Lorainne was feeling ill and very nervous. I just wanted out of there, and it was Sister Genovia who made that possible. She took charge, hustled us out after dinner and the men didn't argue with a nun."

"Anyone else?"

"Um, there were other men around, if that's what you mean. Men at the compound. Men who guarded us or drove us places. Oh, also, one day, two of Juaquim's brothers came to the infirmary. I only knew that because Dr. Villogas introduced them." Wrinkling her nose once more, she added, "They were...kind of... sleazy. I definitely felt as though if I wasn't wearing nursing scrubs and had Dr. Villogas around, then they would be the type to take what they wanted. Um...if you know what I mean."

Cam growled once more, giving her another shoulder squeeze.

Luke had been typing while Miriam gave her responses and said, "This is good information."

"So, any ideas?" she asked tentatively, her eyes darting around the room.

"The caller had a Hispanic accent, you said? But their English was clear?" Bart asked.

She nodded and said, "And it didn't sound...like they were having trouble speaking."

"Good to know," Blaise added. "So it probably wasn't one of workers or guards, who would have no idea how to get ahold of you and would not be speaking distinct English."

"Could be Juaquim or someone who works for him. Someone who knows what happened and would like to get in good with him," Chad added.

"One of his brothers?" Marc asked as they all brainstormed.

Jack would have preferred to brainstorm when Miriam was not with them, but since she was the only one who heard the voice, he needed her input.

"It could have been," she said, trying to remember exactly how the voice sounded. "The caller spoke in an exaggerated manner, so that makes it hard to tell who it was even if I knew them."

Her hand nervously twisted on the tabletop and Cam gave Jack a silent signal. Understanding, Jack ended the meeting.

"Miriam, you did good," Jack said, standing. "I know this is hard. We were conferencing earlier with your brother and Tony Alvarez's group to keep them in the loop."

She rose from her seat, Cam's arm still around her. Twisting her head to look up into his face, she said, "So what now? I refuse to keep living in fear. In fact, Bethany was going to take me this afternoon to visit her grandmother. I'd like to see the facility she lives in."

"*Cariña*, I'm not sure—" Cam started.

"You can come or send someone with us," she prodded, her eyes begging.

"Okay, but I'll go," he agreed.

Jack nodded, saying, "We're gonna see what we can find out about Juaquim and his brothers. While the call did not come from Mexico, they will have contacts here in the U.S. and we'll see about following the trail."

With that, Bethany and Miriam followed Cam out to his SUV for the trip to the nursing home.

Days later, Miriam was sitting in the administrative office of the Glen Arbor Nursing Home interviewing for a position. Nervously wiping her palms on her skirt, she waited as Tonya Barlow read over her resume.

Ms. Barlow smiled at Miriam, saying, "You are very well qualified for our position. To be honest, my only concern is that you will find this job to be infinitely more boring than your past positions." She quickly amended, "Not that working here is boring, you understand. But it certainly is not as fast paced as a hospital ER."

"I understand your concern," Miriam admitted honestly. "I had the opportunity to provide some home nursing care to a friend's mom last year and it was wonderful. I also came last week to visit Ann Bridwell, since I now have become friends with her granddaughter." Miriam was not sure how much to share with the administrator, not wanting to announce her notoriety, so she cautiously said, "I also have had recent events which have left me...no longer comfortable with the loud, busy ER in a large hospital. I...um...need a chance to get to know the patients in a calmer environment."

"I can appreciate that, Ms. Delaro. I was also concerned about our facility being a memory care facility with patients suffering from Dementia and Alzheimer's, but I see that you had geriatric nursing in your master's degree program."

"Yes," she said enthusiastically. "It's really what I love, but I confess that when I graduated, the lure of the money of being an ER nurse in a hospital was hard to resist when I had student loans to pay off."

"And now?"

Smiling, she said, "Different time in my life. Different experiences under my belt. I'm ready for this change and ready for Glen Arbor, if you'll have me."

Returning the smile, Ms. Barlow nodded. "I would like to offer you the position of Floor Nurse here at Glen Arbor. I would surmise with your education and experience that you could easily be promoted to nursing supervisor down the road."

Grinning, Miriam stood to shake Ms. Barlow's hand. "Thank you so much! This is just the career change I needed and I cannot wait to begin."

"Well, take the weekend to celebrate and we'll see you here on Monday morning."

Walking out of the office, Miriam looked around. The room was just off the large, well-lit main lobby. To the left was a living area, dark red walls and white wainscoting, with beautiful floral pictures gracing the area. Several sofas and chairs were arranged in a semi-circle facing a gas-powered fireplace. To the right of the main lobby was the dining facility with several of the more lucid patients lined up ready to enter. She knew from her tour with Bethany that two wings held the assisted living apartments and the third wing was specifically for memory care.

Walking out into the sunshine, she saw Cam leaning against his SUV, his large body at ease, with his hands resting on his hips and one leg crossed in front of the other. His closely trimmed hair and beard gave him a dangerous look until his eyes met hers and his expression broke into a wide grin.

She wanted to be sophisticated, but gave into the urge to run down the short sidewalk and jump up into his arms.

He easily took her weight and held her tight as she pressed against him. "I take it you got the job?"

"Yes!" she exclaimed. "I start on Monday! And we need to celebrate this weekend!"

He latched onto her lips and owned the kiss, thrusting his tongue inside her warm mouth, tasting the minty gum she had been nervously chewing before the interview. "You got anything special you want to do?" he murmured against her lips.

"Ummmhmmm," she moaned.

"I mean after that?" he chuckled.

She felt the rumbling in his chest against her breasts and her panties became wet. "Can I answer that after we get home and celebrate the way we're both wanting to right now?"

"Hell, yeah!" he agreed and turned with her still in his arms, opening the door and planting her ass in the seat. Kissing her once more, he said, "I'll get us home quick."

Grinning she watched him as he rounded the front and hauled himself up into the driver's seat. The drive to his place only took fifteen minutes and she calculated how much time it would take her to drive from her place.

"I can make the drive in thirty minutes from my apartment," she remarked.

His smile left and he glanced sideways. "You're staying with me, so it's only half of that."

"Well, for now," she agreed. "But when I go back—"

"Go back?"

She glanced to the side and saw the now familiar

muscle tick in his jaw. "Well...I kind of assumed...um... that I would be moving back..." her voice drifted off as she watched him turn toward her.

By then they had turned into his driveway and he cut the engine. Twisting so that he was facing her, he said, "What do you think is happening here?"

"Happening...?"

"With us, babe?"

"I know we're together but, I mean my living with you was because you felt like I needed protecting. But, Cam, you never mentioned that this was anything other than that."

"Well, we're sure as hell not just roomies," he growled.

"I'm not a mind-reader," she argued. "You never said, 'Let's move in together.' You just came and got me, and got my brother to agree and here I am!"

Heaving a sigh, Cam slowly let out his breath. He could feel the change of the vibe inside the vehicle— from hot and sexy to cool and irritated.

Reaching across the console, he cupped her face. "You're right, Miriam. I never gave you a choice." He watched as her eyes warmed as she leaned into his palm. "I do want you safe and I can do that if you're with me. But the minute we made love on the beach, I wanted you to be mine. Not just mine to protect...but mine to care for."

Gifting him with a small smile, she said, "I'm glad. I've wanted you too but, well, I wasn't sure exactly what you wanted. I guess we both expected each other to read our minds."

His hand moved from her cheek, sliding to her neck, and he pulled her forward as he leaned toward her as well. Meeting in the middle, he kissed her softly. "Gonna lay it out, babe. I want you...in my house, and in my life."

"I want that too, but giving up my apartment is kind of scary. I mean if we don't make it..."

"I've got no crystal ball, but we're not like most couples who get together when everything is good and when the shit happens, then they might not be able to handle it. *Cariña*, we've been through hell to start with. We've seen each other at our worst. And if you're worried that we only got together because of the intensity of the shit-storm around us, then look at where we are now."

"So...what exactly are you saying? I really don't want to make you mad but, Cam, I need to know."

He touched his lips with hers once more, a gentle kiss full of promise. Leaning back, just enough to peer into her eyes, he said, "Okay, here's where we are. You're in my house and you need to stay until we have a better handle on your safety. We'll go tomorrow and get more of your stuff to bring here. We'll even take it slow. You keep your apartment for another month or two if that makes you feel better. But as far as I'm concerned, you're here. As I said, in my home," he kissed her again. "In my life," followed by another kiss. "And in my heart, *mi amor*."

"*Mi amor?*" She had secretly Googled some of the Spanish endearments he used and knew what he was saying. *Or hoped he was saying.*

His eyes molten, his lips curved into smile as he leaned closer. "Yeah. *Mi amor*. I love you, Miriam."

This time when he kissed her, she moaned in his mouth and his dick jumped to life once more. "You ready to take this celebration of your new job inside, babe?"

"Oh, yeah," she giggled as he bolted out of the vehicle and rounded the front before she could get out. He scooped her up before her feet touched the ground and carried her quickly inside. He twisted as soon as they entered, pressing her against the front door as he reset the alarm panel. His intention had been to carry her to the bedroom, but she had other plans.

23

With her back pressed tightly against the door, Miriam wrapped her legs around Cam's waist, nestling her core against his swollen cock. His jeans made for perfect friction but she desperately wanted the offending material to be gone.

Cam's thoughts of taking it slow flew out of his head as soon as she began rocking into his erection with her breasts at face level.

Sealing his mouth over hers, he took command of the kiss. Not gentle. Not soft. This kiss was demanding and unyielding. His tongue invaded her mouth, searching every crevice, tangling with her tongue, dueling for dominance. He leaned his massive body in, touching every inch of the front of hers, chest to knees.

Separating slightly, he slid his hand under her blouse, his fingers continuing their upward path, coming to rest on her breast. Capturing her moans in his mouth, he devoured her lips. Pushing her back against the door, her legs unwound. Lifting his leg slightly so that she was seated on him, he continued to fondle her breasts then quickly divested her of her top, trying not to pop the buttons off. Jerking the material off of her shoulders, he pulled her forward from the door, just enough to toss the blouse onto the floor. She immediately reached back to him, clutching his shoulders as though she were hanging on for her life.

He pulled the tops of her lacy, pink bra cups down, freeing her breasts. Keeping her breasts at his face level, he continued his assault on them with his mouth. Sucking first one nipple in and then moving to the other, he felt her move her crotch against his leg, creating the friction that she needed.

Lowering his leg, he settled her feet back down on the floor so he could divest himself of his shirt. Jerking it off, he leaned back in pressing her against the door once more, recapturing her mouth with his. This time, flesh against flesh, breasts against chest. *Jesus, she feels so good.*

Using his hand to push her skirt up, he found her hands were already there. She broke the kiss long enough to unzip her skirt, sliding it down her legs along with her silky, pink panties. Unsnapping her bra, it was tossed to the floor to join the other clothes in the pile.

Before moving in for another kiss, he stopped for a moment just to stare at the naked beauty presented in front of him. He had seen naked women's bodies over the years, but none of them came to mind. He could not recall their features, their faces, their shapes. All he could see in his mind was the perfection that was standing in front of him, staring at him with her dark, brown eyes. Eyes that were not just warm with lust, but with... *love? Could she have those feelings for me?*

Before he could process the emotions any more, he felt her hands on the button of his jeans. Chuckling, he allowed her to slide the zipper down over his impressive cock. "In a hurry, babe?"

"Yeah," she whispered. "Aren't you?"

Shoving his jeans and boots off quickly, he stood in front of her just as naked, his cock jutting out toward her. He saw her glance down and suck her lips in momentarily before licking them. His cock twitched as though anxious to be seated in her. Seeing her eyes come back up to his, he laughed. "It's got a mind of its own, *cariña*. And right now, it knows what it wants."

Reaching down to snag a condom out of his jean's pocket, he expertly rolled it on quickly.

As he hefted her up again, she wrapped her legs around his waist, this time her sex directly on his dick. Wanting to make sure she was ready, he slid his finger into her wet folds, moving it deeper and deeper, looking for just the right spot to make her scream. "So damn tight, babe. So goddamn wet."

Feeling the pressure building, she knew she was close...so close she could have come just dry humping his jean-clad leg. The feel of his fingers tweaking deep inside of her was making her crazy. She felt him suck her nipple into his mouth, biting down just enough to give a quick pain then smoothing it with his tongue. Feeling her inner muscles clamping down on his fingers as the orgasm washed over her, she dug her fingernails down his back.

Cam looked at the beauty in his arms. Head thrown back against the door in ecstasy, eyes tightly shut, and that smile. *Jesus, I'd walk through hell to see that smile every day.*

Placing his aching cock at her entrance he rasped, "Ready?" A nod was the only answer he received and all he needed. Her sex impaled on his cock, balls deep, he began thrusting. One hand under her ass for support, the other pressed against the door next to her head. Thrust after thrust, he slid in and out of her wet body, the friction nearly taking him over the edge quickly. Forcing his mind to hold back, he wanted her to come again.

Growling, "Mouth, cariña," he sealed his lips over hers when she brought her mouth back to his. Deep. Demanding. His tongue mimicking the movements of his cock.

She felt the pressure building again. The feeling of trying to reach the finish line of a race, knowing that crossing the end would bring the most incredible euphoria. Closer and closer she came. Feeling his hand move between them and tweak her clit did the trick. She finished the race, shattering into a million pieces. Sucking on his tongue before shouting out his name, her inner walls grabbed at his cock.

The feeling of his cock being milked by her sex was all it took for him to lose control. His head reared back also as he powered through his orgasm. Neck muscles straining, face red and tight, he felt himself empty into her waiting body. *Fuck, never. Never. Never have I come that hard.*

Resting his forehead against the door, he felt his heart pounding out of his chest as he tried to catch his breath. He could feel her panting, her breasts pressing against him with every exhalation. Her legs were still wrapped around his waist, the waning tingles of her orgasm still clutching around his dick.

Pulling back slowly, he peered down into her face wanting to make sure she was all right. Fucking her up against the door was not what he meant to do and for a woman like Miriam, he was not sure it had been the right thing.

Her face put his fears to rest. Smiling up at him with kiss-swollen lips, she had the expression of a happy, well-fucked woman.

"You okay?" he asked, wanting to make sure.

"Oh, yeah. That was…" she giggled. "Um, I don't even know what to call that."

Chuckling, he pulled out of her before setting her feet securely on the floor. Their clothes, strewn around, continued to stay there as he took her hand and led her to the bathroom. Running the water in the sink until it was warm, he then took a washcloth and soaked it. Cleaning her gently between her legs, she thought back to what he said earlier and realized he was right. They may have started out due to extreme circumstances but were as strong as any couple she knew.

Sucking in a deep breath, she looked up at his face and saw his questioning expression.

"I guess this seems like kind of a strange time to be saying this, with me standing here naked in your bathroom after we just…um…did it against the front door, but…um—"

"Where you going with this, babe?" he asked, not sure of what she was trying to say.

Giving a little shrug, she said, "I guess I wanted to let you know that I think you're right. I think we're strong. And even though we haven't known each other for a super long time, I'd like to stay here with you…while we find out where this is going."

Smiling down into her warm eyes, pulled under as though he were drowning in them…just like the first time he saw her picture. She was grinning up at him, an expectant look on her face.

He bent over touching his nose with hers before sliding it toward her cheek. "That's good, *cariña*. Because here is exactly where I want you to be."

Capturing her lips once more in a kiss that promised future, he then pulled back, saying, "Get dressed babe, and let me feed you. Then I've got something to give you."

He left her in the bathroom to put her clothes on, knowing that if he stayed he would take her again, and headed to the kitchen. Pulling out the fixings for quick tacos, he was still making dinner as she walked back into the room. Glancing over, he saw that she had dressed in navy yoga pants and one of his old RPD t-shirts that hung to her knees. *That old tee never looked better*, he thought as he tried to keep his mind on the meat in the frying pan.

Moving up behind him, she slipped her arms around

his middle and pressed her body tightly to his. "Mmmm, what smells so good?"

Chuckling, he replied, "Just tacos, babe. And don't get any ideas that my being Hispanic means they're gonna be great. I'm a simple cook and that means I use the packet shit from the grocery store."

She felt his chest rumble and smiled. "Those are fine with me."

As he removed the pan from the stove, he said, "Grab a plate and fix them how you like them."

She sat at the table and grinned as he placed a glass of diet soda with a lemon wedge on top of the ice. "You remembered?"

"Babe, I remember everything you ever told me."

Thirty minutes later, they finished eating and were settled at the table enjoying each other's company. Cam reached into his pocket and pulled out a pendant on a silver chain. "Here's what I got for you."

As he held it up, she could see that it was a Saint medallion and, reaching for it, she noted that it had St. Camillus imprinted. Cocking her head to the side, she looked at him.

"I was named after St. Camillus," he said, giving a little shrug. "The crazy thing is that he was the founder of the original Red Cross and since we met because of your...um...involvement in the Red Cross, I thought it would be fitting for you to have."

"Oh, Cam. That's lovely and the medallion is perfect. Thank you," she said sincerely.

Leaning forward, he clasped the necklace around her neck and the medallion hung between her breasts.

Knowing that it matched the medallion that he wore around his neck filled him with pride. Taking a deep breath, he said, "There's more." Flipping the medallion around, he pointed saying, "On the back is a tracer. It's tied into Jack's security so that we can know where you are at all times."

Seeing that she was about to question him, he quickly added, "It's not invading your privacy, *cariña*. It's just me making sure that you're safe."

He watched her twist her mouth in thought and added more. "And Bethany had one and it was needed when they had to find her. She wears it all the time now."

Nodding slowly, Miriam smiled. "I love it...I really do. I just hope you never have to use it like that."

A flash of fear crossed his expression before he leaned in to kiss her lips. Pulling back, he looked into her eyes and said, "Me too, babe. Me too."

Cam grew increasingly frustrated as the meeting dragged on. Nothing that Luke or any of the other Saints could find showed that Juaquim had anything to do with the phone call, but they knew that the odds of finding a link would be difficult.

"So my woman has to wonder and worry if anything is out there? Constantly looking over her shoulder?" he growled.

Blaise answered, "Right now, we've got no indication

that she's in danger. She gave the DEA nothing new and has stayed out of the spotlight."

"Yeah, but that phone call sounded so personal," Bart argued back. "Who wanted that?"

Cam shook his head before looking over at the others. "According to her, the only man she had any real verbal contact with was the doctor, who had already claimed Sharon was his new mistress. Then Juaquim, who never made any actual requests from her. She met his two brothers, but they're still in Mexico according to your CIA contacts, Marc."

Marc nodded his agreement, looking just as frustrated as Cam. All eyes turned toward Jack.

He rubbed his beard for a moment, then gazed at Cam. "How's she doing?"

Sighing heavily, Cam said, "She still has some nightmares. I'll find her gazing off into the distance at times, then she blinks and pretends that she was right with me the whole time."

"That actually sounds pretty normal," Chad said. "She still not seeing a counselor?"

"No, she says there's no one who can understand what she went through." Cam held Jack's gaze and continued, "Except for Bethany. Those two have gotten close and Bethany seems to be helping."

Jack nodded, giving a hint of a smile. "Yeah, Bethany has mentioned it. I think it helps her as well." He eyed the big man sitting across from him and said, "I think we still need to keep an eye on Miriam. We can back off the twenty-four-seven, but I want us all to keep her on our protection rotation when Cam's not with her."

The men all eagerly agreed and Cam nodded to each of them, grateful for their concern.

———

Miriam sat with Ann, Bethany's grandmother, and listened to her talk about the cabins at Mountville that she and her husband built when they were first married. Ann did not know where she was or that her husband had passed away almost five years earlier and Miriam did not correct her. She finished her nursing shift and enjoyed sitting for a while with Ann, listening to her tales of old.

An hour later, she saw Cam drive up in his truck and she said goodbye to Ann before jogging to the parking lot. After leaning in to kiss him, she immediately asked, "So, was there anything new?"

He shook his head, knowing she was asking about anything the Saints had found. "No," but then he quickly continued when he saw her fearful expression. "That's good, babe. You've had no new threats and it may have just been an effort to scare you. But Jack and the others still want to keep an eye on you when we're not together."

She leaned back in her seat and nodded. "Cam, there's no way I can ask the Saints to watch me! You all have other duties, assignments, and missions."

He turned to face her, saying, "*Cariña*, look at me."

She responded to his gentle command and met his gaze.

"You're not a burden. Yes, there are always other

assignments and mission we're working on, but your safety is my priority. And therefore a priority to my friends."

She smiled wanly and then said, "Are you going to have to leave soon?"

Confused, he replied, "Leave where?"

"To go on anther mission?"

"Nope. Not for a while. I'm being assigned security details and investigations around here."

Her brow crinkled as she said, "Is that because of me? Am I hampering your career?"

Throwing his head back laughing, he admitted, "No, *cariña*. Not at all. After what we went through in Mexico, Jack's not about to assign me something like that for a bit. And since we take your security seriously then I get the best of both worlds. I stay near you and keep doing my job."

He lifted her chin with his fingers as he pulled her in for another kiss. "So you can toss those concerns right out of your head. Okay?"

Gifting him with her smile once more, she agreed and finally relaxed into her seat to enjoy the ride home.

Several days later, Cam brought in a large handful of mail. "Hey, Miriam!" he called. "It looks like the post office finally got your change of address made."

She began sorting through her mail while he and Bart piled up on the sofas to watch football. A few bills that she had already paid online went into one pile.

Magazines into another. Junk mail went directly into the trash. A large cream envelope caught her eye and, as she looked at the return address, she noticed that it was from the Red Cross. Opening it, she sighed as she noticed her shaking hand holding the letter.

Cam may have had the TV on, but was constantly attuned to her and immediately stood up, walking over as he heard her sigh. "What is it?"

"It's an invitation to a Red Cross appreciation reception," she answered glumly.

He squatted next to her chair, cupping her face with his large hand, pulling her gaze to his. "Babe, you don't have to go. You don't have to do anything you're uncomfortable with," he emphasized.

By now, Bart had turned the TV volume down and looked at his best friend holding Miriam. "Cam's right," he interjected. "You take care of you first. To hell with the Red Cross event.

Smiling, she said, "I know I don't have to go. But it's not the Red Cross' fault I got kidnapped. It says it's just a reception for those of us locally who have served in the last year. I won't be singled out."

Cam watched her carefully, seeing the shadow pass across her expression, then reached over and plucked the invitation out of her hands. "That's it. You're not going."

She blinked up in surprise. "You can't just declare I'm not going," she said, irritation showing in her voice.

"When I'm the one holding you at night when you can't sleep from the nightmares or I see you stare off into the distance and know that you're somewhere dark in your mind, then yeah, I can make that decision for you," he growled.

"I am dealing with things the best way I know how, Cam," she argued back. "If it's such a burden being with me, then I can easily move back to my place."

"Don't put words into my mouth—"

"Whoa, you two," Bart interjected. "It's none of my business, but I still gotta jump in. You two have been through a lot, but you've done it together. Don't get mad at each other because you're both trying to make things better."

Cam looked at Bart in surprise, never having seen a sentimental side to him but, before he could speak, Miriam touched his arm gently.

"I'm sorry, Cam. I know you've had to deal with a lot with me."

He turned, forgetting Bart's presence, and lifted his hand to cup her face. "*Mi amour*. I only want what makes you happy." He pulled her gently in so that her face was pressed to his chest, next to his heartbeat.

"You're right. I'm not ready for this event. I'll send my regrets," she declared and felt his approval as he released a deep breath.

"Thank God, you two. Now let's watch some football," Bart said, plopping back down on the sofa.

24

Miriam slid into Bethany's car in the parking lot of Golden Arbor and the two friends headed back to the Saint's compound.

"The men are still meeting and I knew that Cam had dropped you off at work, so I jumped at the chance to visit Gram and pick you up at the same time," Bethany explained.

"I'm glad you did," Miriam replied, smiling. "It's a nice surprise."

For a few minutes, the friends talked about mundane things before falling into a comfortable silence. Miriam noticed that Bethany kept glancing over at her without saying anything.

"You want to tell me what's on your mind?" Miriam asked.

"Sorry," Bethany said. "I do have something to ask you, but I'm...well, quite frankly, I'm kind of scared to bring it up."

Miriam twisted in her seat and said honestly, "I

know we're still new friends, but I'd like to think that we could talk about anything."

Taking a deep breath and letting it out slowly, Bethany began, "You know what happened to me, when...when I was captured by that killer last year. Well, I have found a psychologist who specializes in victim trauma. She practices in Richmond and even runs a group. I want to go...just to check her out and see if it's worth trying, but I really...well, I was thinking—"

"Yes!" Miriam blurted out.

"Really?" Bethany asked, her nervousness now replaced with hope.

"Absolutely. In fact, I was thinking that I needed to do something. Cam and I actually had a fight the other day for the first time about him being there for me." Shaking her head, Miriam said, "That came out wrong. Cam doesn't mind being there for me, but he doesn't want me to make things worse." Then giggling, she added, "Bart was there and actually had to help us stop the argument."

"Bart?" Bethany asked incredulously. "I'm just getting to know all the guys, but he strikes me as the happy-go-lucky, never get involved type of guy. I don't think he would know love unless it came right up and bit him in the ass!"

"Well, it's probably because we were interrupting the football game."

"Yep, that sounds like Bart!"

Pulling into Jack's driveway several minutes later, they saw the men piling out of Jack's house. Cam's eyes landed on the car and a smile lit his face. Miriam bounded out of the car almost before Bethany parked, then was uncertain as to how much public display of affection Cam wanted with his friends around.

She should not have worried. Cam hurried down the last few steps and lifted her off of her feet into a bear hug before she had a chance to greet him. With one arm around her waist and one at the back of her head, he swung her around several times before leaning back to gently kiss her hello.

By the time Miriam was aware of the others, Bethany had snuggled into Jack's embrace and the rest of the Saints were smiling.

With a wave of his hand, he continued to walk-carry her over to his truck, settling her inside. Once they were heading down the road, he nervously glanced over to her, catching her eye.

Huffing, she said, "Bethany was doing the same things earlier. Staring at me like she wanted to say something but was afraid to. Am I that scary?"

"What was it Bethany wanted?" he asked.

"Oh, now you're deflecting. What was it that you wanted to say?" she quipped.

He shifted uncomfortably in his seat for a moment before finally saying, "I got a call from ma earlier. She was tired of not having met you and with us living together, she wanted a big family meal Friday night."

"So soon?" she squeaked. "That's gives me no time to prepare!"

"Yeah, but it also gives you no time to worry either." He glanced over, keeping a pulse on her emotions but, other than being surprised, she did not seem too upset. "*Cariña*, we don't have to if you really don't want to."

"No, it's fine. It really is," she confessed. "I'd like to meet them, but it just seems sudden."

Silence filled the cab for a few minutes, each lost to their own thoughts before Cam asked, "Now what did Bethany want?"

"She said that she knows of a counselor that specializes in trauma victims and there is a group meeting in Richmond. She would like to go for herself and thought I might like it as well."

He turned quickly, once more checking to see her reaction. "What did you say?" he asked cautiously.

Smiling, she faced him and replied, "I said that I'd like to go."

His face registered surprise as he quickly asked, "Are you sure, babe?"

"Yeah. It's time. I'm doing really well, I think, all things considered. But yeah, it's a group of people who have been victims also. Maybe it would be good. And with Bethany there, I won't feel so weird going."

By now, they had reached Cam's house and, as he stopped the truck, she leaned over placing her hand on his face. "Sweetie, you know that you have been the biggest factor in my doing as well as I am."

"I'd do anything for you, *mi amour.*" Holding her gaze, he added, "I love you, Miriam. I think I've loved you since I first laid eyes on you."

Her breath caught in her throat as his words soothed over her, filling her soul. "Oh, I love you too, Cam." Giving a small giggle, she said, "Probably since the moment you leaned in and whispered *Jobe* and I knew you'd come for me. My prince."

Cam pulled her in for a kiss that quickly moved from gentle and sweet to white hot. Mumbling against her lips, he said, "Inside. Now."

With that, they broke apart, each quickly jumping out of the truck and racing to the front door. She jumped into his arms just as he kicked the door closed and he carried her to the bedroom. This time, he forced himself to go slow, letting her body slide down the front of his until her feet were touching the floor.

She grabbed the bottom of his t-shirt, jerking it up as far as her arms would allow before he took over and pulled it the rest of the way over his head. His sculpted chest and abs were clearly defined, capturing her attention.

While he enjoyed her ogling, he deftly pulled her nursing scrub top over her head and added it to the growing pile in the floor.

Sliding her hands along his chest, she flicked her fingertips over his nipples, watching as they pebbled, and enjoyed hearing the hiss intake of his breath.

Bending, Cam hooked his thumbs in her elastic waist scrub bottoms and quickly slid them down her legs, snagging her panties in the process. *Gotta admit her nursing pants are easy to get rid of,* he thought as the prize he had been seeking was presented to him. Her glorious, naked body.

Instantly wet, she knew he wanted to be in charge, but she had a few tricks of her own. Turning him around so that his back was to the bed, she placed her hands on his chest and gave a little push. He went backwards, a surprised look on his face that quickly changed to lust as he realized what she was doing.

She slowly crawled over his body, her breasts hanging delectably in front. She saw his pupils dilate as he feasted upon the sight of her hard nipples coming tantalizingly closer.

He started to sit up on the bed with his arms reaching out, but she held up a finger waving it back and forth. "Oh no, big boy. This part of the show is all mine."

She licked her way up his abs toward his pecs, landing at his nipples where her little, pink tongue darted out to flick the hard nubs. His sharp intake of breath hissed and she grinned at the power she held. Sitting to the side of his hips, she undid his belt buckle and unzipped his pants down over his massive erection. Standing quickly, she leaned over the bed, pulling his pants over his ass and down his legs, allowing her breasts to once again tease and tantalize.

He lifted his hips to assist her in ridding him of the unnecessary clothing and heard the snap of the belt buckle hit the floor as his pants and boxers joined the other clothing scattered there.

Climbing back over him, this time she straddled him before bending to lick his cock from bottom to its glistening tip. Sliding her lips over him, she took as much as she could into her warm mouth while using her hand to grasp the bottom of his shaft, flicking her fingers over his balls.

This time his hiss was loud and sounded almost

painful. She lifted her gaze to his, her lips smiling around his cock.

Fuck. She's killin' me. Knowing he would come too soon if he didn't take over the show, he grabbed her, rolled and pulled her under him. He latched his mouth over one of her engorged nipples, sucking deeply. Immediately he felt her writhe under him, instinctively trying to ease the pressure in her sex by rubbing it on his swollen cock.

Kissing his way from her nipples to the pulse at the base of her throat, over to nibble on her earlobe, he savored every taste. Finally latching onto her lips, he kissed her as though she were the last breath to be had. Their tongues tangled in an age-old dance as he explored every crevice of her mouth.

She loved the taste of him, craving him, angling her head so he could take the kiss deeper. Wetter. Harder. She latched onto his tongue, sucking it into her mouth as she swallowed his groan. For a man as in control as Cam, she loved taking him over the edge.

He left her lips only to slide down her body until his mouth came to the prize between her legs. Using his hands to push her knees apart, he used his fingers to mimic the action with her slick folds. Licking her fully before circling his tongue on her clit had her hips jerking off of the mattress.

Smiling to himself as he relished the taste of her, he pushed his tongue inside over and over until she was screaming his name as she came. *Like fuckin' nectar.*

Miriam lay boneless and panting on the bed. *What that man can do with his tongue!* She was vaguely aware of him kissing his way back up her body, but it was his talented tongue that brought her back to consciousness. He sucked one nipple while his hand fondled the other breast. The tingling sensation from her nipple went straight to her core that was still recovering from the last assault. Spreading her legs wider for him, she welcomed his hard cock into her willing body, feeling it stretching to accommodate his girth.

Plunging in to the hilt, Cam felt connected to her in more ways than just sex. He realized he had been sent to rescue her, but in many ways she rescued him. She was the lifeline that pulled him in, gave him a purpose besides just protection and investigation. *I haven't felt this alive since before I went undercover for the police department years ago.* Looking down at her flushed face, eyes closed, smile playing on her kiss swollen lips, her dark hair flowing on the pillow below—*mi amour.*

His strokes increased in pace as he worshiped her body. Sliding his hand down to her clit, he fingered the swollen nub as he continued to plunge in and out of her tight core. Feeling her inner walls beginning to clench he knew her second orgasm was near. "Come on, *cariña.* Come for me."

She felt the flames grow higher and higher until she gave over to the blaze of her release. Screaming his name once again as her sex grabbed onto his cock, she raked her fingernails down his back, trying to pull him closer to her. Her breasts rising and falling rapidly as her heartbeat pounded, she could feel him as his breathing changed.

Opening her eyes, wanting to see him come, she

watched as he thrust over and over until he threw his head back and roared out his release. His eyes were closed, his neck strained as the veins bulged and she leaned up to lick the spot where she saw his heartbeat pulse.

His eyes opened as he crashed down on her, floored by the force of his orgasm. *Never, Jesus, never have I felt like that.* Knowing that he must be crushing her, he moved to the side, taking her with him so that she was partially on top.

They lay in silence, allowing their pounding hearts to slow and their breathing to even out. She continued to kiss his neck gently, loving the feel and taste of him. With his arms wrapped around her, she was cocooned in warmth and safety.

When he could finally think again, he opened his eyes and stared at the beauty in front of him. Perfect. Absolutely perfect. She fit perfectly tucked into his embrace. He raised up just long enough to lean over, grabbing the covers to pull on top of them. He saw his semen on her thigh.

Fuck! What if she becomes pregnant? A slow smile replaced the first reaction of fear. *A baby with her. That'd be fine by me!*

"What are you smiling about, big boy?" she asked, watching the various emotions play across his face.

His gaze jumped nervously to hers and he cleared his throat before speaking. "Um, babe, I know I should say I'm sorry, but...well, I forgot to use a condom." He saw her eyes widen, but rushed in to add, "I'm clean.

You know I am, and honest to God, *cariña*, if you get pregnant it's all right by me."

Her face gentled into a smile as her hand cupped his face. "I'm back on the pill, Cam. We should be fine." Leaning up, she placed a soft kiss on his lips. "But thank you for that."

Grinning down at her, he nodded, pressing his cheek into her small hand. "I love you, babe," he whispered against her lips.

"I love you, too," came the quiet reply.

The next evening, Miriam looked through her email, surprised to see one from a Red Cross. Opening it immediately, she quickly read the missive.

My dear, I was so pleased to find that you made your way back home. I am now back with the Red Cross and continuing my work. Lorainne went to be with God the night you left and I was allowed to go back to Los Mochis. I am sorry to say that I never saw Sharon again.

I have been invited to the Red Cross event and hope that you will be there as well. It would be good to see you again.

Sister Genovia

. . .

Oh, my God! With shaking hands, she grabbed the Red Cross invitation from the pile of mail on the counter and found the email address for the RSVP. No longer concerned with the publicity or the memories it might provoke, the thought of seeing the kind nun once more was the only thing on her mind. She sent in her reservation, knowing that she would be able to face the crowd with Sister Genovia at her side.

Pouring a glass of wine, she settled on the sofa, her head leaned back as she allowed some of the memories to slide over her. The tragedy of losing Lorainne was sharp, but she knew that she was in a much better place. *So they let Sister Genovia go. I suppose they saw no threat in her, knowing she would stay in Mexico and continue to help those who needed it.* Suddenly thinking of the event, she hoped that Sister Genovia would be allowed to make it. *But if she's back working with the Red Cross now, then I guess they take care of everything.*

Sipping on the wine, she realized that for the first time she was able to process some memories without a panic attack. Closing her eyes once more, she allowed her mind to think of Sharon. *Where is she? Did she stay as a mistress to Dr. Villogas?* Jerking her eyes open, she realized her breath was becoming rapid so she stood quickly to stop the thoughts.

Just then, the front door opened and Cam walked through. Taking one look at her, he crossed the room quickly, pulling her into his arms. "What's wrong, baby?"

He felt her shake her head against his chest before she leaned back to look into his face.

"No, I'm really okay," she said. "I got an email from Sister Genovia who is coming to the Red Cross event. So I emailed my reply back. I'm going to go, Cam."

His eyes narrowed in suspicion, saying, "Are you sure it was her?"

"Yes," she replied. "She said that Lorainne passed away the night we left and that she had not seen Sharon again."

Knowing that Cam was in doubt, she led him by the hand over to her laptop, showing him the email.

"I'm gonna have Luke take a look at this. I want the Saints to follow up and make sure this was from her."

"You think it's false?" she asked, her voice now fearful.

Hating that he put that there, he said, "Don't know. But I'll feel better if we check it out."

Nodding, she smiled, loving his concern and settling back into his embrace.

The Saints worked around the table once more. Assignments were handed out and the new cases were discussed. Bart looked at the calendar and asked, "Jack, would it be okay if I took a few days next week off? It's been a while since I visited my grandmother in Virginia Beach. I've got a cousin there also and I'd like to head out for a family visit. It'll give me a chance to catch up with some SEAL buds stationed there."

"Absolutely," Jack replied, then looked around the table. "Come to think of it, most of you haven't had any sick or vacation days. You want 'em, you put 'em on the calendar and we work around them. Everyone got that?"

Everyone nodded before getting back to business.

Luke said, "I've got some info for Cam, but figure the rest of you would like in on it."

Cam turned his immediate attention to Luke, but a quick glance around indicated that all of the other Saints were on alert.

"Miriam received an invite to a Red Cross appreciation event but had decided to decline. Last evening she received an email from Sister Genovia, now back with the Red Cross, still in Mexico. The email said that she would be at the event and wanted to see Miriam. And according to Cam, she has now replied that she would attend," Luke reported. "As you can imagine, Cam wanted me to do an email trace to see what I could find out."

Sending his information to their tablets, he reported, "The email did come from a computer located at the Red Cross main center in Los Mochis. I contacted them directly and they confirmed that Sister Genovia was returned to the Red Cross center where she has remained working in their main hospital. The storm wiped out more villages that were already damaged from the earthquake and so she's been busy."

"So the cartel let her go?" Bart asked incredulously.

"Apparently," Luke said. "But not willing to take their word for it, I contacted Alberto for direct confirmation. Manuel went and visited her there. According to the Sister, after Miriam escaped and Lorainne died, someone in the cartel must have taken pity on her and allowed her to return to her Red Cross duties in Los Mochis. It could be their belief system, but from what Miriam told us, Sister Genovia was a force to be reckoned with. Perhaps, fearing the wrath of God, assisted in letting her return."

"What about the event?" Jack queried.

"She's got a flight into Richmond on Friday evening and the event is Saturday. I also checked with the Richmond Red Cross and they said the diocese will be taking care of her while she's in the country and then her plans were to return to Mexico to continue her work.

Cam slowly nodded his head, knowing that Luke had thoroughly checked everything. Heaving a deep sigh, he thanked his friend, adding, "Thank fuck. Maybe this nightmare is about over for her."

25

F riday night came faster than Miriam was prepared for. She had spent time with her family since returning from Mexico, but still felt their nervousness around her as though she would disappear at any moment. Cam told her that his family knew he had rescued her thinking that would make her more at ease. Instead, she now fretted, wondering what they must think of her.

Before she had time to convince herself this was a bad idea, they were pulling into the driveway of a neat home in an older neighborhood on the south side of Richmond. *It looks so much like the home I grew up in,* she realized, taking a deep breath.

As the evening progressed, she could not help but smile at the family dynamics. *It not only looks like my home, but they act like my family!*

Henrico and Bonita welcomed her immediately with hugs and kisses before ushering her through the house to the back yard, packed with adults and children. Cam introduced his sisters, Daniella and Bianca, along with their husbands and children. A handsome man, similar in build to Cam with a devilishly wicked smile, was introduced as his brother, Emilio. Emilio immediately took Miriam's hand, kissed her fingers and began leading her toward the chairs set up near the tables laden with food.

"I've been looking forward to seeing if I could steal you away from my brother ever since he showed us the picture of you," Emilio said, a sparkle in his eye.

"Emilio!" Bonita yelled. "Behave!"

Emilio threw his head back and laughed as Cam swooped in, grabbing Miriam's hand while cuffing the back of his brother's head.

Miriam could not help but laugh at the antics that reminded her so much of her family. After the meal, Bonita maneuvered her over to the side as the men talked and her daughters were watching the children.

"*Mi hija*," Bonita said, placing her hand on Miriam's cheek calling her daughter, "I am so sorry for what you suffered."

Miriam blushed, not knowing what to say.

"But you have made me a happy woman, knowing such a *mujer fuerte* loves my son."

Miriam recognized the name of the river and understood that she was being called a strong woman. "I'm the lucky one," she confessed. "The handsome prince not only came to rescue me, but…well, he loves me too."

Bonita laughed, patting Miriam's arm. "Then you are both blessed and in being so, are blessing our family. I wish you *mucha felicidad y larga vida junta.*" Seeing Miriam's questioning gaze, she translated, "Much happiness and long life together."

Cam was watching and took a step toward her, but his father held him back.

"Let your mother speak to her," Henrico said.

"Dad you have no idea," Cam growled. "No idea how much she's been through."

"Your mother will have a care," his father replied.

Cam could not relax until he saw Miriam smile and embrace his mother. Letting out a breath he did not know he was holding, he grinned as she turned her smile toward him.

Saying their goodbyes later in the evening, Bonita proclaimed she wanted to meet Miriam's family and would invite them all over soon.

With thoughts of their two huge, in-their-business families together, Cam and Miriam looked askance at each other before heading home.

Miriam dressed with indecision, trying on and discarding several outfits. *What should I wear to a Red Cross event?* Since her main garb was nursing scrubs, she finally called her sister over for some fashion advice. Rebecca quickly chose long, black, silky pants covered with silk netting over the top. When she walked, the loose material fell perfectly off her ass, flowing down to the floor. An emerald green, silk, wrap-around top with long sleeves completed the classic appearance that

Miriam wanted. A strand of pearls at her neck with matching pearl studs in her ears finished the polished look.

Rebecca stood in the bedroom of Cam's house, smiling as she watched her sister prance in front of the mirror.

Miriam caught Rebecca's smile and cocked her head to the side. "What?"

Rebecca smiled wider, answering, "It's good to see you more like...I don't know...yourself right now."

A shadow passed across Miriam's expression as she walked over, grasping Rebecca's hand. "Have I been difficult?"

"No! Not at all difficult," her sister exclaimed. Looking down at their hands, she continued, "Just different. Kind of lost. Sad." Her gaze jumped back to Miriam. "That's completely understandable, of course, but as your family, we didn't know how to help you." Then, giggling, she added, "Mama's been doing a lot of housework and washing dishes."

Miriam joined in shared laughter knowing their mother prayed during her household chores, saying that for every dish or room she cleaned, she prayed for the person who used it. As the laughter died down, Miriam sighed heavily. "I know everyone was sick with worry when I was gone and then when I returned...I...well, it was hard on everyone."

"Dad kept saying that as long as you were back, we could handle anything you needed from us."

Miriam enveloped her in a hug. "I love you all, you

know? Not being able to be with you while I was gone was the hardest of all."

Rebecca returned the hug, her tears mingling with Miriam's. "But now, you're home, have a new career, and a gorgeous man." Pulling back, she gazed deeply into Miriam's eyes. "I know those things don't take away your memories or terrors, but…"

"Yes, they make everything worthwhile," Miriam finished for her. Turning back to the mirror, she said, "Now what do we do with my hair?"

Clapping her hands, Rebecca quickly dried her tears and the two women continued their afternoon.

Cam drove Miriam into Richmond that evening, parking in the garage near the elegant, restored Richmond Hotel in the revitalized downtown area. He noted her anxiety and clasped her hand in his, entwining their fingers.

"You okay, babe?"

She licked her lips and nodded nervously. "I don't know why I'm anxious. I'm excited to see Sister Genovia again and well…quite frankly, that's the only thing I care about. All of this other stuff makes me self-conscious."

He leaned down and kissed the top of her head. "Just know that you're the most beautiful woman here and I don't mean only on the outside."

She turned her face up toward his, gifting him with her smile. Taking a deep breath and letting it out slowly, she nudged his arm and said, "Okay, big boy. Let's get the show on the road."

The dinner was rather ordinary and their table companions were several older couples who had worked for the local Red Cross blood drives. She deflected their questions as to what she did for the Red Cross but was surprised when the main speaker asked all nurses who had answered the Red Cross calls during the previous disasters to please stand. She hesitated, but then saw that many of the event goers were nurses and no specifications to Mexico were made. Quickly sitting at the end of the applause, she heaved a sigh of relief.

Cam threw his arm over her shoulders and pulled her in closely, whispering, "You're doing fine, *cariña*."

She smiled, feeling for the first time since she was rescued that she was truly going to be fine. "I just wonder where Sister Genovia is," she murmured, her gaze darting around the large, filled room.

Cam found himself searching the room as well, hoping the Sister would be here after Miriam had expressly come to see her. A movement out of the corner of his eye had him quickly turning his head to the left, seeing Manuel Reyes standing near the entrance. He noticed when Manuel's eyes met his and gave a head jerk, silently asking Cam to come to him.

"Babe, I see someone I need to speak with. Stay here and I'll be right back," Cam gently ordered.

What the fuck is he doing here? Knowing that it must be serious for one of the DEA operatives to be seeking him out, he hustled toward Manuel. *Jesus, it must be bad news if he's come to tell me about it.*

Glancing around as Cam stalked toward Manuel, she continued to search for Sister Genovia. Her gaze landed on a woman, dressed in a nun's robes, standing on the far side of the room. The nun turned and Miriam smiled as the woman waved toward her.

"It's her. I see her," she said, pushing her chair back then, remembering that Cam was not there, felt foolish talking to herself. Offering excuses to the dinner tablemates, she wound through the multitude of tables toward her friend.

On the other side of the room, Cam met Manuel and the two men stepped just outside the noisy ballroom to talk.

"What's up? What are you here for?" Cam bit out, worry lacing his voice.

Before Manuel could begin to speak, a few diners passed them and suddenly Cam felt a prick in his neck.

Whirling, he saw a man with a needle standing next to him before he pitched forward and hit the floor, out cold.

On the other side of the ballroom, Sister Genovia was standing near an entrance and as Miriam approached, the nun gasped as she turned and walked down the hall, holding on to the wall for support. Her nursing instincts kicking in, Miriam hurried after the woman.

"Sister Genovia! Are you all right?" she called after her.

The nun turned at her voice and Miriam stopped suddenly within a few feet of her. *What the hell?* Before she could speak, the woman in the nun's robes grabbed her arm as Miriam heard the sound of running foot-steps. As she turned to see who was coming, she felt a prick in her arm. Whirling back, she saw the woman now holding a needle in her hand before her vision faded to black. Then she crumpled to the floor, unconscious.

26

Jack, enjoying a Saturday evening with Bethany as they piled on the sofa watching football, jerked instantly at the sound of his phone. "Yeah," he growled.

"Jack, it's Marc. Got news and it's not good. Alberto called to say that his partner, Manuel, went off the grid. He's not sure but he's got a bad feeling that he's headed into the states and may be after Miriam. Alberto's fuckin' beside himself, now seeing that Manuel was a mole for the cartel."

"Fuck! She's with Cam at the Red Cross event right now."

"I tried to get ahold of Cam but he's not picking up."

Jack jumped up and with a grimace toward Bethany, headed down to the Saint's work area. With Marc still on the phone, Jack fired off the alert to the other men, who quickly called back using their conference connections.

"Bart and Chad, you two are closest to the event hall

in Richmond and I want you on Miriam. Get there now. Luke, head here and see what you can dig up. Monty, use your connections to see what we can dig up on Manuel Reyes. Blaise, you head to the event hall also and we'll send what information we have on Sister Genovia. She may be in danger as well. Marc, stay in contact with Alberto to see what else he may come up with concerning Manuel."

Each man, with their duties, disconnected and headed out into the night. Bart and Chad quickly suited up with the equipment that they kept at their homes. Bart drove while Chad linked up to Luke's intel. "So far no one has reported an incident at the event. Let's hope it stays that way."

After a few minutes of being in the compound, Luke looked over at Jack and Monty. "Got confirmation from Alberto that Manuel is somewhere in the states. He's got no location on him, but I'll bet Monty's FBI can place him in VA."

Monty caught their gaze and said, "Working on it." He continued with his contact as they tried to get a specific location on Manuel.

"Oh, fuck," Luke shouted out, once more turning his body to face Jack. "You're not going to fuckin' believe this."

"What?" Jack asked, running his hands through his hair.

"Alberto's been in contact with the man on the inside of the working camp of the cartel where Cam and Miriam were. The report that Lorainne died is true. But what was left out was that Sister Genovia became ill. She's in a hospital."

"Then who the fuck is meeting with Miriam?"

The three men instantly knew that whoever had pretended to be Sister Genovia must have been convincing if the Red Cross in Los Mochis did not know it was not her. And whoever it was, was now with Miriam.

"Can you reach Cam?" Jack bit out as Monty sent the new info to his FBI contact and Luke relayed the information to Blaise, Bart, and Chad.

"Can't reach him. He's not picking up...or can't."

A thin line of light pierced the darkness as Cam blinked, trying to remember where he was. Consciousness came slowly and with it the realization that the light was coming from under a door. Lifting his head, he felt the cold, hard floor underneath him and moved awkwardly, as his hands were tied behind his back. It was obvious his assailant... *fuck, that was Manuel*...did not care about completely disabling him, but rather keeping him from being able to protect Miriam. *Shit! Have they got her already?*

His mind still slightly groggy, he heard his name being called from a distance. The sound became closer and clearer. *Bart?* Moving his feet toward the door, he began kicking as hard as his drug-induced body would let him. *Surely someone will hear!* He had no sense of how much time had passed, but prayed he was not too late.

His heart pounded in fear, but he willed it under control. His feet continued to kick at the door until he heard a commotion on the other side.

"Cam? Cam?"

"Yeah! I'm in here!" he yelled back.

Within a few seconds the door splintered inwards and Bart, Blaise, and Chad rushed in. Blaise dropped down beside Cam, a pen light in his hand as he immediately began to assess Cam's condition while Bart deftly cut off his restraints.

"Do you know what they gave you?" Blaise barked out.

Shaking his head, he said, "No. Something in a hypodermic needle, but it was just a pin-prick in the neck. Not a full injection."

"Your pupils are slightly dilated. With the way you were kicking the door, it must not have been too potent."

Bart and Chad assisted Cam up, while he roared, "It was Manuel fuckin' Reyes, Alberto's man."

"We know. We got the intel, but it was too late. Do you know where Miriam is?" Bart asked.

The fear that had hold of Cam now threatened to choke the breath out of him. "Oh, fuck. She was looking for Sister Genovia. They must have gotten them both."

The dread in his eyes was replaced by confusion when he saw the glance shared by the other three."

"Bro, the real Sister Genovia is still in Mexico. She became ill and is in a small hospital not associated with the Red Cross. We also got that intel. Someone is impersonating her."

Stumbling out of the closet, Cam tried to get his legs to hold him up, but found that Bart's strong arm supporting him was necessary.

"Richmond PD, DEA, and FBI are here, Cam. We called everyone in as soon as we got here and neither you nor Miriam could be found," Chad reported.

Monty and Marc came running down the hall toward the other Saints. "Got a visual of a woman in a nun's outfit walking out with a woman who appeared intoxicated. There was a Hispanic man with them and we've preliminarily identified him as Manuel."

Cam whirled around drunkenly, grabbing Bart's shoulders to steady himself, gulping air to clear his mind. "No reason to grab her unless they were taking her back."

"Back to Mexico? To who? You think Juaquim wants her?" Blaise asked.

By then the men had made it outside the building, the cold air slapping Cam into sobriety. He continued to breathe deeply, forcing his mind to work the problem. "Maybe. Jesus, I don't fuckin' know. The only one who showed any interest was..." he jerked his head back up. "The fuckin' doctor. Dr. Villogas."

Marc began talking to Luke quickly, who had Alberto on the line as well. A few minutes later, Marc nodded. "Got it." Turning to the group, he said, "CIA has uncovered recent calls between Manuel and Ernesto Villogas. Luke's using her tracer and has her on his radar. Looks like she's heading to the little airport outside of Charlestown.

Fearful his knees would buckle, Cam stiffened his

legs. Bart noticed and grabbed his friend by the shoulders, pulling his face directly in front of his.

"Bro, pull it together. We got this. But she's gotta have you thinkin' and clear. You got me?"

Nodding, Cam pulled in a deep breath before looking into the eyes of the others. "Let's go," he growled.

The Saints rushed to action, each knowing exactly what needed to be done.

Miriam felt her body slightly bouncing as she forced her eyes to open. She had never been drunk and knew that was not what was wrong, but everything was foggy —her vision, her hearing, and her mind. The slight light hurt her eyes, so she squeezed them tightly together.

The sound of faraway voices became clearer. *A man. And a woman's voice. Close by. Very close.* Instinctively recognizing possible danger, she slowed her breathing and tried not to move, mentally assessing her body with a nurse's skill. *Hands tied behind my back. Shoulder pain, but not broken. Ankles tied together also.* She wiggled her fingers and toes, working the circulation back into them. Licking her parched lips, she tried to still her pounding heartbeat. *Who are they? What do they want with me? Oh, Jesus. Please no. I can't go back!*

"He's gonna be surprised when I tell him we got her. He thought there was no way in hell I'd be able to pull it off."

"Well, don't forget who got you this far," the woman's voice said. "Without me stepping in to play the part of the good nun, you'd never have gotten your hands on her."

"Yeah, Yeah. I know and you're being paid well for your part in the charade."

The man continued, "I've been paid shit for a long time, so I'm due. It's about time that my worth was recognized."

Snorting, the woman said, "Your worth? As a double agent? Hell, that just means that you don't have any loyalty to anyone."

"Shut the fuck up, bitch, or I'll take you back with me."

"You wouldn't dare," the woman bit out, anger pouring from her.

"You never know when to keep your trap shut, do you?"

Miriam was glad the two in the front seat were arguing since it gave her time to get her eyes open and her mind clear. *Cam will know I'm gone. He'll come looking for me.* Fear gripped her once more...*if he can get to me in time.*

The vehicle slowed as it made a sharp turn onto a bumpier road, jostling her as she lay in the back seat. Unable to see anything out of the windows except for the stars, she was not gaining clues as to where they were taking her. They finally came to a stop and the man jumped out of the driver's side, leaving the woman in the front still grumbling.

"Come on, doll face," the man said, as he tried to heft

Miriam's body out of the back seat. *"Dios mío.* How much did you give her?"

As the woman climbed out of the front seat, she jerked on her nun's robes. "I hate wearing this," she bit out. Then, turning to see the man struggling with Miriam's body, she added, "Whatever you put in the needle is what I gave her."

"Well, get over here and help me," he growled.

Miriam tried desperately to make her body go limp and appear still drugged. *Don't give yourself away too early.*

With much difficulty, the man finally hefted her over his shoulder and carried her inside a building. Sneaking a quick peek, she could see a small two-seater plane inside. *Oh my God, NO!* She jerked involuntarily and the man roughly laid her down on the hangar floor.

"Well, *mi bonita.* I see you're awake now."

"Where…" she croaked, then swallowed and licked her lips. "Where are you taking me?" The man's face was vaguely familiar.

"Why, back where you belong. You left before *el doctor* had a chance to make you his."

El doctor? Doctor? Ernesto! Her eyes widened in understanding and she immediately began wiggling to loosen her bonds, to no avail.

Just then, the bottom of a nun's robes came into sight. Lifting her eyes, she saw an older woman similar in appearance to Sister Genovia. The woman raised her hand and pulled off the grey wig, leaving her long blonde hair cascading down her back. The theatrical makeup still gave her fake wrinkles, but Miriam could now see the imposter.

Gasping in recognition, she cried out, "Sharon? You?"

Sharon glanced away, a flash of regret in her eyes quickly replaced by determination. Looking back down at Miriam, she said, "I wasn't given much choice. It was either you or me and I'm sorry, but I'll choose me every time."

Manuel jerked Miriam to her feet. "You and me are gonna take a little flight." He saw the struggle in her eyes to recognize him. "You only met me once, *chica*. I work for Alberto..." he grinned before continuing, "and the Guzmans."

"That's what she meant. You're a traitor to both."

Getting his face into hers, he growled, "I work for me, bitch. And this'll get me in good and tight with the good doctor and in turn, Juaquim. What the government pays me to keep an eye on the cartels barely keeps me out of poverty."

Manuel jerked her arm once more toward the plane. "Let's go."

"Stop!" she cried. "I've got to go to the bathroom first."

He looked at her incredulously. "How fuckin' stupid do you think I am?"

"I do. I can't make it without going."

Not wanting to risk her making a mess in the small plane, he shoved her toward Sharon with a nod toward a side door. "Take her and you'd better not fuck it up or your ass will be on the plane instead."

Grimacing, Sharon caught hold of Miriam's arm as she stumbled toward her. "Come on. Let's get this over with."

Having to hop with her ankles taped, she finally made it inside the small toilet. "I can't sit with these clothes on."

Sharon assisted and then pulled Miriam back toward the sink, when she was done.

"Sharon, why? What happened? Why are you doing this?" she begged.

The other woman had the grace to look aside in embarrassment. "I had no choice. It was my only way out."

"I don't understand?"

"Not all of us had some rescuer come in the night, Miriam," Sharon growled.

"If you'd been there, he would have gotten you out too. It wasn't about me—he came to get all of us."

A pained looked crossed Sharon's face before being replaced with indignation. "I made my choice."

Miriam's anger grew as she replied, "Yes. You chose to get in bed with them. So how'd that work out for you?"

"It would have been fine if you'd stayed. After you left, Ernesto got angry and took it out on me. One day I blew up and showed up at his villa. His wife had a fit—it seems he kept his many mistresses from her."

Miriam noticed that Sharon needed to get her story out and tried to keep her talking as she desperately tried to stall the plane from leaving. "So what happened then?"

Sucking in a shaky breath, Sharon continued, "That crazy bitch hit me. Actually walked up and slapped me." Giving an angry huff, she said, "It was her husband that was cheating on her by fucking me, but I was the one who got slapped."

Blinking the tears back, she looked into Miriam's eyes. "He was furious at me. Said that he'd let the men have me or I could help him. So, it's not too hard to figure out what I was going to do. I agreed to impersonate Sister Genovia and then I was told I could stay in the U.S. while you were taken back."

Seeing the look on Miriam's face, she looked away again. "I'm sorry, Miriam, but I'm not going back."

"But you expect me to? Can't you help me? We could both get out of here!"

"I have no choice. He's got a gun and if you go back, Ernesto'll be good to you. You were always the one he wanted anyway. Me? I couldn't become one of the camp whores."

Shaking overtook Miriam as she realized the desperate woman in front of her was not going to help her escape. Just then, the door flew open and Manuel strolled in. "You fuckin' finished?" Once more, he grabbed Miriam by the arm and pulled her along for a few steps before throwing her over his shoulder.

"What about me?" Sharon yelled.

Manuel shouted back, "Let me get this one in the plane and I'll get you the car keys."

Miriam tried to struggle but, with her extremities bound, she was at his mercy. He climbed up on the wing and leaning down, opened the door. Twisting his body, he maneuvered her into the passenger seat of the small plane. Before she could wiggle out of his grasp, he fastened the seat belt around her body. He looked up, an evil expression crossing his face, before he jumped back down to the hanger floor.

Miriam watched in horror as he turned toward Sharon, smiling as he pulled a gun from his back waist-band and pointed it right at her.

"Wha—"

A loud, reverberating sound penetrated inside of the hangar, causing Miriam to duck her head instinctively. Looking back up, she saw Sharon's crumpled body on the floor, a red river oozing from underneath her.

A scream pierced the night before Miriam realized it came from her.

27

C am threw himself into the passenger seat of the SUV, not willing to be in the backseat. Even though he was not driving, the front seat afforded him the radio intel coming from Luke.

"She still there?" he growled, finding his voice unnaturally low as fear choked him.

"Yeah, her tracer has stopped moving."

"What assistance do we have?"

"Marc's got FAA on alert and Monty's pulled in the FBI. They've got agents heading your way right now."

"Not waiting on them," Cam retorted.

"Understood," Jack said, interrupting the call. "Do what you've got to do."

While Blaise drove, Bart and Chad suited up in the back seat, handing Cam his weapons when he was finished with the intel call.

Pulling off of the main road, Blaise turned off his headlights as he followed the bumpy drive toward the hangar. "What is this place?"

"Luke said it was a private hangar, normally used for keeping a crop-dusting plane. Local gang must now use it for drops and pickups."

Close enough now to see a single vehicle next to the hangar, Blaise parked and the men quickly exited. Just as they began to move stealthily toward the hangar, a piercing scream met their ears. Breaking into a run, Cam prayed his legs would hold him up knowing the agonizing sound came from Miriam. *If she screamed, then she's still alive and still here!*

As the Saints rounded the front of the building, a small plane taxied out. The men fired quickly at the tires, but the aircraft leapt forward as the pilot increased the speed. Blaise ran back to their SUV, determined to chase the aircraft down the runway while Bart, Chad, and Cam continued to fire at the tires.

Cam saw Miriam's pale face looking out of the window staring straight at him.

Miriam heard shots fired and, glancing out of the plane's window, saw Cam and some of the others illuminated by the hangar's lights. *He's here! He found me.*

A renewed determination coursed through her veins as she turned back to see what she could do. Rearing back in the seat, she brought her taped ankles up and kicked the control panel as hard as she could.

"Stop it, *perra*," Manual cursed, using his right hand to hit Miriam in the face.

Her head jerked to the side from the force of his

punch, but she refused to succumb to the pain. Nothing but the determination to not be taken again coursed through her blood. Twisting slightly, she kicked the steering wheel causing the plane to move quickly left. Before he could hit her again, she kicked once more as hard as she could, this time kicking his arm at the same time.

Howling in pain, he let go of the wheel, trying to subdue the wildcat in the cockpit, but she was not to be deterred. Kicking repeatedly on the control panel, she was finally causing damage to the planes controls and Manuel found that he could not maneuver the plane down the small, makeshift runway. They continued to taxi to the side, the aircraft jumping off of the asphalt onto the dirt.

He twisted and hit her once more, dodging her feet. Reaching for his gun, he opened the window and pointed the gun in the direction of the men running toward him.

Cam? No! Her shoulder felt wrenched out of its socket but she forced her body around even further than it had been and kicked Manuel in the back, propelling his body forward just as a zing sounded through the window. Blood splattered over Miriam as he screamed out, dropping the gun and grabbing his shoulder.

As the plane lurched to a stop, she tried to lift herself up from the awkward position but found herself pinned down in the seat. Manuel's face, contorted in pain, turned toward her, his eyes burning in fury.

"*Puta!*" he screamed. "I've lost everything because of

331

you!" Letting go of his bloody shoulder, he reached over with his hand, grasping her around the throat, squeezing with what was left of his strength.

"Let her go!" came the order from Cam's lips as he threw open the door of the plane, his pistol aimed at Manuel.

Bart landed on the other wing and jerked open the pilot's door, yelling the same order.

His fingers still squeezing, he looked back at Cam. "Not going to prison over this piece of *chochos*! You're gonna have to kill me, big man."

"No problem, asshole," Cam growled but, before he could fire, Bart grabbed Manuel from behind at the same time that Miriam kicked upward one more time, landing her foot on his injured shoulder.

Manuel howled in pain, screaming obscenities, as Blaise and Bart maneuvered him out of the cockpit. Chad ran up with the FBI in tow, calling for an ambulance and radioing Jack. "Got Miriam and Manuel. Uncertain of injuries," he reported rapidly.

Cam shifted his large frame between the two seats, his knife slicing through the seat belt trapping Miriam. "Babe, tell me what hurts?" he begged, slicing the tape at her feet, horrified at the blood on her. He could see her split lip and swollen eye, bruises already forming on her throat, but was unsure if anything was broken.

"My shoulder," she croaked, tears streaming down her face.

Trying not to move her, he slipped the knife underneath her body, slicing the bonds at her wrists as well, his shaking hands showing his fear.

"Blaise!" Cam called, needing his friend's medical assistance.

"Right here, bro. You gotta move away, Cam, so I can get to her."

Cam found his body unable to let go of Miriam's hand as Blaise attempted to ascertain her injuries in the tiny space.

"Bart!" Blaise called. "You're needed!"

Bart came up behind Cam and pulled his shoulders back.

Cam twisted his head around in anger. "What the fuck?"

"Let's get her out of the plane, man. Then you can hold her while Blaise checks her out."

Bart's calm voice finally penetrated Cam's mind and he bent low over her body. "Baby, I don't want to hurt you but I've got to get you out of here." He kissed her forehead as he lifted her out of the seat and backed through the door, trying to focus solely on moving her gently and not the pounding of his heart or the soft moans coming from her mouth. "Shit, I'm sorry, *cariña.*"

"It's okay," she hissed through gritted teeth, but the pain was secondary. *He came and got me.* As he lay her down on the blankets that Chad had thrown on the ground, she smiled up at Cam. Blaise knelt by her side as Cam knelt on the other, his hand not leaving hers.

Bart and Chad circled around, keeping the FBI at bay and an eye on their friends. Blaise quickly ascertained that the blood on her clothes was Manuel's.

"Thank Christ," Cam breathed, gently brushing her

hair away from her face, wanting to kiss her but afraid to hurt her split lip.

Opening the medical kit from their vehicle, Blaise treated her injuries. "Looks like your shoulder isn't dislocated, Miriam, but it's definitely sprained. I'm gonna fashion a sling and we'll need you to keep this on until you get to the hospital to be checked out."

As soon as Blaise had the sling in place, Cam moved him out of the way, nearly lying on the blanket with his arms around her. She had begun to shake from the cold and shock, but his body heat began to warm her considerably.

With his arms around her, endearments whispered in her ear, she slowly relaxed in his embrace. Cupping his jaw with her hand, she spoke with tears in her eyes, "You came for me."

"*Cariña*, you were fighting him yourself."

"I couldn't go back. And…I couldn't leave you."

Unashamed of the tears in his own eyes, he whispered, "I love you," as he placed a gentle kiss on her lips.

With a smile on her lips she melted, warm and loved in his arms. "Take me home, Cam. Take me home."

He kissed her once more before lifting her in his mighty arms. "Always, *mi amor*," he promised.

2 8

SIX MONTHS LATER

The wedding gazebo at Mountville Cabins that Bethany decorated was breathtaking. The bride and groom danced their first dance together underneath the pine structure covered in ivory sheers with spring flowers tied in bunches at the rails.

Miriam and Cam gazed into each other's eyes as the rest of the party fell away behind them. Wearing a strapless, ivory, knee-length dress with beading over the bodice she took his breath away, just as much as she had done at their actual wedding earlier in the day.

To satisfy both sets of parents, they married in a church, but both wanted the reception to be a casual party for all of their friends. Cam wore dark pants with a white shirt, but eschewed the tie. His arms wrapped around Miriam as they moved back and forth around the gazebo floor.

Rachel and Joseph Delaro stood with Henrico and Bonita Perez, watching their children dance, knowing the miracle that brought them together...and home.

Jobe threw his arm around his wife, MacKenna, and led her to the gazebo now that the first dance was over, twirling her around as well.

Bethany looked on with pride at her wedding venue, pleased that business was picking up and friends wanted to celebrate there. Jack saw her glancing around nervously so, pulling her in tightly, said, "No working tonight, babe. Your staff has it all in hand, so you can just be mine right now," before he pulled her over to the gazebo to dance as well.

Several of the Saints brought dates and the dance floor began to fill up with couples swaying to the music.

Sister Genovia, now well enough to travel, flew in for the wedding. She and Miriam had a tearful reunion several days earlier and now the nun sat at one of the tables on the lawn, watching the sunset over the mountains. Taking a deep breath, she smiled at the glowing bride, thanking God for her deliverance. As her eyes moved to the groom, she chuckled, thanking God once more for sending Miriam such a kind and handsome rescuer.

Cam took his eyes off his bride for just a moment to glance around at the others. Friends, family, co-workers. He could not imagine being happier than he was at that moment and a sudden flash of memory rushed back to him. *Father Martinez. I haven't thought of him in years.* And he remembered the words the priest had said to him that fateful day. *A man can change his destiny.*

Looking back at the beautiful woman in his arms, he felt the words of the priest slam into him. *I would have been in prison or dead. And now?* Receiving one of Miriam's brilliant smiles as a gift, he knew, *My destiny is having this woman in my life.*

He bent his head and took her mouth in a gentle kiss. One that promised everything, sealing his destiny forever.

Two years later

Miriam woke from her nap, thankful for the chance to have an extra hour of sleep. The house was quiet...too quiet. Her breasts were heavy, ready for feeding time. She rose from the bed quickly but before she could make it to the hall, Cam stepped into the bedroom.

"Where's—"

He shushed her with his fingers over her lips and motioned for her to follow him. He led her to the nursery where she peeked in with curiosity. There in the rocking chair sat Sister Genovia holding a cooing Genevieve. The elderly nun lifted her eyes from the tiny two-month old bundle and smiled over her namesake.

Miriam moved into the room as Genevieve began to fuss, taking her from the Sister's arms. Settling down in the rocking chair herself, she opened her gown and began nursing her baby. Cam patted Sister Genovia's shoulder as she left the room before kneeling down next to the chair watching his beautiful wife with their perfect little girl. Genevieve's head was covered in black downy hair and her dark eyes watched her mother carefully.

After she had her fill, her mouth went slack as sleep overtook the infant. Miriam looked over at Cam, enjoying the few minutes of peace. He assisted her up and watched as she lay the sleeping baby back into her crib. Carefully covering her with a blanket, he ushered Miriam back toward their bedroom.

"What are you doing?" she whispered.

"You need to rest," he answered.

"I just took a nap and there's so much to do," she protested.

"Nope," he replied. "Your mom and my mom are downstairs, whipping the house into shape, trying to outdo each other for grandmother of the year. Sister Genovia is also there, keeping an eye on things. Bethany brought over some food for later so there's no meal to fix."

"Humph," she said, sitting on the edge of the bed. "But I'm not sleepy."

"Well," he said, gently laying her back onto the mattress. "You did have your checkup last week and the doctor did say that we could—"

"Cam! We've got our mothers and Sister Genovia downstairs! How can we possibly—"

Interrupting her concerns, he pushed her gently back onto the bed, slipping his arms around her soft body. Moving his lips over hers, he kissed her. Capturing her moan in his mouth, he took the kiss deeper. Wetter. His hands roamed over her body, ripe with curves. He knew she was self-conscious about losing her post-pregnancy weight, but he loved the feel of her body. Her moans increased as his hands continued to work magic, quickly eliciting her hands to seek out his crotch.

Miriam smiled, finding exactly what she knew she would discover. He was more than ready. Suddenly the thought of having this man make love to her overrode every other thought in her mind. Knowing that little Genevieve could awake at any moment hastened her actions. Her hands sought his skin as clothes were tossed to the side.

He felt her ardor increase as their naked bodies clung to each other. He wanted to rediscover her slowly, with long, languid strokes, but fear of interruption had him moving just as quickly as she.

"Now, Cam. I need you now," she cried. "We can take things slow later. Maybe in about twenty years," she added, thinking about the coming years of passion mixing with parenthood.

Chuckling, he complied, plunging inside her warmth as he relished her body, moving in the age-old rhythm that soon brought them clinging to each other as their orgasms rushed over them.

Minutes later, both sated as he pulled the covers back over their cooling bodies, he held her tightly. Her head rested on his broad chest as her breathing slowed. Within a few minutes, they heard the cooing from the baby monitor and she immediately moved to leave the bed.

He pulled her back for one more kiss and as his dark eyes met hers, they both smiled. She placed her hand on his stubbled cheek, saying, "Thank you." Seeing his questioning expression, she continued, "Thank you for saving me."

Another gentle kiss was placed on her lips before she quickly donned her gown and robe. His eyes followed her as she slipped from the room before he moved to claim his clothes as well. Stepping back into the hall, he watched as she held their baby in her arms. And he knew—he was the one rescued. First by the priest and then by this woman's love. Slipping his daughter into his arms, he smiled as he led them downstairs to the waiting grandmothers. The follies of his youth fell away, knowing that Someone was watching over them.

For the next exciting Saints book (Patrick's story) :
Revealing Love

Don't miss any news about new releases! Sign up for my
Newsletter

Cael

Jaxon

Jayden

Asher

Zeke

Cas

Lighthouse Security Investigations

Mace

Rank

Walker

Drew

Blake

Tate

Levi

Clay

Cobb

Hope City (romantic suspense series co-developed

with Kris Michaels

Brock book 1

Sean book 2

Carter book 3

Brody book 4

Kyle book 5

Ryker book 6

Rory book 7

Killian book 8

Torin book 9

Saints Protection & Investigations

(an elite group, assigned to the cases no one else wants...or can solve)

Serial Love

Healing Love

Revealing Love

Seeing Love

Honor Love

Sacrifice Love

Protecting Love

Remember Love

Discover Love

Surviving Love

Celebrating Love

Searching Love

Follow the exciting spin-off series:

Alvarez Security (military romantic suspense)

Gabe

Tony

Vinny

Jobe

SEALs

Thin Ice (Sleeper SEAL)

SEAL Together (Silver SEAL)

Undercover Groom (Hot SEAL)

Also for a Hope City Crossover Novel / Hot SEAL...

A Forever Dad by Maryann Jordan

Letters From Home (military romance)

Class of Love

Freedom of Love

Bond of Love

The Love's Series (detectives)

Love's Taming

Love's Tempting

Love's Trusting

The Fairfield Series (small town detectives)

Emma's Home

Laurie's Time

Carol's Image

Fireworks Over Fairfield

Please take the time to leave a review of this book. Feel free to contact me, especially if you enjoyed my book. I love to hear from readers!

Facebook

Email

Website

ABOUT THE AUTHOR

I am an avid reader of romance novels, often joking that I cut my teeth on the historical romances. I have been reading and reviewing for years. In 2013, I finally gave into the characters in my head, screaming for their story to be told. From these musings, my first novel, Emma's Home, The Fairfield Series was born.

I was a high school counselor having worked in education for thirty years. I live in Virginia, having also lived in four states and two foreign countries. I have been married to a wonderfully patient man for thirty-five years. When writing, my dog or one of my four cats can generally be found in the same room if not on my lap.

Facebook
Email
Website

Made in the USA
Coppell, TX
21 January 2022

72059557R00204